"RENDELL IS AWFULLY GOOD . . . IN ANY RENDELL BOOK YOU KNOW THAT SOMETHING UNUSUAL IS GOING TO HAPPEN."

The New York Times Book Review

"When Rendell writes crime-from-the-criminal-point-of-view, she is gripping and creepy. When she writes straightforward detection starring homely, countryish Inspector Wexford, she is even better. Only P. D. James can rival Rendell for total, no-seams-showing command of the classic genre, and true mystery fans, unlike literary critics, would probably give Rendell extra points for unliterary economy and ease of her irresistible non-stop prose."

The Kirkus Reviews

Sins of the Fathers

Ruth Rendell

(Formerly titled: *A New Lease of Death*)

BALLANTINE BOOKS • NEW YORK

Formerly titled *A New Lease of Death*

Copyright © 1967 by Ruth Rendell

All rights reserved. Published in the United States by Ballantine Books, a division of Random House, Inc., New York.

ISBN 0-345-32740-3

This edition published by arrangement with Doubleday & Company, Inc.

Printed in Canada

First Ballantine Books Edition: December 1970
Fifth Printing: April 1985

for my father and Simon

All the chapter heading quotations
are extracts from
The Book of Common Prayer

1

The laws of the Realm may punish Christian
men with death for heinous and grievous offences.

The Thirty-nine Articles

IT was five in the morning. Inspector Burden had seen
more dawns than most men, but he had never quite
become jaundiced by them, especially summer dawns.
He liked the stillness, the sight of the little country town
in a depopulated state, the hard blue light that was of
the same shade and intensity as the light at dusk but
without dusk's melancholy.

The two men they had been questioning about last
night's fight in one of Kingsmarkham's cafés had
confessed separately and almost simultaneously just
a quarter of an hour before. Now they were locked into
two stark white cells on the ground floor of this incongruously modern police station. Burden stood by
the window in Wexford's office, looking at the sky
which had the peculiar greenish tint of aquamarine. A
flock of birds flying in dense formation crossed it. They
reminded Burden of his childhood when, as at dawn,
everything had seemed bigger, clearer and of more
significance than it did today. Tired and a little sickened, he opened the window to get rid of cigarette
smoke and the sweaty smell of youths who wore
leather jackets in the height of summer.

Outside in the corridor he could hear Wexford saying good night—or good morning—to Colonel Griswold, the Chief Constable. Burden wondered if Gris-

wold had guessed when he arrived just before ten with a long spiel about stamping out hooliganism that he was in for an all-night session. That, he thought unfairly, was where meddling got you.

The heavy front door clanged and Griswold's car started. Burden watched it move off the forecourt, past the great stone urns filled with pink geraniums and into Kingsmarkham High Street. The Chief Constable was driving himself. Burden saw with approval and grudging amusement that Griswold drove at just about twenty-eight miles per hour until he reached the black and white derestriction sign. Then the car gathered speed and flashed away out of sight along the empty country road that led to Pomfret.

He turned round when he heard Wexford come in. The Chief Inspector's heavy grey face was a little greyer than usual, but he showed no other sign of tiredness and his eyes, dark and hard as basalt, showed a gleam of triumph. He was a big man with big features and a big intimidating voice. His grey suit—one of a series of low fastening, double-breasted affairs—appeared more shabby and wrinkled than ever today. But it suited Wexford, being not unlike an extension of his furrowed pachydermatous skin.

'Another job jobbed,' he said, 'as the old woman said when she jobbed the old man's eye out.'

Burden bore with such vulgarisms stoically. He knew that they were meant to horrify him; they always succeeded. He made his thin lips crease into a tight smile. Wexford handed him a blue envelope and he was glad of the diversion to hide his slight embarrassment.

'Griswold's just given me this,' Wexford said. 'At five in the morning. No sense of timing.'

Burden glanced at the Essex postmark.

'Is that the man he was on about earlier, sir?'

'Well, I don't have fanmail from beautiful olde worlde Thringford as a general rule, do I, Mike? This is the Rev. Mr Archery all right, taking advantage of the Old Pals' Act.' He lowered himself into one of the rather flimsy chairs and it gave the usual protesting creak. Wexford had what his junior called a love-hate relationship with those chairs and indeed with all the aggressively modern furnishings of his office. The glossy block floor, the square of nylon carpet, the chairs with their sleek chrome legs, the primrose venetian blinds— all these in Wexford's estimation were not 'serviceable,' they were dust-traps and they were 'chichi'. At the same time he took in them an enormous half-secret pride. They had their effect. They served to impress visiting strangers such as the writer of this letter Wexford was now taking from its envelope.

It too was written on rather thick blue paper. In a painfully authentic upper-class accent, the Chief Inspector said affectedly, 'May as well get on to the Chief Constable of Mid-Sussex, my dear. We were up at Oxford together, don't you know?' He squeezed his face into a kind of snarling grin. 'All among the bloody dreaming spires,' he said. 'I hate that sort of thing.'

'Were they?'

'Were they what?'

'At Oxford together?'

'I don't know. Something like that. It may have been the playing fields of Eton. All Griswold said was, "Now we've got those villains wrapped up, I'd like you to have a look at a letter from a very good friend of mine called Archery. Excellent fellow, one of the best. This enclosure's for you. I'd like you to give him all the help you can. I've a notion it's got something to do with that scoundrel Painter." '

'Who's Painter?'

'Villain who got the chop about fifteen or sixteen years ago,' said Wexford laconically. 'Let's see what the parson has to say, shall we?'

Burden looked over his shoulder. The letter was headed St Columba's Vicarage, Thringford, Essex. The greek e's awakened in him a small hostility. Wexford read it aloud.

' "Dear sir, I hope you will forgive me for taking up your valuable time . . ." Don't have much choice, do

I? ". . . but I regard this matter as being of some urgency. Col. Griswold, the Chief Constable of blah blah blah and so on, has very kindly told me you are the gentleman who may be able to assist me in this problem so I am taking the liberty, having first consulted him, of writing to you." ' He cleared his throat and loosened his crumpled grey tie. 'Takes a hell of a time coming to the point, I must say. Ah, here we go. "You will remember the case of Herbert Arthur Painter . . ." I *will*. "I understand you were in charge of it. I therefore supposed I should come to you before pursuing certain enquiries which, much against my will, I am compelled to make." '

'Compelled?'

'That's what the man says. Doesn't say why. The rest's a load of compliments and can he come and see me tomorrow—no, today. He's going to phone this morning, but he "anticipates my willingness to meet him." ' He glanced at the window to where the sun was coming up over York Street and with one of his distorted quotations said, 'I suppose he's sleeping in Elysium at this moment, crammed with distressful cold mutton or whatever parsons go to bed on.'

'What's it all about?'

'O God, Mike, it's obvious, isn't it? You don't want to take any notice of this "being compelled" and "against his will" stuff. I don't suppose his stipend amounts to much. He probably writes true crime stories in between early Communion and the Mother's Meeting. He must be getting desperate if he reckons on titillating the mass appetite by resurrecting Painter.'

Burden said thoughtfully, 'I seem to remember the case. I'd just left school . . .'

'And it inspired your choice of a career, did it?' Wexford mocked. ' "What are you going to be, son?" "I'm going to be a detective, Dad." '

In his five years as Wexford's right hand man, Burden had grown immune to his teasing. He knew he was a kind of safety valve, the stooge perhaps on whom Wexford could vent his violent and sometimes shocking sense of humour. The people of this little town, indiscriminately referred to by Wexford as 'our customers' had, unless suspected of felony, to be spared. Burden was there to take the overflow of his chief's rage, ridicule and satire. Now he was cast as the sponge to soak up the scorn that was rightly the due of Griswold and Griswold's friend.

He looked shrewdly at Wexford. After a trying, frustrating day and night, this letter was the last straw. Wexford was suddenly tense with irritation, his skin more deeply wrinkled than usual, his whole body flexed with the anger that would not suffer fools gladly. That tension must find release.

'This Painter thing,' Burden said slyly, slipping into his role of therapist, 'a bit run of the mill, wasn't it? I followed it in the papers because it was the big local sensation. I don't remember it was remarkable in any other way.'

Wexford slipped the letter back into its envelope and put it in a drawer. His movements were precise and under a tight control. One wrong word, Burden thought, and he'd have torn it up, chucked the pieces on the floor and left them to the mercy of the cleaner. His words had apparently been as right as possible under the circumstances for Wexford said in a sharp cool voice, 'It was remarkable to me.'

'Because you handled it?'

'Because it was the first murder case I ever handled on my own. It was remarkable to Painter because it hanged him and to his widow, I daresay. I suppose it shook her a bit as far as anything could shake that girl.'

Rather nervously Burden watched him observe the cigarette burn one of the men they had been interviewing had made in the lemon-coloured leather of a chair seat. He waited for the explosion. Instead Wexford said indifferently:

'Haven't you got a home to go to?'

'Too late now,' said Burden, stifling a yawn that threatened. 'Besides, my wife's away at the seaside.'

A strongly uxorious man, he found his bungalow like a morgue when Jean and the children were absent. This was a side of his character that afforded Wexford many opportunities for quips and snide remarks, this coupled with his comparative youth, his stolid stick-in-the-mud nature and a certain primness of outlook. But all Wexford said was, 'I forgot.'

He was good at his job. The big ugly man respected him for that. Although he might deride, Wexford appreciated the advantage of having a deputy whose grave good looks were attractive to women. Seated opposite the ascetic face, warmed by a compassion Wexford called 'softness', they were more inclined to open their hearts than to a majestic fifty-five-year-old heavyweight. His personality, however, was not strong and his superior effaced him. Now, in order to channel off that sharp-edged vitality, he was going to have to risk a rebuke for stupidity.

He risked it. 'If you're going to have to argue the toss with this Archery, wouldn't it be a good idea if we had a re-cap of the facts?'

'We?'

'Well, you then, sir. You must be a bit rusty yourself on the case after so long.'

The outburst came with an undercurrent of laughter. 'God Almighty! D'you think I can't see your brain working? When I want a psychiatrist I'll hire a professional.' He paused and the laughter became a wry grin. 'O.K. it might help me . . .' But Burden had made the mistake of relaxing too soon. 'To get the facts straight for Mr Bloody Archery, I mean,' Wexford snapped. 'But there's no mystery, you know, no cunning little red herrings. Painter did it all right.' He pointed eastwards out of the window. The broad Sussex sky was becoming suffused with rose and gold, bands of soft creamy pink like strokes from a watercolour brush. 'That's as sure as the sun's rising now,' he said. 'There never was any doubt. Herbert Arthur Painter killed his ninety-year-old employer by hitting her over the head with an axe and he did it for two hundred pounds. He was a brutal savage moron. I read in the paper the other day that the Russians call anti-social people "unpersons" and that just about describes him. Funny sort of character for a parson to champion.'

'If he's championing him.'

'We shall see,' said Wexford.

They stood in front of the map that was attached to the yellow 'cracked ice' wallpaper.

'She was killed in her own home, wasn't she?' Burden asked. 'One of those big houses off the Stowerton road?'

The map showed the whole of this rather sleepy country district. Kingsmarkham, a market town of some twelve thousand inhabitants, lay in the centre, it's streets coloured in brown and white, its pastoral environs green with the blotches of dark veridian that denoted woodland. Roads ran from it as from the meshy heart of a spider's web, one leading to Pomfret in the South, another to Sewingbury in the North-east. The scattered villages, Flagford, Clusterwell and Forby, were tiny flies on this web.

'The house is called Victor's Piece,' said Wexford. 'Funny sort of name. Some general built it for himself after the Ashanti Wars.'

'And it's just about here.' Burden put his finger on a vertical strand of the web that led from Kingsmarkham to Stowerton, lying due north. He pondered and light dawned. 'I think I know it,' he said. 'Hideous dump with a lot of green woodwork all over it. It was an old people's home up until last year. I suppose they'll pull it down.'

'I daresay. There are a couple of acres of land to it. If you've got the picture we may as well sit down.'

Burden had moved his chair to the window. There was something consoling and at the same time rejuvenating in watching the unfolding of what was going to be a lovely day. On the fields tree shadows lay long and densely blue and bright new light glinted on the slate roofs of ancient houses. Pity he hadn't been

able to get away with Jean. The sunlight and the fresh
heady air turned his thoughts towards holidays and
prevented him from recalling details of this case that
had long ago shocked Kingsmarkham. He searched
his memory and found to his shame that he could not
even remember the murder woman's name.

'What was she called?' he asked Wexford. 'A foreign
name, wasn't it? Porto or Primo something?'

'Primero. Rose Isabel Primero. That was her married
name. Far from being foreign, she'd been brought up
at Forby Hall. Her people were by way of being squires
of Forby.'

Burden knew Forby well. What tourists there were
in this agricultural country with neither seaside nor
downs, castles nor cathedrals, made a point of going to
Forby. The guide books listed it absurdly as the fifth
prettiest village in England. Every local newsagent's
contained postcard of its church. Burden himself re-
garded it with a certain affection because its inhabitants
had shown themselves almost totally devoid of criminal
tendencies.

'This Archery could be a relative,' he suggested.
'Maybe he wants some gen for his family achives.'

'I doubt it,' Wexford said, basking in the sun like a
huge grey cat. 'The only relatives she had were her
three grandchildren. Roger Primero, the grandson,
lives at Forby Hall now. Didn't inherit it, had to buy
it. I don't know the details.'

'There used to be a family called Kynaston at
Forby Hall, or so Jean's mother says. Mind you, that
was years and years ago.'

'That's right,' Wexford said with a hint of impatience
in his rumbling bass voice. 'Mrs Primero was born
a Kynaston and she was going on for forty when she
married Dr Ralph Primero. I imagine her people
looked on it a bit askance—this was at the turn of the
century, remember.'

'What was he, a G.P.?'

'Some sort of specialist, I think. It was when he re-
tired that they came to live at Victor's Piece. They

weren't all that well-off, you know. When the doctor died in the thirties Mrs Primero was left with about ten thousand pounds to live on. There was one child of the marriage, a son, but he'd died soon after his father.'

'D'you mean she was living alone in that great place? At her age?'

Wexford pursed his lips, reminiscing. Burden knew his chief's almost supernatural memory. When he was sufficiently interested he had the nearest thing to total recall. 'She had one maid,' Wexford said. 'Her name was—is, she's still alive—her name was Alice Flower. She was a good bit younger than her employer, seventy odd, and she'd been with Mrs Primero for about fifty years. A real ancient retainer of the old school. Living like that, you might think they'd have become friends rather than mistress and servant, but Alice kept to her place and they were "Madam" and "Alice" to each other till the day Mrs Primero died. I knew Alice by sight. She was quite a local character when she came into town to do their shopping, particularly when Painter started bringing her in in Mrs Primero's Daimler. D'you remember how nursemaids used to look? No, you wouldn't. You're too young. Well, Alice always wore a long navy coat and what's called a "decent" navy felt hat. She and Painter were both servants, but Alice put herself miles above him. She'd pull her rank on him and give him his orders just like Mrs Primero herself. He was Bert to his wife and his cronies but Alice called him "Beast". Not to his face, mind. She wouldn't have quite dared that.'

'You mean she was frightened of him?'

'In a way. She hated him and resented his being there. I wonder if I've still got that cutting.' Wexford opened the bottom drawer of his desk, the one where he kept personal, semi-official things, grotesqueries that had interested him. He hadn't much hope of finding what he sought. At the time of Mrs Primero's murder Kingsmarkham police had been housed in an old yellow brick building in the centre of the town. That had been pulled down four or five years ago and re-

placed by this block of startling modernity on the out-
skirts. The cutting had very probably got lost in the
move from the high pitch pine desk to this one of
lacquered rosewood. He leafed through notes, letters,
odd little souvenirs, finally surfacing with a grin of
triumph.

'There you are, the "unperson" himself. Good-
looking if you like the type. Herbert Arthur Painter,
late of the Fourteenth Army in Burma. Twenty-five
years old, engaged by Mrs Primero as chauffeur,
gardener and odd-job man.'

The cutting was from the *Sunday Planet,* several
columns of type surrounding a double-column block.
It was a clear photograph and Painter's eyes were
staring straight at the camera.

'Funny, that,' said Wexford. 'He always looked you
straight in the eye. Supposed to denote honesty, if
you've ever heard such a load of rubbish.'

Burden must have seen the picture before, but he
had entirely forgotten it. It was a large well-made
face with a straight though fleshy nose, spread at the
nostrils. Painter had the thick curved lips that on a
man are a coarse parody of a woman's mouth, a flat
high brow and short tightly waving hair. The waves
were so tightly crimped that they looked as if they
must have pulled the skin and pained the scalp.

'He was tall and well-built,' Wexford went on. 'Face
like a handsome overgrown pug, don't you think? He'd
been in the Far East during the war, but if the heat
and the privation had taken it out of him it didn't
show by then. He had a sort of glistening good health
about him like a shire horse. Sorry to use all these
animal metaphors, but Painter was like an animal.'

'How did Mrs Primero come to take him on?'

Wexford took the cutting from him, looked at it for
a moment and folded it up.

'From the time the doctor died,' he said, 'until 1947
Mrs Primero and Alice Flower struggled to keep the
place going, pulling up a few weeds here and there,
getting a man in when they wanted a shelf fixed. You

can imagine the kind of thing. They had a succession of women up from Kingsmarkham to help with the housework but sooner or later they all left to go into the factories. The place started going to rack and ruin. Not surprising when you think that by the end of the war Mrs Primero was in her middle eighties and Alice nearly seventy. Besides, leaving her age out of it, Mrs Primero never touched the place as far as housework went. She hadn't been brought up to it and she wouldn't have known a duster from an antimacassar.'

'Bit of a tartar, was she?'

'She was what God and her background had made her,' Wexford said gravely but with the faintest suspicion of irony in his voice. 'I never saw her till she was dead. She was stubborn, a bit mean, what nowadays is called "reactionary", inclined to be an autocrat and very much monarch of all she surveyed. I'll give you a couple of examples. When her son died he left his wife and kids very badly off. I don't know the ins and outs of it, but Mrs Primero was quite willing to help financially provided it was on her terms. The family was to come and live with her and so on. Still, I daresay she couldn't afford to keep up two establishments. The other thing was that she'd been a very keen churchwoman. When she got too old to go she insisted on Alice going in her place. Like a sort of whipping bow. But she had her affections. She adored the grandson, Roger, and she had one close friend. We'll come to that later.

'As you know, there was an acute housing shortage after the war and a hell of a servant problem too. Mrs Primero was an intelligent old woman and she got to thinking how she could use one to solve the other. In the grounds of Victor's Piece was a coach house with a sort of loft over the top of it. The place for the coach was used to house the aforesaid Daimler. No one had driven it since the doctor died—Mrs Primero couldn't drive and, needless to say, Alice couldn't either. There was precious little petrol about but you

could get your ration, enough to do the shopping and
take a couple of old dears for a weekly jaunt around
the lanes.'

'So Alice was that much of a friend?' Burden put
in.

Wexford said solemnly, 'A lady can be accompanied
by her maid when she goes driving. Anyway, Mrs
Primero put an advert in the Kingsmarkham *Chronicle*
for a young able-bodied man, willing to do the garden,
perform odd jobs, maintain and drive the car in ex-
change for a flat and three pounds a week.'

'*Three pounds?*' Burden was a non-smoker and no
lover of extravagant living, but he knew from doing
his wife's weekend shopping what a little way three
pounds went.

'Well, it was worth a good bit more in those days,
Mike,' Wexford said almost apologetically. 'Mrs Primero had the loft painted up, divided into three rooms
and piped for water. It wasn't Dolphin Square but, God,
people were glad of one room back in 1947! She got
a lot of answers but for some reason—God knows
what reason—she picked Painter. At the trial Alice
said she thought the fact that he had a wife and a
baby daughter would keep him steady. Depends what
you mean steady, doesn't it?'

Burden shifted his chair out of the sun. 'Was the
wife employed by Mrs Primero too?'

'No, just Painter. She's got this little kid, you see.
She was only about two when they came. If she'd
worked up at the house she'd have had to bring the
child with her. Mrs Primero would never have stood
for that. As far as she was concerned between her and
the Painters there was a great gulf fixed. I gathered
she'd hardly exchanged more than a couple of words
with Mrs Painter all the time Painter was there and
as for the little girl—her name was Theresa, I think—
she barely knew of her existence.'

'She doesn't sound a very nice sort of woman,'
Burden said doubtfully.

'She was typical of her age and class,' Wexford said

tolerantly. 'Don't forget she was a daughter of the lord of the manor when lords of the manor still counted for something. To her Mrs Painter was comparable to a tenant's wife. I've no doubt that if Mrs Painter had been ill she'd have sent old Alice over with a bowl of soup and some blankets. Besides, Mrs Painter kept herself to herself. She was very pretty, very quiet and with a sort of deadly respectability about her. She was a bit scared of Painter which wasn't hard to understand, she being so small and Painter such a great hulking brute. When I talked to her after the murder I noticed she'd got bruises on her arm, too many bruises for her just to have got them through the usual kitchen accidents, and I wouldn't mind betting her husband used to knock her about.'

'So, in fact,' Burden said, 'they were two completely separate units. Mrs Primero and her maid living alone at Victor's Piece, the Painter family in their own home at the bottom of the garden.'

'I don't know about "bottom of the garden". The coach house was about a hundred feet from the back door of the big house. Painter only went up there to carry in the coal and receive his instructions.'

'Ah,' said Burden, 'there was some complicated business about coal, I seem to remember. Wasn't it more or less the crux of the whole thing?'

'Painter was supposed to chop wood and carry coal,' Wexford continued. 'Alice was past carrying coal and Painter was supposed to bring a scuttleful at mid-day—they never lit a fire before that—and another one at six-thirty. Now, he never objected to the gardening or the car maintenance, but for some reason he drew the line at the coal. He did it—apart from frequent lapses—but he was always grumbling about it. The mid-day duty cut across his dinner time, he said, and he didn't like turning out on winter evenings. Couldn't he bring two scuttles at eleven? But Mrs Primero wouldn't have that. She said she wasn't going to have her drawing room turned into a railway yard.'

Burden smiled. His tiredness had almost worn off.

Given breakfast, a shave and a shower down, he would be a new man. He glanced at his watch, then across the High Street to where the blinds were going up on the Carousel Café.

'I could do with a cup of coffee,' he said.

'Two minds with but a single thought. Root some-one out and send them over.'

Wexford stood up and stretched, tightened his tie and smoothed back the hair that was too sparse to become untidy. The coffee arrived in wax cups with plastic spoons and little cubes of wrapped sugar.

'That's better,' said Wexford. 'D'you want me to go on?' Burden nodded.

'By September 1950 Painter had been working for Mrs Primero for three years. The arrangement appeared to work pretty well apart from the difficulties Painter made about the coal. He never brought it in without complaining and he was always asking for a rise.'

'I suppose he thought she was rolling in money?'

'Of course, he couldn't have known what she'd got in the bank or in shares or whatever it was. On the other hand it was an open secret she kept money in the house.'

'In a safe, d'you mean?'

'Not on your life. You know these old girls. Some of it was in drawers stuffed into paper bags, some of it in old handbags.'

With a feat of memory Burden said suddenly, 'And one of those handbags contained *the* two hundred pounds?'

'It did,' Wexford said grimly. 'Whatever she might have been able to afford, Mrs Primero refused to raise Painter's wages. If he didn't like the set-up he could go, but that would mean giving up the flat.

'Being a very old woman, Mrs Primero felt the cold and she liked to start fires in September. Painter thought this unnecessary and he made the usual fuss about it. . . .'

He stopped as the telephone rang and he took the

receiver himself. Burden had no idea from Wexford's reiterated, 'Yes, yes . . . all right,' who it could be. He finished his coffee with some distaste. The rim of the wax cup had become soggy. Wexford dropped the phone.

'My wife,' he said. 'Am I dead? Have I forgotten I've got a home of my own? She's run out of housekeeping and she can't find the cheque book.' He chuckled, felt in his pocket and produced it. 'No wonder. I'll have to nip back.' He added with sudden kindness, 'Go home and have a bit of shut-eye, why don't you?'

'I don't like being left in the air,' Burden grumbled. 'Now I know how my kids feel when I break off in the middle of a bedtime story.'

Wexford began bundling things into his briefcase.

'Leaving out all the circumstantial stuff,' he said, 'there isn't much more. I told you it was straight-forward. It was the evening of September 24th it happened, a cold wet Sunday. Mrs Primero had sent Alice off to church. She went at about a quarter past six, Painter being due to bring the coal at half past. He bought it all right and departed two hundred pounds to the good.'

'I'd like to hear the circumstantial stuff,' Burden said.

Wexford was at the door now.

'To be continued in our next,' he grinned, 'You can't say I'm leaving you in suspense.' The grin faded and his face hardened. 'Mrs Primero was found at seven. She was in the drawing room lying on the floor by the fireplace in a great pool of blood. There was blood on the walls and on her armchair, and in the heart was a blood-stained wood chopper.'

2

When sentence is given upon him let him be
condemned . . . let his children be fatherless
and his wife a widow.
Psalm 109, appointed for the 22nd Day

THE nap Wexford had prescribed for him would have
been attractive on a dull day, but not this morning when
the sky was blue and cloudless and the sun promised
tropical heat by mid-day. Moreover, Burden remembered that he had not made his bed for three days.
Better have that shower and that shave instead.

After a canteen breakfast of two eggs and a couple
of rashers of the greenback he liked, he had made up
his mind what he was going to do. An hour could
easily be spared. He drove northwards along the High
Street with all the car windows down, past the shops,
over the Kingsbrook Bridge, past the Olive and Dove
and out on to the Stowerton road. Apart from a new
house here and there, a supermarket on the site of
the old police station, and aggressive road signs all
over the place, things had not changed much in sixteen
years. The meadows, the tall trees burdened with the
heavy foliage of July, the little weatherboard cottages
were much the same as when Alice Flower had seen
them on her shopping trips in the Daimler. There
would have been less traffic, then, he thought. He
braked, pulled in and raised his eyebrows at the youth
on a motor-bike who, overtaking the on-coming stream,
had missed him by inches.

The lane where Victor's Piece was must be somewhere about here. Those circumstantial details Wexford had been so tantalising about were coming back to him from his own memory. Surely he had read about a bus stop and a telephone box at the end of the lane? Would these be the meadows he remembered reading that Painter had crossed, desperate to conceal a bundle of bloodstained clothing?

Here was the phone box now. He indicated left and turned slowly into the lane. For a short way its surface was metalled, then it petered out into a track ending in a gate. There were only three houses: a white-plastered semi-detached pair and opposite them the late Victorian pile he had described as 'a hideous dump'.

He had never been as near to it as this before, but he saw nothing to make him change his opinion. The roof of grey slates had been constructed—tortured almost—into a number of steep gables. Two of these dominated the front of the house, but there was a third on the right hand side and out of it grew another smaller one that apparently overlooked the back. Each gable was criss-crossed with timbering, some of it inexpertly carved into chevrons and all painted a dull bottle green. In places the plaster between the wood had fallen away, exposing rough pinkish brickwork. Ivy, of the same shade of green, spread its flat leaves and its rope-like grey tendrils from the foot of the downstairs windows to the highest gable where a lattice flapped open. There it had crept and burrowed into the mealy wall, prising the window frame away from the bricks.

Burden observed the garden with a countryman's eye. Never had he seen such a fine selection of weeds. The fertile black soil, cultivated and tended for many years, now nourished docks with leaves as thick and glossy as rubber plants, puce-headed thistles, nettles four feet tall. The gravel paths were choked with grass and mildewed groundsel. Only the clarity of the air and the soft brilliance of sunlight prevented the place from being actually sinister.

The front door was locked. No doubt this window

beside it belonged to the drawing room. Burden could not help wondering with a certain wry humour what insensitive administrator had decreed that this scene of an old woman's murder should be for years the home—indeed the last refuge—of other old women. But they were gone now. The place looked as if it had been empty for years.

Through the window he could see a large shadowy room. In the grate of the amber-coloured marble fireplace someone had prudently placed crumpled newspaper to catch the drifts of soot. Wexford had said there had been blood all over that fireplace. There, just in front of the copper kerb, was where the body must have lain.

He made his way round the side, pushing through a shrubbery where elders and strong little birches were threatening to oust the lilac. The panes in the kitchen casement were blurred with dirt and there was no kitchen door, only a back door that apparently opened off the end of the central passage. The Victorians, he reflected, were not too hot on design. Two doors with a straight passage between them! The draught would be appalling.

By now he was in the back garden but he literally could not see the wood for the trees. Nature had gone berserk at Victor's Piece and the coach house itself was almost totally obscured by creeper. He strolled across the shady flagged yard, made cool by the jutting walls of the house, and found himself skirting a conservatory, attached apparently to a kind of morning or breakfast room. It housed a vine, long dead and quite leafless.

So that was Victor's Piece. Pity he couldn't get inside, but he would, in any case, have to get back. Out of long habit—and partly to set a good example—he had closed all the windows of his car and locked the doors. Inside it was like an oven. He drove out of the broken gateway, into the lane and joined the traffic stream on the Stowerton road.

A greater contrast between the building he had left and the building he entered could hardly have been found. Fine weather suited Kingsmarkham Police Station. Wexford sometimes said that the architect of this new building must have designed it while holidaying in the South of France. It was white, boxy, unnecessarily vast and ornamented here and there with frescoes that owed something to the Elgin marbles.

On this July morning its whiteness glared and glistened. But if its façade seemed to welcome and bask in the sun its occupants did not. There was far too much glass. All right, said Wexford, for hothouse plants or tropical fish, but a mixed blessing for an elderly Anglo-Saxon policeman with high blood pressure and a low resistance to heat. The telephone receiver slid about in his large hand and when he had finished talking to Henry Archery he pulled down the venetian blinds.

'Heat wave's coming,' he said to Burden. 'I reckon your wife's picked a good week.'

Burden looked up from the statement he had begun to read. Lean as a greyhound, his face thin and acute, he often had the hound's instinct for scenting the unusual, coupled with a man's eager imagination.

'Things always seem to happen in a heat-wave,' he said. 'Our sort of things, I mean.'

'Get away,' said Wexford. 'Things are always happening around here.' He raised his spiky toothbrush brows. 'What's happening today,' he said, 'is Archery. He's coming at two.'

'Did he say what it's all about?'

'He's leaving that for this afternoon. Very la-di-da manner he's got with him. All part of the mystique of how to be a gentleman on nothing a year. One thing, he's got a transcript of the trial so I shan't have to go through the whole thing again.'

"That'll have cost him something. He must be keen.'

Wexford looked at his watch and rose. 'Got to get over to the court,' he said. 'Polish off those villains who lost me my night's sleep. Look, Mike, I reckon

we deserve a bit of gracious living and I don't fancy
the Carousel's steak pie for my lunch. What about
popping into the Olive and booking a table for one
sharp?'

Burden smiled. It suited him well enough. Once in a
blue moon Wexford would insist on their lunching or
even dining in comparative style.

'It shall be done,' he said.

The Olive and Dove is the best hostelry in Kingsmarkham that can properly be called an hotel. By a
stretch of the imagination the Queen's Head might be
described as an inn, but the Dragon and the Crusader
cannot claim to be more than pubs. The Olive, as locals
invariably call it, is situated in the High Street at the
Stowerton end of Kingsmarkham, facing the exquisite
Georgian residence of Mr Missal, the Stowerton car
dealer. It is partly Georgian itself, but it is a hybrid
structure with lingering relics of Tudor and a wing
that claims to be pre-Tudor. In every respect it con-
forms to what nice middle-class people mean when
they talk about a 'nice' hotel. There are always three
waiters, the chambermaids are staid and often elderly,
the bath water is hot, the food as well as can be
expected and the A.A. Guide has given it two stars.

Burden had booked his table by phone. When he
walked into the dining room just before one he saw
to his satisfaction that he had been placed by the High
Street window. Here it was just out of the sun and the
geraniums in the window box looked fresh and even
dewy. Girls waiting on the other side of the street for
the Pomfret bus wore cotton frocks and sandals.

Wexford marched in at five past. 'I don't know why
he can't get up at half twleve like they do in Sewingbury,' he grumbled. 'He' Burden knew, meant the
chairman of the Kingsmarkham bench. 'God, it was
hot in court. What are we going to eat?'

'Roast duck,' said Burden firmly.

'All right, if you twist my arm. As long as they
don't mix a lot of rubbish up with it. You know what
I mean, sweet corn and bananas.' He took the menu,

scowling. 'Look at that, Polynesian chicken. What do they think we are, aborigines?'

'I went and had a look at Victor's Piece this morning,' said Burden while they waited for the duck to come.

"Did you now? I see it's up for sale. There's a card in the agent's window with a highly misleading photograph. They're asking six thousand. Bit steep when you think Roger Primero got less than two for it in 1951.'

'I suppose it's changed hands several times since then?"

'Once or twice before the old folks moved in. Thanks,' he said to the waiter. 'No we don't want any wine. Two halves of bitter.' He spread his napkin over his capacious lap and to Burden's controlled distaste sprinkled wing and orange sauce liberally with pepper.

'Was Roger Primero the heir?'

'One of the heirs. Mrs Primero died intestate. Remember I told you she'd only got ten thousand to leave and that was divided equally between Roger and his two younger sisters. He's a rich man now, but however he got his money it wasn't from his grandmother. All kinds of pies he's got his finger in—oil, property development, shipping—he's a real tycoon.'

'I've seen him around, I think.'

'You must have. He's very conscious of his status as a landowner since he bought Forby Hall. Goes out with the Pomfret hounds and all that.'

'How old is he?' Burden asked.

'Well, he was twenty-two when his grandmother was killed. That makes him about thirty-eight now. The sisters were much younger. Angela was ten and Isabel nine.'

'I seem to remember he gave evidence at the trial.'

Wexford pushed his plate away, signalled rather imperiously to the waiter and ordered two portions of apple pie. Burden knew that his chief's notion of gracious living was somewhat limited.

'Roger Primero had been visiting his grandmother

that Sunday,' Wexford said. 'He was working in a solicitor's office in Sewingbury at the time and he used to make quite a habit of having Sunday tea at Victor's Piece. Maybe he had his eye on a share of the loot when Mrs. Primero went—God knows he hadn't a bean in those days—but he seemed genuinely fond of her. It's certainly a fact that after we'd seen the body and sent for him from Sewingbury as next of kin, we had to restrain him forcibly from going over to the coach house and laying violent hands on Painter. I daresay his grandmother and Alice made a lot of him, you know, buttered him up and waited on him. I told you Mrs. Primero had her affections. There'd been a family quarrel but apparently it didn't extend to the grandchildren. Once or twice Roger had taken his little sisters down to Victor's Piece and they'd all got on very well together.'

'Old people usually do get on well with kids,' said Burden.

'They had to be the right kind of children, Mike. Angela and Isabel, yes, and she had a very soft spot for young Liz Crilling.'

Burden put down his spoon and stared at the Chief Inspector.

'I thought you said you'd read all this up at the time?' Wexford said suspiciously. 'Don't say it was a long time ago. My customers are always saying that to me and it makes me see red. If you read the account of that trial you must remember that Elizabeth Crilling, aged precisely five at the time, found Mrs Primero's body.'

'I assure you I can't remember, sir.' That must have been the day he'd missed, the day he hadn't bothered with the papers because he'd been nervous about an interview. 'She didn't appear at the trial, surely?'

'Not at that age—there are limits. Besides, although she was actually the first to go into the drawing room and come upon the body, her mother was with her.'

'Digressing a little,' Burden said, 'I don't quite get this stuff about the right kind of children. Mrs. Crilling

lives over there in Glebe Road.' He turned to the
window and waved his hand in the direction of the
least attractive part of Kingsmarkham where long
streets of small terraced brown houses had sprung up
between the wars. 'She and the girl live in half a
house, they haven't a penny to bless themselves
with . . .'

'They've come down a lot,' said Wexford. 'In September 1950 Crilling himself was still alive—he died
of T.B. soon after—and they lived opposite Victor's
Piece.'

'In one of those white semi-detached places?'

'That's right. A Mrs White and her son lived next
door. Mrs. Crilling was about thirty at the time, little
bit over thirty.'

'You're joking,' said Burden derisively. 'That makes
her only in her late forties now.'

'Look, Mike, people can say what they like about
hard work and childbearing and all that. I tell you
there's nothing like mental illness to make a woman
look old before her time. And you know as well as I
do Mrs Crilling's been in and out of mental hospitals
for years.' He paused as their coffee came and pursed
his lips censoriously at the anaemic brown liquid.

'You did say black, sir?' the waiter asked.

Wexford gave a sort of grunt. The church clock
struck the last quarter. As the reverberation died away,
he said to Burden:

'Shall I keep the person waiting ten minutes?'

Burden said neutrally, 'That's up to you, sir. You
were going to tell me how Mrs Primero and the Crilling woman became friends. I suppose they were
friends?'

'Not a doubt of it. Mrs Crilling was ladylike enough
in those days and she had a way with her, sycophantic,
sucking up, *you* know. Besides, Crilling had been an
accountant or something, just enough of a professional
man, anyway, in Mrs Primero's eyes to make his wife
a lady. Mrs Crilling was always popping over to Victor's Piece and she always took the child with her. God

knows, they must have been pretty close. Elizabeth
called Mrs Primero "Granny Rose" just as Roger and
his sisters did.'

'So she "popped over" that Sunday night and found
Granny Rose dead?' Burden hazarded.

'It wasn't as simple as that. Mrs. Crilling had been
making the kid a party frock. She finished it by about
six, dressed Elizabeth up and wanted to take her over
and show her off to Mrs Primero. Mind you, she and
Alice Flower were always at loggerheads. There was a
good bit of jealousy there, spheres of influence and
so on. So Mrs Crilling waited until Alice had gone off
to church and went over alone, intending to go back
and fetch the child if Mrs Primero was awake. She
dozed a good bit, you see, being so old.

'That first time—it was about twenty past six—
Mrs Primero *was* asleep and Mrs Crilling didn't go in.
She's just tapped on the drawing room window. When
the old woman didn't stir she went back and returned
again later. By the way, she saw the empty scuttle
through the window so she knew Painter hadn't yet
been in with the coal.'

'You mean that Painter came in and did the deed
between Mrs Crilling's visits?' Burden said.

'She didn't go back again till seven. The back door
had to be left unlocked for Painter, so she and the
child went in, called out "yoo-hoo" or some damn'
thing, and marched into the drawing room when they
didn't get an answer. Elizabeth went first—more's the
pity—and Bob's your uncle!'

'Blimey,' said Burden, 'that poor kid!'

'Yes,' Wexford murmured, 'yes . . . Well, much as
I should like to while away the rest of the afternoon,
reminiscing over the coffee cups, I do have to see this
clerical bloke.'

They both got up. Wexford paid the bill, leaving a
rather obviously exact ten per cent for a tip.

'I can't see where the parson comes into it at all,'
Burden said when they were in the car.

'He can't be an abolitionist because they've done

away with the death penalty. As I say, he's writing a book, expects to make a big thing out of it and that's why he's laid out good money on a transcript.'

'Or he's a prospective buyer of Victor's Piece. He's a haunted house merchant and he thinks he's got another Borley Rectory.'

An unfamiliar car stood on the forecourt of the police station. The numberplate was not local and beside it was a little metal label that bore the name Essex with the county coat of arms of three scimitars on a red field.

'We shall soon know,' said Wexford.

3

There are false witnesses risen up against me
and such as speak wrong.
> *Psalm 27, appointed for the 5th Day*

IN general Wexford disliked the clergy. To him the dog collar was like a slipped halo, indicating a false saintliness, probably hypocrisy and massive self-regard. As he saw it vicars were not vicarious enough. Most of them expected you to worship God in them.

He did not associate them with good looks and charm. Henry Archery, therefore, caused him slight surprise. He was possibly not much younger than Wexford himself, but he was still slim and exceedingly good-looking, and he was wearing an ordinary rather light-coloured suit and an ordinary collar and tie. His hair was thick enough and fair enough for the grey not to show much, his skin was tanned and his features had a pure evenly cut regularity.

During the first preliminary small-talk remarks Wexford had noticed the beauty of his voice. You felt it would be a pleasure to hear him read aloud. As he showed him to a chair and sat down opposite him, Wexford chuckled to himself. He was picturing a group of tired ageing female parishioners working their fingers to the bone for the pitiful reward of this man's smile. Archery was not smiling now and he looked anything but relaxed.

'I'm familiar with the case, Chief Inspector,' he began. 'I've read the official transcript of the trial and I've discussed the whole thing with Colonel Griswold.'

"What exactly do you want to know, then?' Wexford asked in his blunt way.

Archery took a deep breath and said rather too quickly:

'I want you to tell me that somewhere in your mind there is just the faintest doubt, the shadow of a doubt, of Painter's guilt.'

So that was it, or part of it. Burden with his theories that the parson was a Primero relative or seeking to buy the Primero house couldn't have been more wrong. This man, whatever axe he might be grinding, was bent on whitewashing Painter.

Wexford frowned and after a moment said, 'Can't be done. Painter did it all right.' He set his jaw stubbornly, 'If you want to quote me in your book you're quite welcome. You can say that after sixteen years Wexford still maintains that Painter was guilty beyond the shadow of a doubt.'

'What book is this?' Archery inclined his handsome head courteously. His eyes were brown and now they looked bewildered. Then he laughed. It was a nice laugh and it was the first time Wexford had heard it. 'I don't write books,' he said. 'Well, I did once contribute a chapter to a work on Abyssinian cats but that hardly . . .'

Abyssinian cats. Bloody great red cats, thought Wexford. Whatever next? 'Why are you interested in Painter, Mr Archery?'

Archery hesitated. The sun showed up lines on his

face that Wexford had not realised were there. Funny, he thought ruefully, how dark women age slower than fair ones but the reverse was true of men.

'My reasons are very personal, Chief Inspector. I can't suppose that they would interest you. But I can assure you that there's no possibility of my publishing anything you tell me."

Well, he had promised Griswold—as to that, he didn't have much choice. Hadn't he, in any case, already resigned himself to giving up most of the afternoon to this clergyman? Weariness was at last beginning to gain a hold on him. He might be equal to reminiscing, going over past familiar words and scenes; on this hot afternoon he was quite unequal to anything more exacting. Probably the personal reasons—and he confessed mentally to an almost childish curiosity about them—would emerge in due course. There was something frank and boyish in his visitor's face which made Wexford think he would not be particularly discreet.

'What d'you want me to tell you?' he asked.

'Why you are so determined Painter was guilty. Of course I don't know any more about this sort of thing than the average layman, but it seems to me there were a good many gaps in the evidence. There were other people involved, people who had quite definite interests in Mrs Primero's death.'

Wexford said coldly, 'I'm fully prepared to go over any points with you, sir.'

'Now?'

'Certainly now. Have you got that transcript with you?'

Archery produced it from a very battered leather briefcase. His hands were long and thin but not womanish. They reminded Wexford of saints' hands in what he called 'churchy' paintings. For five minutes or so he scanned the papers in silence, refreshing his memory on tiny points. Then he put them down and raised his eyes to Archery's face.

'We have to go back to Saturday, September 23rd,' he said, 'the day before the murder. Painter didn't appear with the coal at all that evening. The two old women waited until nearly eight o'clock when the fire was almost out, and Mrs Primero said she would go to bed. Alice Flower was incensed at this and went out to get what she called "a few lumps".'

'That was when she hurt her leg,' Archery said eagerly.

'It wasn't a serious injury but it made Mrs Primero angry and she blamed Painter. At about ten on the following morning she sent Alice down to the coach house to tell Painter she wanted to see him at eleven thirty sharp. He came up ten minutes late, Alice showed him into the drawing room and afterwards she heard him and Mrs Primero quarrelling.'

'This brings me to the first point I want to raise,' Archery said. He flipped through the transcript and, putting his finger at the beginning of a paragraph, passed it to Wexford. 'This, as you know, is part of Painter's own evidence. He doesn't deny the quarrel. He admits that Mrs Primero threatened him with dismissal. He also says here that Mrs Primero finally came round to see his point of view. She refused to give him a rise because she said that would put ideas into his head and he would only ask for another increase in a few months' time. Instead she'd give him what she understood was called a bonus.'

'I remember all that well,' Wexford said impatiently. 'He said she told him to go upstairs and into her bedroom where he'd find a handbag in her wardrobe. He was to bring that handbag down to her and this, he said, he did. There was about two hundred pounds in the handbag and this he could have, take it away in the handbag and look upon it as a bonus on condition he was absolutely circumspect about bringing the coal at the required times.' He coughed. 'I never believed a word of it and neither did the jury.'

'Why not?' Archery asked quietly.

God, thought Wexford, this was going to be a long session.

'Firstly, because the stairs at Victor's Piece run up

between the drawing room and the kitchen. Alice Flower was in the kitchen cooking the lunch. She had remarkably good hearing for her age, but she never heard Painter go up those stairs. And, believe me, he was a big heavy lout if ever there was one.' Archery winced faintly at this but Wexford went on, 'Secondly, Mrs. Primero would never have sent the gardener upstairs to poke about in her bedroom. Not unless I'm very mistaken in her character. She would have got Alice to have fetched the money on some pretext or other.'

'She might not have wanted Alice to know about it.'

'That's for sure,' Wexford retorted sharply. 'She wouldn't have. I said on some pretext or other.' That made the parson draw in his horns. Wexford said very confidently, 'In the third place Mrs Primero had a reputation for being rather mean. Alice had been with her for half a century but she'd never given Alice anything bar her wages and an extra pound at Christmas.' He jabbed at the page. 'Look, she says so here in black and white. We know Painter wanted money. The night before when he hadn't brought the coal he'd been drinking up at the Dragon with a pal of his from Stowerton. The pal had a motor-bike to sell and he'd offered it to Painter for a bit less than two hundred pounds. Apparently Painter hadn't a hope of getting the money but he asked his friend to hold on to the bike for a couple of days and he'd contact him the minute anything came up. You're saying he got the money before noon on Sunday. I say he stole it after he brutally murdered his employer in the evening. If you're right, why didn't he get in touch with his friend on Sunday afternoon? There's a phone box at the bottom of the lane. We checked with the pal, he didn't move out of his house all day and the phone never rang.'

It was a very tempest of fact and Archery yielded, or appeared to yield, before it. He said only:

'You're saying, I think, that Painter went to the

wardrobe after he'd killed Mrs. Primero in the evening. There was no blood on the inside of the wardrobe.'

'For one thing he wore rubber gloves to do the deed. Anyway, the prosecution's case was that he stunned her with the flat side of the axe blade, took the money, and when he came downstairs, finished her off in a panic.'

Archery gave a slight shiver. 'Doesn't it strike you as odd,' he then said, 'that if Painter did it he should have been so transparent about it?'

'Some are. They're stupid, you see.' Wexford said it derisively, his mouth curling. He still had no notion what Archery's interest in Painter might be, but that he was pro-Painter was apparent. 'Stupid,' he said again, intent on flicking the clergyman on the raw. Another wince from Archery rewarded him. 'They think you'll believe them. All they've got to say is it must have been a tramp or a burglar and you'll go away satisfied. Painter was one of those. That old tramp thing,' he said. 'When did you last *see* a tramp? More than sixteen years ago, I'll bet.'

'Let's come to the murder itself,' Archery said quietly.

'By all means.' Again Wexford took the transcript, gathering with a quick glance the information he needed. 'Now, then,' he began, 'Painter said he went over to fetch the coal at half six. He remembered the time—twenty-five past six when he left the coach house—because his wife said five minutes to go before the child's bedtime. The time's not all that important, anyway. We know it was between twenty past six and seven o'clock that she was killed. Painter went over, chopped some wood and cut his finger. Or so he said. He certainly did cut his finger—cut it deliberately.'

Archery ignored this last. 'He and Mrs Primero belonged to the same blood group,' he said.

'They were both Group O. They weren't quite so accurate about the minute grouping of blood sixteen years ago as they are now. It was handy for Painter, that. But it didn't do him any real good.'

The clergyman crossed his legs and leaned back. Wexford could see he was trying to appear relaxed and making a poor job of it. 'I believe you personally went to interview Painter after the crime was discovered?'

'We were round at the coach house by a quarter to eight. Painter was out. I asked Mrs Painter where he was and she said he'd come back from the big house some time after six-thirty, washed his hands and gone straight out again. He'd told her he was going to Stowerton to see his friend. We'd only been there about ten minutes when he came in. His story didn't stand up, there was far too much blood around to have come from a cut finger and—well, you know the rest. It's all down there. I charged him on the spot.'

The transcript fluttered a little in Archery's hand. He could not keep his fingers quite steady. 'In evidence,' he said, speaking slowly and evenly, 'Painter said he hadn't been to Stowerton. "I waited at the bus stop at the end of the lane, but the bus never came. I saw the police cars turn into the lane and I wondered what was up. Presently I felt a bit faint on account of my finger bleeding a lot. I came back to my flat. I thought my wife might know what it was all about." ' After a pause, he added with a kind of pleading eagerness, 'That doesn't sound like the evidence of the complete moron you make him out to be.'

Wexford answered him patiently as if he were talking to a precocious teenager. 'They edit these things, Mr Archery. They condense them, make them sound coherent. Believe me. You weren't in court and I was. As to the truth of that statement. I was in one of those police cars and I was keeping my eyes open. We overtook the Stowerton bus and turned left into the lane. There wasn't anyone waiting at that bus stop.'

'I imagine you mean that while he said he was at the bus stop he was in fact hiding some clothes.'

'Of course he was hiding the clothes! When he was

working he habitually wore a raincoat. You'll see that in Mrs Crilling's evidence and in Alice's. Sometimes it hung in the coach house and sometimes on a hook behind the back door of Victor's Piece. Painter said he had worn it that evening and had left it hanging on the back door. That raincoat couldn't be found. Both Alice and Roger Primero said they remembered having seen it on the back door that afternoon, but Mrs Crilling was certain it wasn't there when she brought Elizabeth in at seven.'

'You finally found the raincoat rolled up in a ball under a hedge two fields away from the bus stop.'

'The raincoat plus a pullover,' Wexford retorted, 'and a pair of rubber gloves. The lot was sodden with blood.'

'But anyone could have worn the raincoat and you couldn't identify the pullover.'

'Alice Flower went so far as to say it looked like one Painter sometimes wore.'

Archery gave a deep sigh. For a time he had been firing questions and statements briskly at Wexford, but suddenly he had fallen silent. Little more than indecision showed on his face. Wexford waited. At last, he thought, Archery had reached a point where it was going to become necessary to reveal those 'personal reasons'. A struggle was going on within him and he said in an artificial tone:

'What about Painter's wife?'

'A wife cannot be compelled to give evidence against her husband. As you know, she didn't appear at the trial. She and the child went off somewhere and a couple of years later I heard she'd married again.'

He stared at Archery, raising his eyebrows. Something he had said had made the clergyman's mind up for him. A slight flush coloured Archery's even tan. The brown eyes were very bright as he leaned forward, tense again.

'That child . . .'

'What of her? She was asleep in her cot when we

searched Painter's bedroom and that's the only time I saw her. She was four or five.'

Archery said jerkily, 'She's twenty-one now and she's a very beautiful young woman.'

'I'm not surprised. Painter was a nice enough looking fellow if you like the type, and Mrs Painter was pretty.' Wexford stopped. Archery was a clergyman. Had Painter's daughter taken after her father and somehow come into his care as a result of her transgressions? Archery could be a prison visitor. It was right up his street, Wexford thought nastily. Anger rose in his throat as he wondered if all this sparring discussion had been engineered merely because Archery wanted his help in getting the right psychological approach to a convicted thief or confidence woman. 'What about her?' he snapped. Griswold could go to hell! 'Now come on, sir, you'd better tell me and have done.'

'I have a son, Chief Inspector, an only child. He also is twenty-one . . .'

'Well?'

Obviously the clergyman had difficulty in framing the words. He hesitated and pressed his long hands together. At last he said diffidently and in a low voice, 'He wishes to marry Miss Painter.' When Wexford started and stared at him, he added, 'or Miss Kershaw, as her legal name now is.'

Wexford was all at sea. He was astonished, a rare thing for him, and he felt a sharp-edged excitement. But he had shown all the surprise he thought consistent with policy and now he spoke soberly.

'You must excuse me, Mr Archery, but I can't see how your son, the son of an Anglican clergyman, came to meet a girl in Miss Painter's—er, Miss Kershaw's —position.'

'They met at Oxford,' Archery said easily.

'At the *university?*'

'That is so. Miss Kershaw is quite an intelligent young woman.' Archery gave a slight smile. 'She's reading Modern Greats. Tipped for a First, I'm told.'

4

If any of you know cause or just impediment
why these two persons should not be joined together in holy matrimony, ye are to declare it.

The Banns of Marriage

If he had been asked to predict the future of such a
one as Theresa Painter, what would he have foreseen
for her? Children like her, Wexford reflected as he
recovered from his second shock, children like Painter's
little girl started life with a liability and a stain. The
surviving parent, well-meaning relatives and cruel
schoolfellows often made matters worse. He had hardly thought about the fate of the child until today. Now,
thinking quickly, he supposed he would have counted
her lucky to have become an anonymous manual
worker with perhaps already a couple of petty con-
victions.

Instead to Theresa Painter had apparently come the
greatest blessings of civilised life: brains, advanced
education, beauty, friendship with people like this
vicar, an engagement to this vicar's son.

Wexford cast his mind back to the first of only
three encounters with Mrs Painter. A quarter to eight
it had been on that Sunday in September. He and the
sergeant with him had knocked on the door at the
foot of the coach house stairs and Mrs Painter had
come down to let them in. Whatever might have been
fashionable in London at that time, the young women
of Kingsmarkham were still doing their hair in a big
pile on the forehead with tight curls falling to the

34

shoulders. Mrs Painter was no exception. Hers was
naturally fair, her face was powdered and her mouth
painted diffidently red. Respectable provincial matrons
did not go in for eye make-up in 1950 and Mrs Painter
was of all things respectable. There seemed to be very
little else to her. On her dry fine skin lines had already
begun to form, little indentations which marked a
regular prudish pursing of the lips, a setting of the
chin that accompanied an outraged flounce.

She had the same attitude to the police as others
might have to bugs or mice. When they came upstairs
she alternated her replies to their questions with reiterated remarks that it was a disgrace to have them
in the house. She had the blankest, most obtuse blue
eyes he had ever seen on anyone. At no time, even
when they were about to take Painter away, did she
show the least pity or the least horror, only this fixated
dread of what people would think if they found the
police had been questioning her husband.

Perhaps she had not been so stupid as he had
thought. Somewhere in that pretty respectable mouse
and that great hunk of sub-humanity, her husband,
must have been the spring from which their daughter
drew her intelligence. 'Quite an intelligent girl,' Archery had said casually. Good God, thought Wexford,
remembering how he had boasted when his own daughter got eight O Level passes. Good God! What were
Modern Greats, anyway? Were they the same as Mods
and did that mean Modern Languages? He had a vague
idea that this might be the esoteric and deliberately
deceptive name given to Philosophy and Political
Economy. He wouldn't show his ignorance to Archery.
Philosophy! He almost whistled. Painter's daughter
reading—yes, that was the term, reading—philosophy!
It made you think all right. Why, it made you doubt . . .

'Mr Archery,' he said, 'you're quite sure this *is*
Herbert Arthur Painter's girl?'

'Of course I'm sure, Chief Inspector. She told me.'
He looked almost defiantly at Wexford. Perhaps he
thought the policeman would laugh at his next words.

'She is as good as she is beautiful,' he said. Wexford's expression remained unaltered. 'She came to stay with us at Whitsun. It was the first time we'd seen her, though naturally our son had written to us and told us about her. We took to her at once.

'Chief Inspector, times have changed since I was at college. I had to face the possibility that my son would meet some girl at Oxford, perhaps want to marry her at an age when I'd thought of myself as still a boy and when Orders were a lifetime away. I'd see my friends' children marry at twenty-one and I was prepared to try and manage something for him, give him something to start life on. All I hoped was that the girl would be someone we could like and understand.

'Miss Kershaw—I'll use that name if you don't mind —is just what I would have chosen for him myself, beautiful, graceful, well-mannered, easy to talk to. Oh, she does her best to hide her looks in the uniform they all wear nowadays, long shaggy hair, trousers, great black duffel coat—you know the kind of thing, But they all dress like that. The point is she can't hide them.

'My wife is a little impulsive. She was hinting about the wedding before Theresa had been with us for twenty-four hours. I found it hard to understand why the young people were so diffident about it. Charles's letters had been paeans of praise and I could see they were deeply in love. Then she told us. She came out with it quite baldly. She said—I remember the very words—"I think you ought to know something about me, Mrs Archery. My father's name was Painter and he was hanged for killing an old woman."

'At first my wife didn't believe it. She thought it was some sort of a game. Charles said, "It's true. It doesn't matter. People are what they are, not what their parents did." Then Theresa—we call her Tess—said, "It would matter if he had done it, only he didn't. I told you *why* he was hanged. I didn't mean he'd done it." Then she began to cry.'

'Why does she call herself Kershaw?'

'It's her stepfather's name. He must be a very remarkable man, Chief Inspector. He's an electrical engineer, but . . .' You needn't come that rude mechanicals stuff with me, thought Wexford crossly. '. . . but he must be a most intelligent, perceptive and kind person. The Kershaws have two children of their own, but as far as I can gather, Mr. Kershaw has treated Tess with no less affection than his own son and daughter. She says it was his love that helped her to bear—well, what I can only call the stigma of her father's crime when she learnt about it at the age of twelve. He followed her progress at school, encouraged her in every way and fostered her wish to get a County Major Scholarship.'

'You mentioned "the stigma of her father's crime". I thought you said she thinks he didn't do it?'

'My dear Chief Inspector, she *knows he didn't do it.*'

Wexford said slowly, 'Mr Archery, I'm sure I don't have to tell a man like yourself that when we talk of somebody *knowing* something we mean that what they know is a fact, something that's true beyond a reasonable doubt. We mean that the majority of other people *know* it too. In other words, it's history, it's written down in books, it's common knowledge.' He paused. 'Now I and the Law Lords and the official records and what your son means when he talks about the Establishment, know beyond any reasonable doubt, that Painter did kill Miss Rose Primero.'

'Her mother told her so,' said Archery. 'She told her that she had absolute irrefutable personal knowledge that Tess's father did not kill Mrs Primero.'

Wexford shrugged and smiled. 'People believe what they want to believe. The mother thought it was the best thing for her daughter. If I'd been in her shoes I daresay I'd have said the same.'

'I don't think it was like that,' Archery said stubbornly. 'Tess says her mother is a very unemotional woman. She never talks about Painter, never discusses him at all. She just says quite calmly, "Your father never killed anybody" and beyond that she won't say any more.'

'Because she can't say any more. Look, sir, I think you're taking a rather romantic view of this. You're visualising the Painters as a devoted couple, kind of merry peasants, love in a cottage and all that. It wasn't like that. Believe me, Painter was no loss to her. I'm certain in my own mind he was in the habit of striking her just when the fancy took him. As far as he was concerned, she was just his woman, someone to cook his meals, wash his clothes and—well,' he added brutally, 'someone to go to bed with.'

Archery said stiffly, 'I don't see that any of that's material.'

'Don't you? You're picturing some sort of declaration of innocence plus incontrovertible proof made to the one person he loved and whom he knew would believe in him. Forgive me, but that's a load of rubbish. Apart from the few minutes when he came back to the coach house to wash his hands—and incidentally hide the money—he was never alone with her. And he couldn't have told her then. He wasn't supposed to know about it. D'you understand me? He could have told her he had done it, he couldn't have told her he had *not*.

'Then we came. We found blood flecks in the sink and faint blood marks on the kitchen wall where he'd stripped off that pullover. As soon as he came back he took the bandage off his hand to show us the cut and he handed the bandage to his wife. But he didn't speak to her, didn't even appeal to her for support. He made just one reference to her . . .'

'Yes?'

'We found the handbag with the money in it under the mattress in their double bed. Why hadn't Painter told his wife if he'd been given that money in the morning? Here it is, find it in your transcript. "I knew the wife would want to get her hooks on it. She was always nagging me to buy things for the flat." That's all he said and he didn't even look at her. We charged him and he said, "O.K., but you're making a big mistake. It was a tramp done it." He came straight down the stairs with us. He didn't kiss his wife and he didn't ask to go in and see his child.'

'She must have seen him in prison?'

'With a prison officer present. Look, sir, you appear to be satisfied and so do all the parties concerned. Surely that's the main thing. You must forgive me if I can't agree with you."

Silently Archery took a snapshot from his wallet and laid it on the desk. Wexford picked it up. Presumably it had been taken in the vicarage garden. There was a great magnolia tree in the background, a tree as tall as the house it partly concealed. It was covered with waxen cup flowers. Under its branches stood a boy and a girl, their arms round each other. Tht boy was tall and fair. He was smiling and he was plainly Archery's son. Wexford wasn't particularly interested in him.

The girl's face was in sad repose. She was looking into the camera with large steady eyes. Light-coloured hair fell over her forehead in a fringe and down to the shoulders of a typical undergraduate's shirtwaister, faded, tightly belted and with a crumpled skirt. Her waist was tiny, her bust full. Wexford saw the mother again, only this girl was holding a boy's hand instead of a bloody rag.

'Very charming,' he said dryly. "I hope she'll make your son happy.' He handed the photograph back. 'No reason why she shouldn't.'

A mixture of emotions, anger, pain, resentment, flared in the clergyman's eyes. Interestedly, Wexford watched him.

'I do not know what or whom to believe,' Archery said unhappily, 'and while I'm in this state of uncertainty, Chief Inspector, I'm not in favour of the marriage. No, that's putting it too coolly.' He shook his head vehemently. 'I'm bitterly, bitterly against it,' he said.

'And the girl, Painter's daughter?'

'She believed—perhaps accepts is the better word
—in her father's innocence, but she realises others
may not. When it comes to it, I don't think she would
marry my son while his mother and I feel as we do.'

'What are you afraid of, Mr. Archery?'

'Heredity.'

'A very chancy thing, heredity.'

'Have you children, Chief Inspector?'

'I've got two girls.'

'Are they married?'

'One is.'

'And who is her father-in-law?'

For the first time Wexford felt superior to this
clergyman. A kind of *schadenfreude* possessed him.
'He's an architect, as a matter of fact, Tory councillor
for the North Ward here.'

'I see.' Archery bowed his head. 'And do your
grandchildren already build palaces with wooden bricks,
Mr Wexford?' Wexford said nothing. The only sign
of his first grandchild's existence was so far envinced
in its mother's morning sickness. 'I shall watch mine
from their cradle, waiting to see them drawn towards
objects with sharp edges.'

'You said if you objected she wouldn't marry him.'

'They're in love with each other. I can't . . .'

'Who's going to know? Palm Kershaw off as her
father.'

'I shall know,' said Archery. 'Already I can see
Painter when I look at her. Instead of her mouth and
her eyes I can see his thick lips and his bloodlust. It's
the same blood, Chief Inspector, the blood that mingled with Mrs Primero's, on the floor, on the clothes,
down the water pipes. That blood will be in my grandchild.' He seemed to realise that he had allowed himself to be carried away, for he stopped suddenly,
blushed, and shut his eyes briefly as if wincing at the
sight he had described.

Wexford said gently, 'I wish I could help you, Mr
Archery, but the case is closed, over, finished. There
is nothing more I can do.'

Archery shrugged and quoted softly, almost as if he could not stop himself, ' "He took water and washed his hands before the multitude, saying, I am innocent of the blood of this just person . . ." ' Then he jumped up, his expression suddenly contrite. 'Forgive me, Chief Insperor. That was an appalling thing to say. May I tell you what I intend to do?'

'Pontius Pilate, that's me,' said Wexford. 'So see you show more respect in future.'

Burden grinned. 'What exactly did he want, sir?'

'Firstly to tell him Painter may have been unjustly executed, which I can't. Damn it all, it would be tantamount to saying I didn't know my job. It was my first murder case, Mike, and it was fortunate for me it was so straightforward. Archery's going to do a spot of enquiry on his own. Hopeless after sixteen years but it's useless telling him. Secondly, he wanted my permission to go around hunting up all the witnesses. Wanted my support if they come round here, complaining and foaming at the mouth.'

'And all he's got to go on,' said Burden thoughtfully, 'is Mrs Painter's sentimental belief in her husband's innocence?'

'Aah, that's nothing! That's a load of hooey. If you got the chop, wouldn't Jean tell John and Pat you were innocent? Wouldn't my wife tell the girls? It's natural. Painter didn't make any last-minute confessions—you know what the prison authorities are like for watching out for things like that. No, she dreamed it up and convinced herself.'

'Has Archery ever met her?'

'Not yet, but he's making a day of it. She and her second husband live in Purley and he's got himself an invite for tea.'

'You say the girl told him at Whitsun. Why has he waited so long? It must be a couple of months.'

'I asked him that. He said that for the first couple of weeks he and his wife just let it ride. They thought the son might see reason. But he wouldn't. He got his father to get hold of a transcript of the trial, nagged him into working on Griswold. Of course he's an only child and as spoilt as they come. The upshot was that Archery promised to start poking his nose into it as soon as he got his fortnight's holiday.'

'So he'll be back?'

'That will depend on Mrs Painter,' said Wexford.

5

. . . That they may see their children christian-
ly and virtuously brought up.
The Solemnisation of Matrimony

THE Kershaws' house was about a mile from the town centre, separated from shops, station, cinema and churches by thousands of other large suburban villas. For number 20 Craig Hill was large, half-heartedly Georgian and built of raspberry red brick. The garden was planted with annuals, the lawn was clover-free and the dead heads had been nipped off the standard rose bushes. On the concrete drive a boy of about twelve was washing down a large white Ford.

Archery parked his car at the kerb. Unlike Wexford he had not yet seen the coach house at Victor's Piece, but he had read about it and it seemed to him that Mrs. Kershaw had climbed high. Sweat started on his forehead and his upper lip as he got out of the car. He told himself that it was unusually hot and that he had always been prone to feel the heat.

'This is Mr Kershaw's house, isn't it?' he asked the boy.

'That's right.' He was very like Tess, but his hair

was fairer and his nose was freckled. 'The front door's open. Shall I give him a shout?'

'My name is Archery,' said the clergyman and he held out his hand.

The boy wiped his hands on his jeans. 'Hallo,' he said.

By now a little wrinkled man had come down the porch steps. The bright hot air seemed to hang between them. Archery tried not to feel disappointment. What had he expected? Certainly not someone so small, so unfinished looking and so wizened as this scrawny creature in old flannels and tieless knitted shirt. Then Kershaw smiled and the years fell from him. His eyes were a bright sparkling blue, his uneven teeth white and clean.

'How do you do?'

'Good afternoon, Mr Archery. I'm very happy to meet you. As a matter of fact I've been sitting in the window, looking for you.'

In this man's presence it was impossible not to feel hope, cheerfulness almost. Archery detected at once a rare quality in him, a quality he had come upon perhaps only half a dozen times in his life. This was a man who was interested in all things. Energy and enthusiasm radiated from him. On a winter's day he would warm the air. Today, in this heat, his vitality was overwhelming.

'Come inside and meet my wife.' His voice was a hot breeze, a cockney voice that suggested fish and chips, eels and mash and East End pubs. Following him into the square panelled hall, Archery wondered how old he was. Perhaps no more than forty-five. Drive, the fire of life, lack of sleep because sleep wasted time, could prematurely have burnt away his youth. 'We're in the lounge,' he said, pushing open a reeded glass door. 'That's what I like about a day like this. When I get home from work I like to sit by the french windows for ten minutes and look at the garden. Makes you feel all that slogging in the winter was worthwhile.'

'To sit in the shade and look upon verdure?' After the words were out Archery was sorry he had spoken. He didn't want to put this suburban engineer in a false position.

Kershaw gave him a quick glance. Then he smiled and said easily, 'Miss Austen certainly knew what she was talking about, didn't she?' Archery was overcome. He went into the room and held out his hand to the woman who had got up from an armchair.

'My wife. This is Mr Archery, Rene.'

'How do you do?'

Irene Kershaw said nothing, but holding out her hand, smiled a tight bright smile. Her face was Tess's face as it would be when time had hardened it and finished it. In her youth she had been blonde. Now her hair, evidently set that day and perhaps in his honour, was dyed a dull leaf-brown and arranged in unreal feathery wisps about her forehead and ears.

'Sit down, Mr Archery,' said Kershaw. 'We won't keep you a minute for your tea. Kettle's on, isn't it, Rene?'

Archery sat in an armchair by the window. Kershaw's garden was full of experimental rose pergolas, eruptions of rockery and stone sporting geraniums. He gave the room a quick glance, noting at once its cleanliness and the enormous mass of things which had to be kept clean. Books abounded, Readers' Digests, encyclopaedias, dictionaries, works on astronomy, deep sea fishing, European history. There was a tank of tropical fish on a corner table, several model aircraft on the mantelpiece; stacks of sheet music covered the grand piano, and on an easel was a half-finished, rather charming, portrait in oils of a young girl. It was a large room, conventionally furnished with Wilton carpet and chintz covers, but it expressed the personality of the master of the house.

'We've had the pleasure of meeting your Charlie,' said Kershaw. 'A nice unassuming boy. I liked him.' Charlie! Archery sat very still, trying not to feel affronted. Charles's eligibility, after all, was not in question.

Quite suddenly Rene Kershaw spoke. 'We all like him,' she said. Her accent was just the same as Wexford's. 'But I'm sure I don't know how they plan to manage, what with everything being such an awful price—the cost of living, you know—and Charles not having a job in line . . .' Archery felt amazement. Was she really concerned with this trivia? He began to wonder how he would broach the subject that had brought him to Purley. 'I mean where will they live?' Mrs Kershaw asked primly. 'They're just babies really. I mean, you've got to have a home of your own, haven't you? You've got to get a mortgage and . . .'

'I think I can hear the kettle, Rene,' said her husband.

She got up, holding her skirt modestly down to cover her knees. It was a very suburban skirt of some permanently pleated material banded in muted blue and heather pink and of dead sexless respectability. With it she wore a short-sleeved pink jumper and around her neck a single string of cultured pearls. If cultured meant tended and nurtured, Archery thought he had never seen such obviously cultured pearls. Each night, he was sure, they were wrapped in tissue and put away in the dark. Mrs Kershaw smelt of talcum powder, some of which lingered in the lines of her neck.

'I don't think we've got to the mortgage stage yet,' said Kershaw when she had gone. Archery gave a wry smile. 'Believe me, Mr Archery, I know you haven't come here just for an in-laws' get-together over the tea cups.'

'I'm finding it more awkward than I thought possible.'

Kershaw chuckled. "I daresay. I can't tell you anything about Tess's father that isn't common knowledge, that wasn't in the papers at the time. You know that?'

'But her mother?'

'You can try. At times like this women see things through a cloud of orange blossom. She's never been very keen on Tess being an educated woman. She wants to see her married and she'll do her best to see nothing stands in her way.'

'And you, what do you want?'

'Me? Oh, I want to see her happy. Happiness doesn't necessarily begin at the altar.' Suddenly he was brisk and forthright. 'Frankly, Mr Archery, I'm not sure if she can be happy with a man who suspects her of homicidal tendencies before she's even engaged to him.'

'It isn't like that!' Archery hadn't expected the other man to put him on the defensive. 'Your stepdaughter is perfect in my son's eyes. I'm making the inquiries, Mr. Kershaw. My son knows that, he wants it for Tess's sake, but he doesn't even know I'm here. Put yourself in my position . . .'

'But I *was* in your position. Tess was only six when I married her mother.' He looked quickly at the door, then leaned closer to Archery. 'D'you think I didn't watch her, look out for the disturbance to show itself? When my own daughter was born Tess was very jealous. She resented the baby and one day I found her leaning over Jill's pram striking her on the head with a celluloid toy. Luckily, it *was* a celluloid toy.'

'But, good heavens . . . !' Archery felt the pallor drawing at his face muscles.

'What could I do? I had to go to work and leave the children. I had to trust my wife. Then we had a son —I think you bumped into him outside cleaning the car—and Jill resented him in just the same way and with just the same violence. All children behave like this, that's the point.'

'You never saw any more—any more of these tendencies?'

'Tendencies? A personality isn't made by heredity, Mr Archery, but by environment. I wanted Tess to have the best sort of environment and I think I can say, with all due modesty, that she has.'

The garden shimmered in the heat haze. Archery saw things he hadn't noticed at first, chalk lines on the lawn, where, regardless of herbaceous borders, the grass had been marked out for a tennis court; a shambles of rabbit hutches attached to the garage wall; an ancient swing. Behind him on the mantelpiece he saw propped against ornaments two party invitations. A framed photograph above it showed three children in shirts and jeans sprawled on a haystack. Yes, this had been the best of all possible enviroments for the murderer's orphan.

The door was pushed open and the girl in the portrait came in pushing a tea trolley. Archery who was too hot and troubled to feel hungry, saw with dismay that it was laden with homebaked pastries, strawberries in glass dishes, fairy cakes in paper cases. The girl looked about fourteen. She was not so beautiful as Tess and she wore a bunchy school tunic, but her father's vitality illumined her face.

'This is my daughter Jill.'

Jill sprawled in a chair, showing a lot of long leg.

'Now sit, nicely, dear,' said Mrs Kershaw sharply. She gave the girl a repressive look and began to pour tea, holding the pot with curled fingers. 'They don't realise they're young women at thirteen these days, Mr Archery.' Archery was embarrassed but the girl didn't seem to care. 'You must have one of these cakes. Jill made them.' Unwillingly he took a pastry. 'That's right. I've always said to both my girls, schooling is all very well in its way, but algebra won't cook the Sunday dinner. Tess and Jill are both good plain cooks . . .'

'Mummy! I'm not plain and Tess certainly isn't.'

'You know what I mean. Now don't take me up on everything. When they get married their husbands won't be ashamed to have anybody for a meal.'

'This is my managing director, darling,' said Jill pertly. 'Just cut a slice off him and put it under the grill, will you?'

Kershaw roared with laughter. Then he took his wife's hand. 'You leave Mummy alone.' All this jollity and family intimacy was making Archery nervous. He forced a smile and knew it looked forced.

'What I really mean is, Mr Archery,' said Mrs

Kershaw earnestly, 'is that even if your Charlie and my Tessie have their ups and downs at first, Tess hasn't been brought up to be an idle wife. She'll put a happy home before luxuries.'

'I'm sure she will.' Archery looked helplessly at the lounging girl, firmly entrenched in her chair and devouring strawberries and cream. It was now or never. 'Mrs Kershaw, I don't doubt Theresa's suitability as a wife . . .' No, that wasn't right. That was just what he did doubt. He floundered. 'I wanted to talk to you about . . .' Surely Kershaw would help him? Jill's brows drew together in a small frown and her grey eyes stared steadily at him. Desperately he said, 'I wanted to speak to you alone.'

Irene Kershaw seemed to shrink. She put down her cup, laid her knife delicately across her plate and, folding her hands, in her lap, looked down at them. They were poor hands, stubby and worn, and she wore just one ring, her second wedding ring.

'Haven't you got any homework to do, Jill?' she asked in a whisper. Kershaw got up, wiping his mouth.

'I can do it in the train,' said Jill.

Archery had begun to dislike Kershaw, but he could not help admiring him. 'Jill, you know all about Tess,' Kershaw said, 'what happened when she was little. Mummy has to discuss it with Mr Archery. Just by themselves. We have to go because, although we're involved, it's not quite our business. Not like it is theirs. O.K.?'

'O.K.' said Jill. Her father put his arm round her and took her into the garden.

He had to begin, but he was hot and stiff with awkwardness. Outside the window Jill had found a tennis racquet and was practising shots against the garage wall. Mrs Kershaw picked up a napkin and dabbed at the corners of her mouth. She looked at him, their eyes met, and she looked away. Archery felt suddenly that they were not alone, that their thoughts concentrated on the past, had summoned from its

prison grave a presence of brute strength that stood
behind their chairs, laying a bloody hand on their
shoulders and listening for judgment.

'Tess says you have something to tell me,' he said
quietly. 'About your first husband.' She was rolling
the napkin now, squashing it, until it was like a golf-
ball. 'Mrs Kershaw, I think you ought to tell me.'

The paper ball was tipped soundlessly on to an
empty plate. She put her hand up to her pearls.

'I never speak of him, Mr Archery. I prefer to let the
past be the past.'

'I know it's painful—it must be. But if we could
discuss it just once and get it over, I promise I'll never
raise the subject again.' He realised that he was speaking as if they would meet again and often, as if they
were already connected by marriage. He was also
speaking as if he had confidence in her word. 'I've
been to Kingsmarkham today and . . .'

She clutched at the straw. 'I suppose they've built
it all up and spoiled it.'

'Not really,' he said. Please God, don't let her
digress!

'I was born near there,' she said. He tried to stifle a
sigh. 'A funny little sleepy place it was, my village. I
reckon I thought I'd live and die there. You can't tell
what life will bring forth, can you?'

'Tell me about Tess's father.'

She dropped her hands from fidgeting with the pearls
and rested them in her respectable blue lap. When she
turned to him her face was dignified, almost ridiculously prim and shuttered. She might have been a mayoress,
taking the chair at some parochial function, clearing her
throat preparatory to addressing the Townswomen's
Guild. 'Madam chairman, ladies . . .' she should have
begun. Instead she said:

'The past is the past, Mr Archery.' He knew then
that it was hopeless. 'I appreciate your difficulty, but
I really can't speak of it. He was no murderer, you'll
have to take my word. He was a good kind man who
wouldn't have harmed a fly.' It was curious, he thought,

how she jumbled together old village phrases with platform jargon. He waited, then burst out:

'But how do you know? How *can* you know? Mrs Kershaw, did you see something or hear something . . . ?'

The pearls had gone up to her mouth and her teeth closed over the string. As it snapped pearls sprayed off in all directions, into her lap, across the tea things, on to the carpet. She gave a small refined laugh, petulant and apologetic. 'Look what I've done now!' In an instant she was on her knees, retrieving the scattered beads and dropping them into a saucer.

'I'm very keen on a white wedding.' Her face bounced up from behind the tea trolley. Politeness demanded that he too should get on his knees and help in the hunt. 'Get your wife to back me up, will you? Oh, thanks so much. Look, there's another one, just by your left foot.' He scrambled round after her on all fours. Her eyes met his under the overhanging cloth. 'My Tess is quite capable of getting married in jeans if the fancy takes her. Would you mind if we had the reception here? It's such a nice big room.'

Archery got up and handed her three more pearls. When the tennis ball struck the window he jumped. The sound had been like a pistol shot.

'Now, that's quite enough, Jill,' said Mrs Kershaw sharply. Still holding the saucer full of pearls, she opened the window. 'If I've told you once, I've told you fifty times, I don't want any more breakages.'

Archery looked at her. She was annoyed, affronted, even slightly outraged. He wondered suddenly if this was how she had looked on that Sunday night long ago when the police had invaded her domain at the coach house. Was she capable of any emotion greater than this, of mere irritation at disturbance of her personal peace?

'You just can't settle to a quiet discussion with children about, can you?' she said.

Within an instant, as if at a cue, the whole family was upon them, Jill truculent and protesting, the boy he had encountered on the drive now demanding tea, and Kershaw himself, vibrant as ever, his little lined face showing a certain dry acuteness.

'Now, you're to come straight out and give me a hand with these dishes, Jill.' The saucer was transferred to the mantelpiece and stuck between an Oxfam collecting box and a card inviting Mrs Kershaw to a coffee morning in aid of Cancer Relief. 'I'll say good-bye now, Mr Archery.' She held out her hand. 'You've such a long way to go I know you'll want to be on your way.' It was almost rude, yet it was queenly. 'If we don't meet again before the great day—well, I'll see you in church.'

The door closed. Archery remained standing.

'What am I to do?' he said simply.

'What did you expect?' Kershaw countered. 'Some sort of inconvertible evidence, an alibi that only she can prove?'

'Do *you* believe her?' Archery cared.

'Ah, that's another matter. I don't care, you see. I don't care one way or the other. It's so easy *not* to ask, Mr Archery, just to do nothing and accept.'

'But I care,' said Archery. 'If Charles goes ahead and marries your stepdaughter, I shall have to leave the church. I don't think you realise the sort of place I live in, the sort of people . . .'

'Aah!' Kershaw wrinkled up his mouth and spread his hands angrily fanwise. 'I've no patience with that sort of out-dated rubbish. Who's to know? Everybody round here thinks she's my kid.'

'I shall know.'

'Why the hell did she have to tell you? Why couldn't she keep her mouth shut?'

'Are you condemning her for her honesty, Kershaw?'

'Yes, by God I am!' Archery winced at the oath and shut his eyes against the light. He saw a red haze. It was only eyelid membrane, but to him it seemed like a lake of blood. 'It's discretion, not honesty, that's the best policy. What are you worrying about, anyway? You know damn' well she won't marry if you don't want it.'

Archery snapped back, 'And what sort of a relationship should I have with my son after that?' He controlled himself, softened his voice and his expression.
'I shall have to try to find a way. Your wife is so sure?'

'She's never weakened.'

'Then I shall go back to Kingsmarkham. It's rather
a forlorn hope, isn't it?' He added with an absurdity
he realised after the words had come, 'Thanks for
trying to help and—and for an excellent tea.'

6

> Yet forasmuch as in all appearance the time of
> his dissolution draweth near, so fit and prepare
> him . . . against the hour of death.
>   *The Visitation of the Sick*

THE man lay on his back in the middle of the zebra
crossing. Inspector Burden, getting out of the police
car, had no need to ask where he was or to be taken to
the scene of the accident. It was all there before his
eyes like a horrible still from a Ministry of Transport
warning film, the kind of thing that makes women
shudder and turn quickly to the other channel.

An ambulance was waiting, but nobody was making
any attempt to move the man. Inexorably and with a
kind of indifference the twin yellow beacons went on
winking rhythmically. Up-ended, with its blunt nose
poking into the crushed head of a bollard, was a white
Mini.

'Can't you get him away?' asked Burden.

The doctor was laconic. 'He's had it.' He knelt
down, felt the left wrist and got up again, wiping blood
from his fingers. 'I'd hazard a guess the spine's gone

and he's ruptured his liver. The thing is he's still more
or less conscious and it'd be hell's own agony to try
to shift him.'

'Poor devil. What happened? Did anybody see it?'

His eye roved across the knot of middle-aged women
in cotton dresses, late homegoing commuters and
courting couples on their evening stroll. The last of the
sun smiled gently on their faces and on the blood that
gilded the black and white crossing. Burden knew that
Mini. He knew the stupid sign in the rear window
that showed a skull and the words: *You have been
Mini-ed*. It had never been funny and now it was
outrageous, cruel in the way it mocked the man in the
road.

A girl lay sprawled over the steering wheel. Her hair
was short, black and spiky, and she had thrust her
fingers through it in despair of remorse. The long red
nails stuck out like bright feathers.

'Don't worry about her,' said the doctor contemp-
tuously. 'She's not hurt.'

'You, madam . . .' Burden picked out the calmest and
least excited looking of the bystanders. 'Did you happen to see the accident?'

'Ooh, it was awful! Like a beast she was, the little
bitch. Must have been doing a hundred miles an hour.'

Picked a right one there, thought Burden. He turned
to a white-faced man holding a sealyham on a lead.

'Perhaps you can help me, sir?'

The lead was jerked and the sealyham sat down at
the kerb.

'That gentleman . . .' Blanching afresh, he pointed
towards the crumpled thing lying on the stripes. 'He
looked right and left like you're supposed to. But
there was nothing coming. You can't see all that well
on account of the bridge.'

'Yes, yes. I get the picture.'

'Well, he started to cross to the island like, when
that white car came up out of nowhere. Going like a
mad thing she was. Well, not a hundred, but sixty, I
reckon. Those Minis can go at a terrible lick when

they've had their engines hotted up. He sort of hesitated and then he tried to go back. You know, it was
all in a flash. I can't rightly go into details.'

'You're doing very well.'

'Then the car got him. Oh, the driver slammed on
her brakes for all she was worth. I'll never forget the
noise to my dying day, what with the brakes screaming
and him screaming too, and sort of throwing up his
arms and going down like a ninepin.'

Burden set a constable to take names and addresses,
turned away and took a step in the direction of the
white car. A woman touched his arm.

'Here,' she said, 'he wants a priest or something. He
kept on asking before you came. Get me Father Chiverton, he says, like he knew he was going.'

'That right?' said Burden sharply to Dr Crocker.

Crocker nodded. The dying man was covered now, a
folded mac under his head, two policemen's jackets
across his body. 'Father Chiverton is what he said.
Frankly, I was more concerned for his physical than
his spiritual welfare.'

'R.C. then, is he?'

'God, no. Bunch of atheists, you cops are. Chiverton's the new vicar here. Don't you ever read the
local rag?'

'*Father?*'

'He's very high. Genuflecting and Sung Eucharist
and all that jazz.' The doctor coughed. 'I'm a Con-
gregationalist myself.'

Burden walked over to the crossing. The man's face
was blanched a yellowish ivory, but his eyes were open
and they stared back. With a little shock Burden
realised he was young, perhaps no more than twenty.

'Anything you want, old chap?' He knew the doctor
had given him a pain-killing injection. With his own
bent body he shielded him from the watchers. 'We'll
get you away from here in a minute.' He lied. "Anything we can get you?'

'Father Chiverton . . .' it was a toneless whisper, as

detached and inhuman as a puff of wind. 'Father
Chiverton . . .' A spasm crossed the waning face. 'Confess . . . atone . . . spare Thou them which are peni-
tent.'

'Bloody religion,' said the doctor. 'Can't even let a
man die in peace.'

'You must be an asset to the Congregationalists,'
Burden snapped. He got up, sighing. 'He obviously
wants to confess. I suppose they do have confession
in the Church of England?'

'You can have it if you want it but you needn't if
you don't fancy it. That's the beauty of the C of E.'
When Burden looked murderous, he added, 'Don't get
in a tiz with me. We've been on to Chiverton, but he
and his curate are off at some conference."

'Constable Gates!' Burden beckoned impatiently to
the man noting down addresses. 'Nip into Stowerton
and fetch me a—a vicar.'

'We've tried Stowerton, sir.'

'O God,' said Burden quietly.

'Excuse me, sir, but there's a clergyman got an
appointment with the Chief Inspector now. I could
get on to the station and . . .'

Burden raised his eyebrows. Kingsmarkham police
station had apparently become the battleground of the
Church Militant.

'You do that, and quick . . .'

He murmured something useless to the boy, and
moved towards the girl who had begun to sob.

She was not crying because of what she had done,
but because of what she had seen two hours before. It
was two or three years now since she had what she
called a waking nightmare—though at one time they
were more real than reality—and she was crying because the nightmares were going to begin again and
the remedy she had tried had not erased the picture
from her mind.

She had seen it in the estate agent's window when

she was coming home from work. It was a photograph of a house, but not as it was now, dirty and weathered, set in a tangled wilderness. The estate agents deceived you, they meant you to think it was like it had once been long ago . . . You? As soon as she found she was addressing herself as 'You' she knew it was beginning again, the re-telling of the nightmare. So she had got into the Mini and driven to Flagford, away from associations and memories and the hateful You voice, to drink and drink and try to send it away.

But it would not go away and you were back in the big house, listening to the voices that went on coaxing, cajoling, arguing until you were bored, so bored until you went out into the garden and met the little girl.

You went up to her and you said, 'Do you like my dress?'

'It's pretty,' she said, and she didn't seem to mind that it was much nicer than her own.

She was playing with a heap of sand, making pies in an old cup without a handle. You stayed and played and after that you came to the sand every day, down there out of sight of the big windows. The sand was warm and nice and you could understand it. You could understand the little girl too, even though she was the only little girl you had ever known. You knew a lot of grown-ups, but you could not understand them, nor the ugly words and the funny wheedling way the talk was always about money, so that you seemed to see coins dropped out of wriggling lips and sliding dirtily through twitching fingers.

The little girl had some magic about her, for she lived in a tree. Of course it was not really a tree but a house inside a kind of bush all shivering with leaves.

The sand was not dry like the desert you lived in now, but warm and moist, like beach sand washed by a tepid sea. It was dirty too and you were afraid of what would happen if you got it on your dress . . .

You cried and stamped your foot, but you never cried as you were crying now as the good-looking inspector came up to the car, his eyes full of anger.

Did he seriously imagine he was going to find anything new after so long? Archery considered Wexford's question. It was, he decided, more a matter of faith than of any real belief in Painter's innocence. But faith in what? Not, surely, in Mrs Kershaw. Perhaps it was just a childlike certainty that such things could not happen to anyone connected with him, Archery. The child of a murderer could not be as Tess was, Kershaw would not have loved her, Charles would not want to marry her.

'It can't do any harm to see Alice Flower,' he said. He felt he was pleading, and pleading weakly. 'I'd like to talk to the Primero grandchildren, particularly the grandson.'

For a moment Wexford said nothing. He had heard of faith moving mountains, but this was simply absurd. To him it was almost as ridiculous as if some crank had come to him with the suggestion that Dr Crippen was the innocent victim of circumstances. From bitter experience he knew how difficult it was to hunt a killer when only a week had elapsed between a murder and the beginning of an investigation. Archery was proposing to open an enquiry a decade and a half too late and Archery had no experience at all.

'I ought to put you off,' he said at last. 'You don't know what you're attempting.' It's pathetic, he thought, it's laughable. Aloud he said, 'Alice Flower's in the geriatric ward at Stowerton Infirmary. She's paralysed. I don't even know if she could make herself understood.'

It occurred to him that Archery must be totally ignorant of the geography of the place. He got up and lumbered over to the wall map.

'Stowerton's there,' he said, pointing with the sheathed tip of a ballpoint pen, 'and Victor's Piece is about here, between Stowerton and Kingsmarkham.'

'Where can I find Mrs. Crilling?'

Wexford made a wry face. 'In Glebe Road. I can't recall the number off-hand, but I'll get it looked up or you could find it on the electoral register.' He turned round ponderously and fixed Archery with a grey glare. 'You're wasting your time, of course. I'm sure I don't have to tell you to be very careful when it comes to throwing out a lot of unfounded accusations.'

Under those cold eyes it was difficult for Archery not to drop his own. 'Chief Inspector, I don't want to find someone else guilty, just prove that Painter was innocent.'

Wexford said briskly, 'I'm afraid you may find the former consequent upon the latter. It would be a wrong conclusion, of course—I don't want trouble.' At a knock on the door he spun round testily. 'Yes, what is it?'

Sergeant Martin's bland face appeared. 'That fatal on the zebra in the High Street, sir?'

'What of it? It's hardly my province.'

'Gates has just been on, sir. A white Mini, LMB 12M, that we've had our eye on—it was in collision with a pedestrian. It appears they want a clergyman and Gates recalled that Mr Archery was . . .'

Wexford's lips twitched. Archery was in for a surprise. In the courtly manner he sometimes assumed, he said to the vicar of Thringford, 'It looks as if the secular arm needs some spiritual assistance, sir. Would you be so good . . .?'

'Of course I will.' Archery looked at the sergeant. 'Someone has been knocked down and is—is *dying?*'

'Unfortunately, yes, sir," said Martin grimly.

'I think I'll come with you,' said Wexford.

As a priest of the Anglican Church Archery was obliged to hear confession if a confessor was needed. Until now, however, his only experience of this mystery concerned a Miss Baylis, an elderly female parishioner of his who, having been (according to Mrs. Archery) for many years in love with him, demanded he should listen to a small spate of domestic sins mumbled out each Friday morning. Hers was a masochistic, self-abasing need, very different from the yearning of the boy who lay in the road.

Wexford shepherded him across the black and white lines to the island. Diversion notices had been placed in the road, directing the traffic around Queen Street, and the crowd had been induced to go home. There were several policemen buzzing and pacing. For the first time in his life Archery realised the aptness of the term "bluebottles'. He glanced at the Mini and averted his eyes hastily from the bright bumper with its ribbon of blood.

The boy looked at him doubtfully. He had perhaps five minutes to live. Archery dropped to his knees and put his ear to the white lips. At first he felt only fluttering breath, then out of the soft sighing vibration came something that sounded like 'Holy orders . . .', with the second word rising on a high note of enquiry. He bent closer as the confession began to flow out, jerky, toneless, spasmodic, like the gulping of a sluggish stream. It was something about a girl, but it was utterly incoherent. He could make nothing of it. *We fly unto Thee for succour*, he thought, *on behalf of this Thy servant, here lying under Thy hand in great weakness of body . . .*

The Anglican Church provides no order quite comparable to that of Extreme Unction. Archery found himself saying urgently over and over again, 'It will be all right, it will be all right.' The boy's throat rattled and a stream of blood welled out of his mouth, splashing Archery's folded hands. *'We humbly commend the soul of this Thy servant, our dear brother, into Thy hands . . .'* He was tired and his voice broke with compassion and with horror. *'Most humbly beseeching Thee that it may be precious in Thy sight . . .'*

It was the doctor's hand that appeared, mopping with a handkerchief at Archery's fingers, then feeling a still heart and an inert pulse. Wexford looked at the doctor, gave an infinitesimal shrug. Nobody spoke. Across the silence came the sound of brakes, a horn braying and an oath as a car, taking the diversion too late, veered into Queen Street. Wexford pulled the coat up over the dead face.

Archery was shattered and cold in the evening heat. He got up stiffly, feeling an utter loneliness, a terrible desire to weep. The only thing to lean on now the bollard was gone was the rear of that lethal white car. He leaned on it, feeling sick.

Presently he opened his eyes and moved slowly along the body of the car to where Wexford stood contemplating a girl's shaggy black head. This was no business of his, Archery's. He wanted no hand in it, only to ask Wexford where he could find an hotel for the night.

Something in the other man's expression made him hesitate. The big Chief Inspector's face was a study in irony. He watched Wexford tap on the glass. The window was slid back and the girl inside lifted to them a face drowned in tears.

'This is a bad business,' he heard Wexford say, 'a very bad business, Miss Crilling.'

'God moves in a mysterious way,' said Wexford as he and Archery walked over the bridge, 'His wonders to perform.' He hummed the old hymn tune, apparently liking the sound of his rather rusty baritone.

'That's true,' said Archery very seriously. He stopped, rested his hand on the granite parapet and looked down into the brown water. A swan sailed out from under the bridge, dipping its long neck into the drifting weed. 'And that is really the girl who found Mrs. Primero's body?'

'That's Elizabethan Crilling, yes. One of the wild young things of Kingsmarkham. A boy friend—a very *close* friend, I may add—gave her the Mini for her twenty-first and she's been a menace in it ever since.'

Archery was silent. Tess Kershaw and Elizabeth Crilling were the same age. Their lives had begun together, almost side by side. Each must have walked with her mother along the grass verges of the Stowerton Road, played in the fields behind Victor's Piece. The Crillings had been comfortably off, middle-class people; the Painters miserably poor. In his mind's eye he saw again that tear-wrecked face down which grease and mascara ran in rivulets, and he heard again the ugly words she had used to Wexford. Another face superimposed itself on Elizabeth Crilling's, a fair aquiline face with steady intelligent eyes under a page-boy's blonde fringe. Wexford interrupted his thoughts.

'She's been spoilt, of course, made too much of. Your Mrs. Primero had her over with her every day, stuffing her with sweets and what-have-you, by all accounts. After the murder Mrs Crilling was always taking her to psychiatrists, wouldn't let her go to school till they had the kid-catcher down on her. God knows how many schools she *has* been to. She was what you might call the female lead in the juvenile court here.'

But it was Tess whose father had been a murderer, Tess who might have been expected to grow up like that. 'God knows how many schools she's been to . . .' Tess had been to one school and to one ancient, distinguished university. Yet the daughter of the innocent friend had become a delinquent; the killer's child a paragon. Certainly God moved in a mysterious way.

'Chief Inspector, I want very much to talk to Mrs Crilling.'

'If you care to attend the special court in the morning, sir, she'll in all likelihood be there. Knowing Mrs Crilling, I'd say you might again be called upon in your professional capacity and then, who knows?'

Archery frowned as they walked on. 'I'd rather it was all above-board. I don't want to do anything underhand.'

'Look, sir,' said Wexford in a burst of impatience, 'if you're coming in on this lark you'll have to be underhand. You've no real authority to ask questions of innocent people and if they complain I can't protect you.'

'I'll explain everything frankly to her. May I talk to her?'

Wexford cleared his throat. 'Are you familiar with *Henry the Fourth,* Part One, sir?'

Slightly puzzled, Archery nodded. Wexford stopped

under the arch that led to the coaching yard of The Olive and Dove. 'The quotation I had in mind is Hotspur's reply to Mortimer when he says he can call spirits from the vast deep.' Startled by Wexford's deep voice, a little cloud of pigeons flew out from the beams, fluttering rusty grey wings. 'I've found that reply very useful to me in my work when I've been a bit too optimistic.' He cleared his throat and quoted, ' "And so can I and so can any man. But will they come when you do call to them?" Good night, sir. I hope you find the Olive comfortable.'

7

Into how high a dignity . . . ye are called, that is to say to be Messengers, Watchmen and Stewards . . .

The Ordering of Priests

Two people sat in the public gallery of Kingsmarkham court, Archery and a woman with sharp, wasted features. Her long grey hair, oddly fashionable through carelessness rather than intent, and the cape she wore gave her a medieval look. Presumably she was the mother of this girl who had just been charged with manslaughter, the girl whom the clerk had named as Elizabeth Anthea Crilling, of 24A Glebe Road, Kingsmarkham in the County of Sussex. She had a look of her mother and they kept glancing at each other, Mrs. Crilling's eyes flicking over her daughter's string-thin body or coming to rest with maudlin watery affection on the girl's face. It was a well-made face, though gaunt but for the full mouth. Sometimes it seemed to

become all staring dark eyes as a word or a telling
phrase awakened emotion, sometimes blank and shuttered like that of a retarded child with an inner life of
goblins and things that reach out in the dark. An invisible thread held mother and daughter together but
whether it was composed of love or hatred Archery
could not tell. Both were ill-dressed, dirty-looking, a
prey, he felt, to cheap emotion, but there was some
quality each had—passion? Imagination? Seething
memory?—that set them apart and dwarfed the other
occupants of the court.

He had just enough knowledge of the law to know
that this court could do no more than commit the girl
to the Assizes for trial. The evidence that was being
laboriously taken down on a typewriter was all against
her. Elizabeth Crilling, according to the licensee of The
Swan at Flagford, had been drinking in his saloon bar
since six-thirty. He had served her with seven double
whiskies and when he had refused to let her have another, she had abused him until he had threatened to
call the police.

'No alternative but to commit you for trial at the
Assizes at Lewes,' the chairman was saying. '. . . Nothing to hope for from any promise of favour, and nothing
to fear from any threat which may be . . .'

A shriek came from the public gallery. 'What are
you going to do to her?' Mrs Crilling had sprung up,
the tent-like cape she wore billowing out and making
a breeze run through the court, 'You're not going to
put her in prison?'

Hardly knowing why he did so, Archery moved
swiftly along the form until he was at her side. At the
same time Sergeant Martin took half a dozen rapid
strides towards her, glaring at the clergyman.

'Now, madam, you'd far better come outside.'

She flung herself away from him, pulling the cape
around her as if it were cold instead of suffocatingly
hot.

'You're not going to put my baby in gaol!' She
pushed at the sergeant who stood between her and

her view of the bench. 'Get away from me, you dirty sadist!'

'Take that woman outside,' said the magistrate with icy calm. Mrs Crilling spun round to face Archery and seized his hands. 'You've got a kind face. Are you my friend?'

Archery was horribly embarrassed. 'You can ask for bail, I think,' he muttered.

The policewoman who stood by the dock came over to them. 'Come along now, Mrs Crilling . . .'

'Bail, I want bail! This gentleman is an old friend of mine and he says I can have bail. I want my rights for my baby!'

'We really can't have this sort of thing.' The magistrate cast an icy scornful look upon Archery who sat down, wrenching his hands from Mrs Crilling's. 'Do I understand you wish to ask for bail?' He turned his eyes on Elizabeth who nodded defiantly.

'A nice cup of tea, Mrs Crilling,' said the policewoman. 'Come along now.' She shepherded the demented woman out, her arm supporting her waist. The magistrate went into conference with the clerk and bail was granted to Elizabeth Crilling in her own recognisance of five hundred pounds and that of her mother for a similar sum.

'Rise, please!' said the warrant officer. It was over.

On the other side of the court Wexford shovelled his papers into his briefcase.

'A friend in need, that one,' he said to Burden, glancing in Archery's direction. 'You mark my words, he'll have a job getting out of old Mother Crilling's clutches. Remember when we had to cart her off to the mental unit at Stowerton that time? You were her friend then. Tried to kiss you, didn't she?'

'Don't remind me,' said Burden.

'Funny affair altogether last night, wasn't it? Him being on hand, I mean, to show that poor kid his way to heaven.'

'It was lucky.'

'I only remember that happening once before, except

in the case of R.C.s, of course.' He turned as Archery slipped between the wooden forms and came up to them. 'Good morning, sir. I hope you slept well. I was just saying to the inspector, there was a fellow killed out Forby way soon after I came here. Must be all of twenty years. I've never forgotten it. He was just a kid too and got it in the neck from an army lorry. But he wasn't quiet, he was screaming. All about a girl and a kid it was.' He paused. 'Did you speak, sir? Sorry, I thought you did. He wanted a clergyman, too.'

'I hope and trust he got what he wanted.'

'Well, no he didn't as a matter of fact. He died—unshriven is the word, I think. The vicar's car broke down on the way. Funny, I've never forgotten it. Grace was his name, John Grace. Shall we go?'

The Crillings had departed. As they came out into the sunshine, the policewoman came up to Wexford.

'Mrs Crilling left a note with me, sir. She asked me to give it to a Mr Archery.'

'Take my advice,' said Wexford. 'Tear it up. She's as mad as a hatter.' But Archery had already slit open the envelope.

Dear Sir, he read.

They tell me that you are a man of God. Blessed is he that sitteth not in the seat of the scornful. God has sent you to me and my baby. I will be at home this afternoon, waiting to thank you in person.

Your affectionate friend,   Josephine Crilling

Archery's bedroom combined charmingly the best of old and new. The ceiling was beamed, the walls painted pink and decorated with a tooled design of chevrons, but there was also a fitted carpet, an abundance of lights on walls and bedhead and a telephone. He rinsed his hands at the pink washbasin (a private bathroom he felt to be an unwarranted extravagance), lifted the receiver and asked for a call to Thringford in Essex.

'Darling?'

'Henry! Thank heaven you've phoned. I've been trying over and over again to get you at that Olive Branch place or whatever it's called.'

'Why, what's the matter?'

'I've had a dreadful letter from Charles. Apparently poor darling Tess phoned her people late yesterday afternoon and now she's told Charles the engagement's definitely off. She says it wouldn't be fair on him or us.'

'And . . . ?'

'And Charles says if Tess won't marry him he's going to come down from Oxford and go out to Africa to fight for Zimbabwe.'

'How utterly ridiculous!'

'He says if you try and stop him he'll do something dreadful and get sent down.'

'Is that all?'

'Oh, no. There's lots and lots of it. Let me see. I've got the letter here. ". . . What's the use of Father always ballsing on"—sorry, darling, does that mean something awful?—"on about faith and taking things on trust if he won't take Tess's word and her mother's? I've been into the whole fiasco of the case myself and it's full of holes. I think Father could get the Home Secretary to have the case reopened if he would only make some sort of effort. For one thing there was an inheritance involved but it never came up at the trial. Three people inherited vast sums and at least one of them was buzzing around the place the day Mrs. Primero died . . ." '

'All right,' said Archery wearily. 'If you remember, Mary, I have a transcript of the trial myself and it cost me two hundred pounds. How are things apart from that?'

'Mr Sims is behaving rather oddly.' Mr Sims was Archery's curate. 'Mis Bayliss says he keeps the communion bread in his pocket, and this morning she got a long blonde hair in her mouth.'

Archery smiled. The parish chit-chat was more in his wife's line than solving murders. It brought her to him visually, a handsome strong woman who minded the lines on her face that he never noticed. He was beginning to miss her mentally and physically.

'Now, listen, darling. Write back to Charles—be diplomatic. Tell him how well Tess is behaving and say I'm having some very interesting talks with the police. If there's the slightest chance of getting the case reopened I'll write to the Home Secretary.'

'That's wonderful, Henry. Oh, there go your second lot of pips. I'll ring off. By the way, Rusty caught a mouse this morning and left it in the bath. He and Tawny are missing you.'

'Give them my love,' said Archery to please her.

He went downstairs into the dark cool dining room, ordered something called a *Navarin d'agneau,* and in a burst of recklessness, a half-bottle of Anjou. All the windows were open but on some of them the green shutters had been closed. A table in one of these embrasures reminded him with its white cloth, its tilted cane chairs and its vaseful of sweet peas of a Dufy that hung on the walls of his study at home. Filtered sunlight lay in primrose-pale bars across the cloth and the two places laid with silver.

But for himself and half a dozen elderly residents, the dining room was deserted, but presently the door from the bar opened and the head waiter ushered in a man and a woman. Archery wondered if the management would object to the apricot poodle the woman fondled in her arms. But the head waiter was smiling deferentially and Archery saw him pat the tiny woolly head.

The man was small and dark and would have been good-looking but for his glassy, red-rimmed eyes. Archery thought he might be wearing contact lenses. He sat down at the Dufy table, ripped open a packet of Peter Stuyvesant and poured the contents into a gold cigarette case. In spite of the man's obvious polish—his sleek hair, svelt suit, taut bone-smooth skin—there was something savage in the way his white fingers tore the paper. A wedding ring and a big bold signet gleamed in the soft light as he tossed the mutilated packet on to the cloth. Archery was amused to see how much jewellery he wore, a sapphire tie pin and a watch as well as the rings.

By contrast the woman wore none. She was plainly dressed in a cream silk suit that matched her hair, and everything about her from the gauzy hat and hair to her crossed ankles was the colour of faint sunlight, so that she seemed to glow with a pale radiance. Outside the cinema and the pictures in Mary's magazines, she was the most beautiful woman he had seen for years. Compared to her Tess Painter was just a pretty girl. Archery was reminded of an ivory orchid or a tea rose which, when lifted from the florist's cube of cellophane, still retains its patina of dew.

He gave himself a little shake and applied himself determinedly to his *Navarin*. It had turned out to be two lamb chops in a brown sauce.

Between Kingsmarkham High Street and the Kingsbrook Road lies an estate of ugly terraced houses covered with that mixture of mortar and grit builders call pebble dashing. On a hot day when the roads are dusty and flickering with heat mirage these rows of dun-coloured houses look as if they have been fashioned out of sand. A giant's child might have built them, using his crude tools unimaginatively.

Archery found Glebe Road by the simple and traditional expedient of asking a policeman. He was getting into the habit of asking policemen and this one was low in the hierarchy, a young constable directing traffic at the crossroads.

Glebe Road might have been designed by the Romans, it was so straight, so long and so uncompromising. The sand houses had no woodwork about them. Their window frames were of metal and their porch canopies excrescences of pebbly plaster. After every fourth house an arch in the façade led into the back and through these arches sheds, coal bunkers and dustbins could be seen.

The street was numbered from the Kingsbrook Road

end and Archery walked nearly half a mile before he found twenty-four. The hot pavements running with melted tar made his feet burn. He pushed open the gate and saw that the canopy covered not one front door but two. The house had been converted into two surely tiny flatlets. He tapped the chromium knocker on the door marked 24A and waited.

When nothing happened he tapped again. There was a grinding trundling sound and a boy on roller skates came out from under the arch. He took no notice at all of the clergyman. Could Mrs Crilling be asleep? It was hot enough for a siesta and Archery felt languid himself.

He stepped back and looked through the arch. Then he heard the door open and slam shut. So somebody was at home. He rounded the sandy wall and came face to face with Elizabeth Crilling.

At once he sensed that she had not answered, nor probably even heard, his knock. Evidently she was going out. The black dress had been changed for a short blue cotton shift that showed the outlines of her prominent hip bones. She wore backless white mules and carried a huge white and gilt handbag.

'What d'you want?' It was obvious she had no idea who he was. He thought she looked old, finished, as if somehow she had been used and wrecked. 'If you're selling something,' she said, 'you've come to the wrong shop.'

'I saw your mother in court this morning,' Archery said. 'She asked me to come and see her.'

He thought she had rather a charming smile, for her mouth was well-shaped and her teeth good. But the smile was too brief.

'That,' she said, 'was this morning.'

'Is she at home?' He looked helplessly at the doors. 'I—er—which one is it, which flat?'

'Are you kidding? It's bad enough sharing a house with her. Only a stone-deaf paralytic could stick living *underneath* her.'

'I'll go in, shall I?'

'Suit yourself. She's not likely to come out here.' The bag strap was hoisted on to the right shoulder, pulling the blue stuff tight across her breasts. Without knowing why, Archery remembered the exquisite woman in the dining room of the Olive and Dove, her petal skin and her easy grace.

Elizabeth Crilling's face was greasy. In the bright afternoon light the skin had the texture of lemon peel. 'Well, go on in,' she said sharply, unlocking the door. She pushed it open and turned away, her mules flapping and clacking down the path. 'She won't bite you,' she said over her shoulder. 'At least, I shouldn't think so. She bit me once, but there were—well, extenuating circumstances.'

Archery went into the hall. Three doors led off it but they were all closed. He coughed and said tentatively, 'Mrs Crilling?' The place was stuffy and silent. He hesitated for a moment, then opened the first part of the doors. Inside was a bedroom divided into two by a hardboard partition. He had been wondering how the two women managed. Now he knew. The middle room must be where they lived. He tapped on the door and opened it.

Although the french windows were ajar the air was thick with smoke and the two ashtrays on a gateleg table were filled with stubs. Every surface was covered with papers and debris and the debris with dust. As he entered a blue budgerigar in a tiny cage broke into a stream of high brittle chatter. The cage swung furiously.

Mrs. Crilling wore a pink nylon dressing gown that looked as if it had once been designed for a bride. The honeymoon, Archery thought, was long over, for the dressing gown was stained and torn and hideous. She was sitting in an armchair looking through the window at a fenced-in piece of land at the back. It could hardly be called a garden for nothing grew in it but nettles, three feet high, rose-pink firewood, and brambles that covered everything with fly-infested tendrils.

'You hadn't forgotten I was coming, Mrs Crilling?'

The face that appeared round the wing of the chair was enough to intimidate anyone. The whites of the eyes showed all the way round the black pupils. Every muscle looked tense, taut and corrugated as if from some inner agony. Her white hair, fringed and styled like a teenager's, curtained the sharp cheekbones.

'Who are you?' She dragged herself up, clinging to the chair arm and came slowly round to face him. The vee at the dressing gown front showed a ridged and withered valley like the bed of a long-dried stream.

'We met in court this morning. You wrote to me . . .' He stopped. She had thrust her face within inches of his and seemed to be scrutinising it. Then she stepped back and gave a long chattering laugh which the budgerigar echoed.

'Mrs Crilling, are you all right? Is there anything I can do?'

She clutched her throat and the laugh died away in a rising wheeze. 'Tablets . . . asthma . . .' she gasped. He was puzzled and shocked, but he reached behind him for the bottle of tablets on the littered mantelpiece. "Give me my tablets and then you can . . . you can get out!'

'I'm sorry if I've done anything to distress you.'

She made no attempt to take a tablet but held the bottle up against her quaking chest. The movement made the tablets rattle and the bird, fluttering its wings and beating against the bars, began a frenzied crescendo, half song and half pain.

'Where's my baby?' Did she mean Elizabeth? She must mean Elizabeth.

'She's gone out. I met her in the porch. Mrs Crilling, can I get you a glass of water? Can I make you a cup of tea?'

'Tea? What do I want with tea? That's what she said this morning, that police girl. Come and have a cup of tea, Mrs Crilling.' A terrible spasm shook her and she fell back against the chair, fighting for breath. 'You . . . my baby . . . I thought you were my friend . . . Aaah!'

Archery was really frightened now. He plunged from the room into the dirty kitchen and filled a cup with water. The window ledge was stacked with empty chemist's bottles and there was a filthy hypodermic beside an equally dirty eye dropper. When he came back she was still wheezing and jerking. Should he make her take the tablets, dare he? On the bottle label were the words: *Mrs J. Crilling. Take two when needed.* He rattled two into his hands and, supporting her with his other arm, forced them into her mouth. It was all he could do to suppress the shudder of distaste when she dribbled and choked over the water.

'Filthy . . . nasty,' she mumbled. He half-eased, half-rolled her into the chair and pulled together the gaping edges of the dressing gown. Moved with pity and with horror, he knelt down beside her.

'I will be your friend if you want me to be,' he said soothingly.

The words had the opposite effect. She made a tremendous effort to draw breath. Her lips split open and he could see her tongue rising and quivering against the roof of her mouth.

'Not my friend . . . enemy . . . police friend! Take my baby away . . . I saw you with them . . . I watched you come out with them.' He drew back from her, rising. Never would he have believed her capable of screaming after that spasm and when the scream came, as clear and ear-splitting as a child's, he felt his hands go up to his face. '. . . Not let them get her in there! Not in the prison! They'll find it out in there. She'll tell them . . . my baby . . . She'll have to tell them!' With a sudden galvanic jerk she reared up, her mouth open and her arms flailing. 'They'll find it all out. I'll kill her first, kill her . . . D'you hear?'

The french windows stood open. Archery staggered back into the sun against a stinging prickling wall of weeds. Mrs Crilling's incoherent gasps had swollen into a stream of obscenity. There was a gate in the wire netting fence. He unlatched it, wiping the sweat from his forehead, and stepped into the cool dark cave of the sand-walled arch.

'Good afternoor, sir. You don't look very well. Heat affecting you?'

Archery had been leaning over the bridge parapet, breathing deeply, when the detective inspector's face appeared beside him.

'Inspector Burden, isn't it?' He shook himself, blinking his eyes. There was comfort in this man's steady gaze and in the shoppers who flowed languidly across the bridge. 'I've just come from Mrs Crilling's and . . .'

'Say no more, sir. I quite understand.'

'I left her in the throes of an asthma attack. Perhaps I should have got a doctor or an ambulance. Frankly, I hardly knew what to do.'

There was a crumb of stony bread on the wall. Burden flicked it into the water and a swan dived for it.

'It's mostly in the mind with her, Mr Archery. I should have warned you what to expect. Threw one of her scenes on you, did she?' Archery nodded. 'Next time you see her I daresay she'll be as nice as pie. That's the way it takes her, up one minute, down the next. Maniac-depressive is the term. I was just going into Carousel for a cup of tea. Why don't you join me?'

They walked up the High Street together. Some of the shops sported faded striped sunblinds. The shadows were as black as night, the light cruelly bright under a Mediterranean blue sky. Inside the Carousel it was darkish and stuffy and it smelt of aerosol fly spray.

'Two teas, please,' said Burden.

'Tell me about the Crillings.'

'There's plenty to tell, Mr Archery. Mrs Crilling's husband died and left her without a penny, so she moved into town and got a job. The kid, Elizabeth, was always difficult and Mrs. Crilling made her worse. She took her to psychiatrists—don't ask me where the money came from—and then when they made her send her to school it was one school after another. She was in St Catherine's, Sewingbury for a bit but she got expelled. When she was about fourteen she came up before the juvenile court here as being in need of care and protection and she was taken away from her mother. But she went back eventually. They usually do.'

'Do you think all this came about because she found Mrs Primero's body?'

'Could be.' Burden looked up and smiled as the waitress brought the tea. 'Thanks very much, miss. Sugar, Mr Archery? No, I don't either.' He cleared his throat and went on, 'I reckon it would have made a difference if she'd had a decent home background, but Mrs Crilling was always unstable. In and out of jobs, by all accounts, until she ended up working in a shop. I think some relative used to give them financial assistance. Mrs Crilling used to take days off from work ostensibly on account of the asthma but really it was because she was crazy."

'Isn't she certifiable?'

'You'd be surprised how difficult it is to get anyone certified, sir. The doctor did say that if ever he saw her in one of her tantrums he could get an urgency order, but they're cunning, you see. By the time the doctor gets there she's as normal as you or me. She's been into Stowerton once or twice as a voluntary patient. About four years ago she got herself a man friend. The whole place was buzzing with it. Elizabeth was training to be a physiotherapist at the time. Anyway, the upshot of it all was that the boyfriend preferred young Liz.'

'*Mater pulchra, filia pulchrior,*' Archery murmured.

'Just as you say, sir. She gave up her training and went to live with him. Mrs Crilling went off her rocker again and spent six months in Stowerton. When she came out she wouldn't leave the happy couple alone, letters, phone calls, personal appearances, the lot. Liz couldn't stand it so eventually she went back to mother. The boyfriend was in the car trade and he gave her that Mini.'

Archery sighed. 'I don't know if I ought to tell you this, but you've been very kind to me, you and Mr. Wexford . . .' Burden felt the stirring of guilt. It wasn't what he would call kind. 'Mrs Crilling said that if Elizabeth—she calls her her baby—went to prison . . . it might mean prison, mightn't it?'

'It might well.'

'Then she'd tell you something, you or the prison authorities. I got the impression she'd feel compelled to give you some information Mrs Crilling wanted kept secret.'

'Thank you very much, sir. We shall have to wait and see what time brings forth.'

Archery finished his tea. Suddenly he felt like a traitor. Had he betrayed Mrs Crilling because he wanted to keep in with the police?

'I wondered,' he said, justifying himself, 'if it could have anything to do with Mrs Primero's murder. I don't see why Mrs Crilling couldn't have worn the raincoat and hidden it. You admit yourself she's un-balanced. She was there, she had just as much oppor-tunity as Painter.'

Burden shook his head. 'What was the motive?'

'Mad people have motives which seem very thin to normal men.'

'But she dotes on her daughter in her funny way. She wouldn't have taken the kid with her.'

Archery said slowly, 'At the trial she said she went over the first time at twenty-five past six. But we've only her word for it. Suppose instead she went at twenty to seven when *Painter had already been and gone*. Then she took the child back later because no one would believe a killer would wittingly let a child discover a body she knew was there.'

'You've missed your vocation, sir,' said Burden, get-ting up. 'You should have come in on our lark. You'd have been a superintendent by now.'

'I'm letting my fancy run away with me,' Archery said. To avoid a repetition of the gentle teasing, he added quickly, changing the subject, 'Do you happen to know the visiting times at Stowerton Infirmary?'

'Alice Flower's next on your list, is she? I'd give the matron a ring first, if I were you. Visiting's seven till seven-thirty.'

8

The days of our age are threescore years and ten; and though men be so strong that they come to fourscore years, yet is their strength then but labour and sorrow.

Psalm 90. The Burial of the Dead

ALICE Flower was eighty-seven, almost as old as her employer had been at the time of her death. A series of strokes had battered her old frame as tempests batter an ancient house, but the house was strong and sturdily built. No gimcrack refinements of decoration or delicacy had ever belonged to it. It had been made to endure wind and weather.

She lay in a narrow high bed in a ward called Honeysuckle. The ward was full of similar old women in similar beds. They had clean pink faces and white hair through which patches of rose-pink scalp showed. Every bed trolley held at least two vases of flowers, the sops to conscience, Archery supposed, of visiting relatives who only had to sit and chat instead of handing bedpans and tending bed-sores.

'A visitor for you, Alice,' said the sister. 'It's no use trying to shake hands with her. She can't move her hands but her hearing's perfectly good and she'll talk the hind leg off a donkey.'

A most un-Christian hatred flared in Archery's eyes. If she saw it the sister took no notice.

'Like a good gossip, don't you, Alice? This is the Reverend Archery.' He winced at that, approached the bed.

'Good evening, sir.'

Her face was square with deeply ridged rough skin. One corner of her mouth had been drawn down by the paralysis of the motor nerves, causing her lower jaw to protrude and reveal large false teeth. The sister bustled about the bed, pulling the old servant's nightgown higher about her neck and arranging on the coverlet her two useless hands. It was terrible to Archery to have to look at those hands. Work had distorted them beyond hope of beauty, but disease and oedema had smoothed and whitened the skin so that they were like the hands of a misshapen baby. The emotion and the feel for the language of 1611 that was with him always welled in a fount of pity. Well done, thou good and faithful servant, he thought. Thou has been faithful over a few things, I will make thee ruler over many things . . .

'Would it upset you to talk to me about Mrs Primero, Miss Flower?' he asked gently, easing himself into a bentwood chair.

'Of course it wouldn't,' said the sister, 'she loves it.'

Archery could bear no more. 'This is rather a private matter, if you don't mind.'

'Private! It's the whole ward's bedtime story, believe me.' She flounced away, a crackling navy and white robot.

Alice Flower's voice was cracked and harsh. The strokes had affected her throat muscles or her vocal cords. But her accent was pleasant and correct, learnt, Archery supposed, in the kitchens and nurseries of educated people.

'What was it you wanted to know, sir?'

'First tell me about the Primero family.'

'Oh, I can do that. I always took an interest.' She gave a small rattling cough and turned her head to hide the twisted side of her mouth. 'I went to Mrs. Primero when the boy was born . . .'

'The boy?'

'Mr Edward, her only child he was.'

Ah, thought Archery, the father of rich Roger and his sisters.

'He was a lovely boy and we always got on a treat, him and me. I reckon it really aged me and his poor mother when he died, sir. But he'd got a family of his own by then, thanks be to God, and Mr Roger was the living spit of his father.'

'I suppose Mr Edward left him pretty well off, did he?'

'Oh, no, sir, that was the pity of it. You see, old Dr Primero left his money to madam, being as Mr Edward was doing so well at the time. But he lost everything on something in the city and when he was taken Mrs Edward and the three kiddies were quite badly off.' She coughed again, making Archery wince. He fancied he could see a terrible vain effort to raise those hands and cover the rattling lips. 'Madam offered to help— not that she had more than she needed—but Mrs Edward was that proud, she wouldn't take a penny from her mother-in-law. I never shall know how she managed. There was the three of them, you see. Mr Roger he was the eldest, and then there was the two little mites, ever so much younger than their brother, but close together if you take my meaning. No more than eighteen months between them.'

She rested her head back on the pillows and bit at her lip as if trying to pull it back into place. 'Angela was the oldest. Time flies so I reckon she'd be twenty-six now. Then there was Isabel, named after madam. They was just babies when their Daddy died and it was years before we saw them.

'It was a bitter blow to madam, I can tell you, not knowing what had become of Mr Roger. Then one day just out of the blue he turned up at Victor's Piece. Fancy, he was living in digs just over at Sewingbury, studying to be a solicitor with a very good firm. Somebody Mrs Edward knew had got him in. He hadn't no idea his granny was still alive, let alone in Kingsmarkham, but he was looking up somebody in the phone book, in the line of business, sir, and there it was; Mrs Rose Primero, Victor's Piece. Once he'd come over there was no stopping him. Not that we wanted to stop him, sir. Pretty nearly every Sunday he came and once or twice he fetched his little sisters all the way from London and brought them with him. Good as gold they were.

'Mr Roger and madam, they used to have some laughs together. All the old photographs they'd have out and the tales she used to tell him!' She stopped suddenly and Archery watched the old face swell and grow purple. 'It was a change for us to have a nice gentlemanlike young fellow about the place after that Painter.' Her voice changed to a shrill whistling shriek. 'That dirty murdering beast!'

Across the ward another old woman in a bed like Alice Flower's smiled a toothless smile as of one hearing a familiar tale retold. The ward's bedtime story, the sister had said.

Archery leant towards her. 'That was a dreadful day, Miss Flower,' he said, 'the day Mrs Primero died.' The fierce eyes flickered, red and spongey blue. 'I expect you feel you'll never forget it ...'

'Not to my dying day,' said Alice Flower. Perhaps she thought of the now useless body that had once been so fine an instrument and was already three-quarters dead.

'Will you tell me about it?'

As soon as she began he realised how often she must have told it before. It was likely that some of these other old women were not absolutely bedridden, that sometimes in the evenings they got up and gathered round Alice Flower's bed. A tale, he thought, paraphrasing, to draw children from play and old women from the chimney corner.

'He was a devil,' she said, 'a terror. I was scared of him but I never let him know it. Take all and give nothing, that was his motto. Six pounds a year, that was all I got when I first went out into service. Him, he had his home and his wages, a lovely motor to drive. There's some folks want the moon. You'd think a big strong young fellow like that'd be only too glad to fetch the coal in for an old lady, but not Mr Bert Painter. Beast Painter was what I called him.

'That Saturday night when he never come and he never come madam had to sit all by herself in the icy cold. Let me go over and speak to him, madam, I said, but she wouldn't have it. The morning's time enough, Alice, she said. I've said to myself over and over again, if he'd come that night I'd have been in there with them. He wouldn't have been able to tell no lies then.'

'But he did come the next morning, Miss Flower . . .'

'She told him off good and proper. I could hear her giving him a dressing down.'

'What were you doing?'

'Me? When he come in first I was doing the vegetables for madam's lunch, then I popped on the oven and put in the meat tin. They asked me all that at the court in London, the Old Bailey it was.' She paused and there was suspicion in the look she gave him. 'You writing a book about it all, are you, sir?'

'Something like that,' said Archery.

'They wanted to know if I was sure I could hear all right. My hearing's better than that judge's, I can tell you. Just as well it is. If I'd been hard of hearing we might have all gone up in smoke that morning.'

'How was that?'

'Beast Painter was in the drawing room with madam and I'd gone into the larder to get the vinegar for the mint sauce, when all of a sudden I heard a kind of a plop and sizzle. That's that funny old oven, I said, and sure enough it was. I popped back quick and opened the oven door. One of the potatoes had kind of spat out, sir, and fallen on the gas. All in flames it was and sizzling and roaring like a steam engine. I turned it off quick and then I did a silly thing. Poured water on it. Ought to have known better at my age. Ooh, the racket and the smoke! You couldn't hear yourself think.'

There had been nothing about that in the trial transcript. Archery caught his breath in the excitement. 'You couldn't hear yourself think . . .' While you were choked with smoke and deafened by hissing you might not hear a man go upstairs, search a bedroom and come down again. Alice's evidence in this matter had been one of the most important features of the case. For if Painter had been offered and had taken the two hundred pounds in Mrs Primero's presence in the morning, what motive could he have had for killing her in the evening?

'Well, we had our lunch and Mr Roger came. My poor old leg was aching from where I'd bruised it the night before getting a few lumps in on account of Beast Painter being out on the tiles. Mr Roger was ever so nice about it, kept asking me if there was anything he could do, wash up or anything. But that isn't man's work and I always say it's better to keep going while you can.

'It must have been half past five when Mr Roger said he'd have to go. I was up to my neck what with the dishes and worrying if Beast would turn up like he'd promised. "I'll let myself out, Alice", Mr Roger said, and he come down to the kitchen to say goodbye to me. Madam was having a little snooze in the drawing room, God rest her. It was the last she had before her long sleep.' Aghast, Archery watched two tears well into her eyes and flow unchecked down the ridged sunken cheeks. 'I called out, "Cheeri-by, Mr. Roger dear, see you next Sunday", and then I heard him shut the front door. Madam was sleeping like a child, not knowing that ravening wolf was lying in wait for her.'

'Try not to upset yourself, Miss Flower.' Doubtful as to what he should do—the right thing is the kind thing, he thought—he pulled out his own clean white handkerchief and gently wiped the wet cheeks.

'Thank you, sir. I'll be all right now. You do feel

a proper fool not being able to dry your own tears.'
The ghastly cracked smile was almost more painful to
witness than the weeping. 'Where was I? Oh, yes. Off
I went to church and as soon as I was out of the way
along comes Madam Crilling, poking her nose in . . .'

'I know what happened next, Miss Flower,' Archery
said very kindly and quietly. 'Tell me about Mrs
Crilling. Does she ever come to see you in here?'

Alice Flower gave a kind of snort that would have
been comical in a fit person. 'Not she. She's kept out
of my way ever since the trail, sir. I know too much
about her for her liking. Madam's best friend, my
foot! She'd got one interest in madam and one only.
She wormed that child of hers into madam's good books
on account of she thought madam might leave her
something when she went.'

Archery moved closer, praying that the bell for the
end of visiting would not ring yet.

'But Mrs Primero didn't make a will.'

'Oh, no, sir, that's what worried Mrs Clever Crilling. She'd come out into my kitchen when madam
was sleeping. "Alice,' she'd say, "we ought to get dear
Mrs Primero to make her last will and testament. It's
our duty, Alice, it says so in the Prayer Book." '

'Does it?'

Alice looked both shocked and smug. 'Yes, it does,
sir. It says, "But men should often be put in remem-
brance to take order for the settling of their temporal
estates whilst they are in health." Still I don't hold
with everything that's in the Prayer Book not when it
comes to downright interference—saving your presence, sir. "It's in your interest too, Alice," she says.
"You'll be turned out into the streets when she goes."

'But madam wouldn't have it, anyway. Everything
was to go to her natural heirs, she said, them being
Mr Roger and the little girls. It'd be theirs automati-
cally, you see, without any nonsense about wills and
lawyers.'

'Mr. Roger didn't try to get her to make a will?'

'He's a lovely person is Mr Roger. When Beast

Painter had done his murdering work and poor madam was dead Mr Roger got his bit of money—three thousand it was and a bit more. "I'll take care of you, Alice," he said, and so he did. He got me a nice room in Kingsmarkham and gave me two pounds a week on top of my pension. He was in business on his own then and he said he wouldn't give me a lump sum. An allowance, he called it, bless his heart, out of his profits.'

'Business? I thought he was a solicitor.'

'He always wanted to go into business on his own, sir. I don't know the ins and outs of it, but he came to madam one day—must have been two or three weeks before she died—and he said a pal of his would take him in with him if he could put up ten thousand pounds. "I know I haven't got a hope," he said, speaking ever so nice. "It's just a castle in the air, Granny Rose."

' "Well, it's no good looking at me," says madam. "Ten thousand is all I've got for me and Alice to live on and that's tucked away in Woolworth's shares. You'll get your share when I'm gone." I don't mind telling you, sir, I thought then, if Mr. Roger liked to do his little sisters down he could try getting round madam to make that will and leave him the lot. But he never did, never mentioned it again, and he'd always made a point of bringing the two mites just whenever he could. Then Beast Painter killed madam and the money went like she said it would, to the three of them.

'Mr. Roger's doing very well now, sir, very well indeed, and he comes to see me regular. I reckon he got the ten thousand from somewhere or maybe another pal came up with something else. It wasn't for me to ask, you see.'

A nice man, Archery thought, a man who had needed money perhaps desperately, but would do nothing underhand to get it; a man who provided for his dead grandmother's domestic while he was struggling to get a business going, who still visited her and who doubtless listened patiently over and over again to the tale Archery had just heard. A very nice man. If love, praise and devotion could reward such a man, he had his reward.

'If you should see Mr Roger, sir, if you want to see him about the story you're writing, would you give him my best respects?'

'I won't forget, Miss Flower.' He put his hand over her dead one and pressed it. 'Good-bye and thank you.' Well done, thou good and faithful servant.

It was gone eight when he got back to the Olive and Dove. The head waiter glared at him when he walked into the dining room at a quarter past. Archery stared about him at the empty room, the chairs arranged against the walls.

'Dance on tonight, sir. We did make a point of asking residents to take their dinner at seven sharp, but I expect we can find you something. In here, if you please.'

Archery followed him into the smaller of the two lounges that led off the dining room. The tables had been crammed in and people were hastily gobbling their meal. He ordered, and through the glass doors, watched the band take its place on the dais.

How was he to spend this long hot summer evening? The dancing would probably go on until half-past twelve or one and the hotel would be unbearable. A quiet stroll was the obvious thing. Or he could take the car and go and look at Victor's Piece. The waiter came back with the braised beef he had ordered, and Archery, resolutely economical, asked for a glass of water.

He was quite alone in his alcove, at least two yards from the next table, and he jumped when he felt something soft and fluffy brush against his leg. Drawing back, he put his hand down, lifted the cloth and met a pair of bright eyes set in a golden woolly skull.

'Hallo, dog,' he said.

'Oh I'm so sorry. Is he being a nuisance?'

He looked up and saw her standing beside him. They had evidently just come in, she, the man with the glassy eyes and another couple.

'Not a bit.' Archery's poise deserted him and he found himself almost stammering. 'I don't mind, really. I'm fond of animals.'

'You were here at lunch, weren't you? I expect he recognised you. Come out, Dog. He doesn't have a name. We just call him Dog because he is one and it's just as good a name as Jock or Gyp or something. When you said, "Hallo, dog," he thought you were a personal friend. He's very intelligent.'

'I'm sure he is.'

She gathered the poodle up in her arms and held him against the creamy lace of her dress. Now that she wore no hat he could see the perfect shape of her head and the high unshadowed brow. The head waiter minced over, no longer harassed.

'Back again, Louis, like the proverbial bad pennies,' said the glassy-eyed man heartily. 'My wife took a fancy to come to your hop, but we must have a spot of dinner first.' So they were married, these two. Why hadn't it occurred to him before, what business was it of his and, above all, why should it cause him this faint distress? 'Our friends here have a train to catch, so if you can go all out with the old speed we'll be eternally grateful.'

They all sat down. The poodle mooched between diners' legs, scavenging for crumbs. Archery was faintly amused to see how quickly their dinner was brought to them. They had all ordered different dishes, but there was little delay and at the same time little hustle. Archery lingered over his coffee and his bit of cheese. Surely he was no bother to anyone in his small corner. People were coming in to dance now, passing his table and leaving in their wake the faint scent of cigars and floral perfume. In the dining room, a ballroom now, the garden doors had been opened and couples stood on the terrace listening to the music in the tranquillity of the summer night.

The poodle sat on the threshold, bored, watching the dancers.

'Come here, Dog,' said his owner. Her husband got up.

'I'll take you to the station, George,' he said. 'We've only got ten minutes, so get a wiggle on, will you?' He seemed to have a variety of expressions to imply the making of haste. 'You don't have to come, darling. Finish your coffee.'

The table was veiled in smoke. They had smoked throughout the courses. He would be gone perhaps only half an hour but he bent over and kissed his wife. She smiled at him, lit another cigarette. When they had gone, she and Archery were alone. She moved into her husband's chair from where she could watch the dancers, many she seemed to know, for she waved occasionally and nodded as if promising she would soon join them.

Archery suddenly felt lonely. He knew no one in this place except two rather hostile policemen. His stay might be for the whole fortnight. Why hadn't he asked Mary to join him? It would be a holiday for her, a change, and—heaven knew—she needed a change. In a minute, when he had finished his second cup, he would go upstairs and telephone her.

The girl's voice startled him. 'Do you mind if I have your ashtray? Ours are all full.'

'Of course not, take it.' He lifted the heavy glass plate and as he handed it to her the tips of her cool dry fingers touched his own. The hand was small, childlike, with short unpainted nails. 'I don't smoke,' he added rather foolishly.

'Are you staying here long?' Her voice was light and soft, yet mature.

'Just a few days.'

'I asked,' she said, 'because we come here so often and I hadn't seen you before today. Most of the people are regulars.' She put out the cigarette carefully, stubbing it until the last red spark was dead. 'They have these dances once a month and we always come. I love dancing.'

Afterwards Archery wondered what on earth had induced him, a country vicar nearly fifty years old, to say what he did. Perhaps it was the mingled scents, the descending twilight or just that he was alone and out of his environment, out of his identity almost.

'Would you like to dance?'

It was a waltz they were playing. He was sure he could waltz. They waltzed at church socials. You simply had to make your feet go one, two, three in a sort of triangle. And yet, for all that, he felt himself blush. What would she think of him at his age? She might suppose he was doing what Charles called 'picking her up.'

'I'd love to,' she said.

Apart from Mary and Mary's sister, she was the only woman he had danced with in twenty years. He was so shy and so overcome by the enormity of what he was doing, that for a moment he was deaf to the music and blind to the hundred or so other people who circled the floor. Then she was in his arms, a light creature of scent and lace whose body so incongruously touching his had the fluidity and the tenuousness of a summer mist. He felt that he was dreaming and because of this, this utter unreality, he forgot about his feet and what he must make them do, and simply moved with her as if he and she and the music were one.

'I'm not very good at this sort of thing,' he said when he found his voice. 'You'll have to overlook my mistakes.' He was so much taller than she that she had to lift her face up to him.

She smiled. 'Hard to make conversation when you're dancing, isn't it? I never know what to say but one must say something.'

'Like "Don't you think this is a good floor?"' Strange, he remembered that one from undergraduate days.

'Or "Do you reverse?" It's absurd really. Here we

are dancing together and I don't even know your name.' She gave a little deprecating laugh. 'It's almost immoral.'

'My name's Archery. Henry Archery.'

'How do you do, Henry Archery?' she said gravely. Then as they moved into a pool of sunset light, she looked steadily at him, the glowing colour falling on her face. 'You really don't recognise me, do you?' He shook his head, wondering if he had made some terrible *faux pas*. She gave a mock sigh. 'Such is fame! Imogen Ide. Doesn't it ring a bell?'

'I'm awfully sorry.'

'Frankly, you don't look as if you spend your leisure perusing the glossy magazines. Before I married I was what they call a top model. The most photographed face in Britain.'

He hardly knew what to say. The things that came to mind all had some reference to her extraordinary beauty and to speak them aloud would have been impertinent. Sensing his predicament, she burst out laughing, but it was a companionable laugh, warm and kind.

He smiled down at her. Then over her shoulder he caught sight of a familiar face. Chief Inspector Wexford had come on to the floor with a stout pleasant-looking woman and a young couple. His wife, his daughter and the architect's son, Archery supposed, feeling a sudden pang. He watched them sit down and just as he was about to avert his eyes, Wexford's met his. The smiles they exchanged were slightly antagonistic and Archery felt hot with awkwardness. Wexford's expression held a mocking quality as if to say that dancing was a frivolity quite out of keeping with Archery's quest. Abruptly he looked away and back to his partner.

'I'm afraid I only read *The Times*,' he said, feeling the snobbishness of the remark as soon as the words were out.

'I was in *The Times* once,' she said. 'Oh, not my picture. I was in the High Court bit. Somebody men-

tioned my name in a case and the judge said, 'Who is
Imogen Ide?" '

'That really is fame.'

'I've kept the cutting to this day.'

The music that had been so liquid and lullaby-like
suddenly jerked into a frightening tempo with a stormy
undertone of drums.

'I haven't a hope of doing this one,' Archery said
helplessly. He released her quickly, there in the middle
of the floor.

'Never mind. Thank you very much, anyway. I've
enjoyed it.'

'So have I, very much indeed.'

They began to thread their way between couples
who were shuddering and bounding about like savages.
She was holding his hand and he could hardly with-
draw it without rudeness.

'Here's my husband back,' she said. 'Won't you
join us for the evening if you've nothing better to do?'

The man called Ide was coming up to them, smiling.
His evenly olive face, dead black hair and almost fem-
inine standard of grooming gave him the look of a
waxwork. Archery had the absurd notion that if you
came upon him at Madame Tussaud's the old joke of
the naive spectator mistaking a model for a flesh and
blood attendant would be reversed. In this case you
would pass the real man by, thinking him a figure in
wax.

'This is Mr Archery, darling. I've been telling him
he ought to stay. It's such a beautiful night.'

'Good idea. Perhaps I can get you a drink, Mr
Archery?'

'Thank you, no.' Archery found himself shaking
hands, astonished because of his fantasy at the warmth
of Ide's hand. 'I must go. I have to phone my wife.'

'I hope we shall see you again,' said Imogen Ide. 'I
enjoyed our dance.' She took her husband's hand and
they moved away into the centre of the floor, their
bodies meeting, their steps following the intricate
rhythm. Archery went upstairs to his bedroom. Earlier

he had supposed that the music would annoy him but
here in the violet-coloured dusk it was enchanting,
disturbing, awakening in him forgotten, undefined
longings. He stood at the window, looking at the sky
with its long feather scarves of cloud, rose pink as
cyclamen petals but less substantial. The strains of
the music had softened to match this tranquil sky and
now they seemed to him like the opening bars of an
overture to some pastoral opera.

Presently he sat down on the bed and put his hand
to the telephone. It rested there immobile for some
minutes. What was the point of ringing Mary when he
had nothing to tell her, no plans even for what he
would do in the morning? He felt a sudden distaste for
Thringford and its small parochial doings. He had
lived there so long, so narrowly, and outside all the
time there had been a world of which he knew little.

From where he sat he could see nothing but sky,
broken continents and islands on a sea of azure. 'Here
will we sit and let the sound of music creep in our
ears . . .' He took his hand from the telephone and
lay back, thinking of nothing.

9

The words of his mouth were softer than but-
ter, having war in his heart: his words were
smoother than oil, and yet be they very swords.
Psalm 55, appointed for the Tenth Day

'I SUPPOSE there isn't anything in it?'
'In what, Mike? Liz Crilling having some dark secret her mother doesn't want extorted from her under
the third degree?'

Burden lowered the blinds against the brazen morning sky.

'Those Crillings always make me uneasy,' he said.

'They're no more kinky than half our customers,' Wexford said breezily. 'Liz'll turn up at the Assizes all right. If not for any other reason simply because Mrs Crilling doubts her ability to get a thousand quid out of her brother-in-law, or whoever it is supports them. And then if she's got something to tell us, she'll tell us.'

Burden's expression, though apologetic, was obstinate.

'I can't help feeling it's got some connection with Painter,' he said.

Wexford had been leafing through a thick orange-coloured trade directory. Now he dropped it on the desk with a deliberate bang.

'By God, I won't have any more of this! What is it, anyhow, some sort of conspiracy to prove I can't do my job?'

'I'm sorry, sir, you know I didn't mean that.'

'I don't know a damn' thing, Mike. I only know the Painter case was an open and shut affair, and nobody's got a hope in hell of showing he didn't do it.' He began to calm down slowly, and he spread his hands in two large implacable fans on the directory cover. 'Go and question Liz by all means. Or tell Archery to do it for you. He's a fast worker that one.'

'Is he? What makes you say so?'

'Never mind. I've got work to do if you haven't and . . .' said Wexford, splendidly co-ordinating his metaphors, 'I'm fed up to my back teeth with having Painter rammed down my throat morning, noon and night.'

Archery had slept deeply and dreamlessly. It occurred to him that he had done all his dreaming while he was awake and there was none left for sleep. The telephone roused him. It was his wife.

'Sorry it's so early, darling, but I've had another letter from Charles.'

There was a cup of cold tea by the bed. Archery wondered how long it had been there. He found his watch and saw that it was nine.

'That's all right. How are you?'

'Not so bad. You sound as if you're still in bed.'

Archery grunted something.

'Now, listen. Charles is coming down tomorrow and he says he's coming straight over to Kingsmarkham.'

'Coming *down?*'

'Oh, it's all right, Henry. He's going to cut the last three days of term. Surely it can't matter much.'

'As long as it isn't the thin end of the wedge. Is he coming to The Olive?'

'Well, naturally. He's got to stay somewhere. I know it's expensive, darling, but he's got himself a job for August and September—something in a brewery. It sounds awful but he's going to get sixteen pounds a week and he says he'll pay you back.'

'I hadn't realised I made such an avaricious impression on my son.'

'You know he doesn't mean that. You *are* touchy this morning . . .'

After she had rung off he still held the receiver for some moments in his hand. He wondered why he hadn't asked her to join him as well. He had meant to last night and then . . . Of course, he had been so drowsy while she was speaking that he hardly knew what he was saying. The operator's voice broke in.

'Have you finished or did you want to make a call?'

'No thank you. I've finished.'

The little sandy houses in Glebe Road seemed to have been bleached and dried up by the sun. This morning they looked even more like desert dwellings, each surrounded by its own scanty oasis.

Burden went first to number a hundred and two. An old acquaintance of his lived there, a man with a long record and a nasty sense of humour called by some

'Monkey' Matthews. Burden thought it more than likely that he was responsible for the home-made bomb, a bizarre affair of sugar and weed killer stuffed into a whisky bottle that a blonde woman of easy virtue had received that morning through her letter box. The bomb had done no more than wreck the hall of her flat, she and her current lover being still in bed, but Burden thought it might amount to attempted murder just the same.

He knocked and rang but he was sure the bell didn't work. Then he went round the back and found himself ankle-deep in garbage, pram wheels, old clothes, newspapers and empty bottles. He looked through the kitchen window. There was a packet of weed killer—sodium chlorate crystals—on the window sill and the top had been torn off. How confident could you get, or how stupid? He went back up the street to a call box and told Bryant and Gates to pick up the occupant of a hundred and two Glebe Road.

Twenty-four was on the same side. Now he was so near there would be no harm in having a chat with Liz Crilling. The front door was closed but the latch was down. He coughed and walked in.

In the back room a plastic transistor was playing pop music. Elizabeth Crilling sat at the table reading the Situations Vacant in last week's local paper and she was wearing nothing but a slip, its broken shoulder strap held together with a safety pin.

'I don't remember inviting you in.'

Burden looked at her distastefully. 'D'you mind putting something on?' She made no move but kept her eyes on the paper. He glanced around the dismal, untidy room, and from the various miscellaneous heaps of clothes, selected something that might have been a dressing gown, a pink floppy thing whose flounces recalled withered petals. 'Here,' he said, and he wondered if she were not quite well, for she shuddered as she put the dressing gown round her. It was far too big, obviously not her own.

'Where's your mother?'

'I don't know. Gone out somewhere. I'm not her keeper.' She grinned suddenly, showing her beautiful teeth. 'Am I my mother's keeper? That's good, don't you think? Which reminds me . . .' The smile died and she exclaimed sharply, 'What's that clergyman doing here?'

Burden never answered a question if he could help it.

'Looking for a new post, are you?'

She gave a sulky pout. 'I phoned my firm yesterday when I got back from that bloody court and they gave me the push. I've got you lot to thank for that.' Burden inclined his head politely. 'Well, I've got to have a job, haven't I? They want girls at the raincoat factory and they say you can pick up twenty quid a week with overtime.'

Burden remembered her education, the expensive schools the Crilling relatives had paid for. She stared at him boldly.

'I may as well go and see them,' she said. 'What's the harm? Life's hell anyway.' She gave a strident laugh, walked to the mantelpiece and leaned against it, looking down at him. The open dressing gown, the tatty underclothes were provocative in a raw, basic way, that seemed to go with the hot weather and the dishevelled room. 'To what do I owe the honour of this visit? Are you lonely, Inspector? I hear your wife's away.' She took a cigarette and put it between her lips. Her forefinger was rusty with nicotine, the nail yellow, the cuticle bitten. 'Where the hell are the matches?'

There was something in the quick wary look she gave over her shoulder that impelled him to follow her to the kitchen. Once there, she turned to face him, grabbed a box of matches and stood as if barring his way. He felt a thrill of alarm. She thrust the matches into his hand.

'Light it for me, will you?'

He struck the match steadily. She came very close to him and as the flame shrivelled the tobacco, closed her fingers over his hand. For a split second he felt what his rather prudish nature told him was vile, then that nature, his duty and a swift suspicion took over. She was breathing hard, but not, he was certain, because of his nearness to her. From long practice he sidestepped neatly, freeing the long bare leg from between his own, and found himself confronting what she perhaps had hoped to hide from him.

The sink was crammed with dirty crocks, potato peelings, tea leaves, wet paper, but the Crillings were long past middle-class concealment of squalor.

'You could do with a few days off, I should think,' he said loudly. 'Get this place in some sort of order.'

She had begun to laugh. 'You know, you're not so bad-looking on the other side of a smoke-screen.'

'Been ill, have you?' He was looking at the empty pill bottles, the one that was half full and the syringe. 'Nerves, I daresay.'

She stopped laughing. 'They're hers.'

Burden read labels, saying nothing.

'She has them for her asthma. They're all the same.' As he put out his hand to find the hypodermic she seized his wrist. 'You've no business to turn things over. That amounts to searching and for searching you need a warrant.'

'True,' said Burden placidly. He followed her back to the living room and jumped when she shouted at him:

'You never answered my question about the clergyman.'

'He's come here because he knows Painter's daughter,' said Burden guardedly.

She went white and he thought she looked like her mother.

'Painter that killed the old woman?'

Burden nodded.

'That's funny,' she said. 'I'd like to see her again.' He had a queer feeling she was changing the subject, and yet her remark was not inconsequential. She turned her eyes towards the garden. But it wasn't, he thought, the nettles, the brambles and the mean wire fence she could see. 'I used to go over to the coach house and play with her,' she said. 'Mother never knew. She said Tess wasn't my class. I couldn't understand that. I thought, how can she have a class if she doesn't go to school?' She reached up and gave the birdcage a vicious push. 'Mother was always with the old woman —talk, talk, talk, I'll never forget it—and she used to send me into the garden to play. There wasn't anything to play with and one day I saw Tessie, mucking about with a heap of sand . . . Why are you looking at me like that?'

'Am I?'

'Does she know about her father?' Burden nodded. 'Poor kid. What does she do for a living?'

'She's some kind of a student.'

'*Student?* My God, I was a student once.' She had begun to tremble. The long worm of ash broke from her cigarette and scattered down the pink flounces. Looking down at it, she flicked uselessly at old stains and burn marks. The movement suggested the uncontrollable jerking of chorea. She swung round on him, her hate and despair striking him like a flame. 'What are you trying to do to me?' she shouted. 'Get out! Get out!'

When he had gone she grabbed a torn sheet from a stack of unironed linen and flung it over the birdcage. The sudden movement and the gust of breeze it had caused fluttered the thing her mother called a negligee but that she had never feared until it touched her own skin. Why the hell did he have to come here and rake it all up again? Perhaps a drink would help. True, it hadn't done so the other day . . . There never was a drink in this house, anyway.

Newspapers, old letters and unpaid bills, empty cigarette packets and a couple of old laddered stockings tumbled out when she opened the cupboard door. She rummaged in the back among dusty vases, Christmas wrapping paper, playing cards with dog-eared

corners. One vase had an encouraging shape. She
pulled it out and found it was the cherry brandy Uncle
had given her mother for her birthday. Filthy, sweet
cherry brandy . . . She squatted on the floor among the
debris and poured some of it into a grimy glass. In a
minute she felt a lot better, almost well enough to get
dressed and do something about the bloody job. Now
she had begun she might as well finish the bottle—it
was wonderful how little it took to do the trick provided you started on an empty stomach.

The neck of the bottle rattled against the glass. She
was concentrating on keeping her hand steady, not
watching the liquid level rise and rise until it over-
brimmed, spilt and streamed over the spread pink
flounces.

Red everywhere. Good thing we're not houseproud,
she thought, and then she looked down at herself, at
red on pale pink . . . Her fingers tore at the nylon until
they were red and sticky too. O God, God! She tram-
pled on it, shuddering as if it were slimy, alive, and
threw herself on the sofa.

. . . You had nothing pretty on now, nothing to
show to Tessie. She used to worry in case you got
yourself dirty and one day when Mummy was indoors
with Granny Rose and the man they called Roger she
took you upstairs to see Auntie Rene and Uncle Bert,
and Auntie Rene made you put an old apron on over
your frock.

Uncle Bert and Roger. They were the only men you
knew apart from Daddy who was always ill—'ailing'
Mummy called it. Uncle Bert was rough and big and
once when you came upstairs quietly you heard him
shouting at Auntie Rene and then you saw him hit her.
But he was kind to you and he called you Lizzie.
Roger never called you anything. How could he when
he never spoke to you, but looked at you as if he
hated you?

It was in the Autumn that Mummy said you ought
to have a party frock. Funny really, because there
weren't any parties to go to, but Mummy said you

could wear it on Christmas day. Pink it was, three layers of pale pink net over a pink petticoat, and it was the most beautiful dress you had ever seen in your life . . .

Elizabeth Crilling knew that once it had begun it would go on and on. Only one thing could stop it now. Keeping her eyes from the pink thing, all spattered with red, she stumbled out into the kitchen to find her temporary salvation.

Irene Kershaw's voice on the telephone sounded cold and distant. 'Your Charlie seems to have had a bit of a tiff with Tessie, Mr Archery. I don't know what it's all about, but I'm sure it can't be her fault. She worships the ground he treads on.'

'They're old enough to know what they're doing,' said Archery insincerely.

'She's coming home tomorrow and she must be upset if she's cutting the last days of term. All the people round here keep asking when the wedding is and I just don't know what to say. It puts me in a very awkward position.'

Respectability, always respectability.

'Did you ring me up about something special, Mr Archery, or was it just for a chat?'

'I wondered if you'd mind giving me your husband's business number?'

'If you two think you can go together,' she said more warmly, 'and have a go at patching things up, that would suit me down to the ground. I really can't contemplate the idea of my Tess being—well, thrown over.' Archery did not answer. 'The number's Uplands 62234,' she said.

Kershaw had an extension of his own and a bright cockney secretary.

'I want to write to Painter's commanding officer," Archery said when the civilities had been exchanged.

Kershaw seemed to hesitate, then said in his usual eager, vital voice, 'Don't know the bloke's name, but it was the Duke of Babraham's Light Infantry he was in. Third Battalion. The War Office'll tell you.'

'The defence didn't call him at the trial, but it might help me if he could give Painter a good character.'

'If. I wonder why the defence didn't call him, Mr Archery?'

The War Office was helpful. The Third Battalion had been commanded by a Colonel Cosmo Plashet. He was an old man now and living in retirement in Westmorland. Archery made several attempts to write to Colonel Plashet. The final letter was not what he would have wished, but it would have to do. After lunch he went out to post it.

He strolled up towards the Post Office. Time hung heavy on his hands and he had no notion what to do next. Tomorrow Charles would come, full of ideas and extravagant plans, but comforting, an assistant. Or, knowing Charles, a director. He badly needed someone to direct him. Police work is for policemen, he thought, experts who are trained and have all the means for detection at their disposal.

Then he saw her. She was coming out of the florist's next door to the Post Office and her arms were full of white roses. They matched and mingled with the white pattern on her black dress so that you could not tell which were real and which a mere design on silk.

'Good afternoon, Mr Archery,' said Imogen Ide.

Until now he had hardly noticed the beauty of the day, the intense blue of the sky, the glory of perfect holiday weather. She smiled.

'Would you be very kind and open the car door for me?'

He jumped to do her bidding like a boy. The poodle, Dog, was sitting on the passenger seat and when Archery touched the door, he growled and showed his teeth.

'Don't be such a fool,' she said to the dog and dumped him on the back seat. 'I'm taking these up to Forby cemetery. My husband's ancestors have a sort of vault there. Very feudal. He's in town so I said I'd do it. It's an interesting old church. Have you seen much of the country round here yet?'

'Very little, I'm afraid.'

'Perhaps you don't care for clerestories and fonts and that sort of thing.'

'Quite the contrary, I assure you. I'll get the car and go over to Forby tonight if you think it's worth seeing.'

'Why not come now?'

He had meant her to ask him. He knew it and he was ashamed. Yet what was there to be ashamed about? In a way he was on holiday and holiday acquaintances were quickly made. He had met her husband and it was only by chance her husband was not with her now. In that case he would have accepted without a qualm. Besides, in these days there was no harm in a man going on a little excursion with a woman. How many times had he picked up Miss Baylis in Thringford village and driven her into Colchester to do her shopping? Imogen Ide was much farther removed from him in age than Miss Baylis. She couldn't be more than thirty. He was old enough to be her father. Suddenly he wished he hadn't thought of that, for it put things in an unpleasant perspective.

'It's very good of you,' he said. 'I'd like to.'

She was a good driver. For once he didn't mind being driven, didn't wish he was at the wheel. It was a beautiful car, a silver Lancia Flavia, and it purred along the winding roads. All was still and they passed only two other cars. The meadows were rich green or pale yellow where they had been shorn of hay, and between them and a dark ridge of woodland ran a glittering brown stream.

'That's the Kingsbrook,' she said, 'the same one that passes under the High Street. Isn't it strange? Man can do almost anything, move mountains, create seas, irrigate deserts, but he can't prevent the flow of water. He can dam it, channel it, pass it through pipes, make bridges over it . . .' He watched her, remembering with wonder that she had been a photographic model. Her lips were parted and the breeze blew her hair. 'But still it springs from the earth and finds its way to the sea.'

He said nothing and hoped she could sense if not see his nod. They were coming into a village. A dozen or so cottages and a couple of big houses surrounded a sprawling green; there was a little inn and through a mass of dark green foliage Archery could see the outlines of the church.

The entrance to the churchyard was by way of a kissing gate. He followed Imogen Ide and he carried the roses. The place was shady and cool but not well-tended and some of the older gravestones had tumbled over on their backs into the tangle of nettles and briars.

'This way,' she said, taking the left hand path. 'You mustn't go widdershins around a church. It's supposed to be unlucky.'

Yews and ilexes bordered the path. Underfoot it was sandy, yet green with moss and the delicate tufts of arenaria. The church was very old and built of rough-hewn oaken logs. Its beauty lay in its antiquity.

'It's one of the oldest wooden churches in the country.'

'There's one like it in my county,' said Archery. 'At Greensted. I believe it's ninth century.'

'This one's Nine something. Would you like to see the leper squint?'

They knelt down side by side and, bending forward, he peered through the small triangular gap at the base of the log wall. Although it was not the first of its kind he had seen, it pained him to think of the outcast, the unclean, who came to this tiny grille and listening to the Mass, received on his tongue the bread that some believe is the body of God. It made him think of Tess, herself an outcast, condemned like the leper to an undeserved disease. Within he could see a little stone aisle, wooden pews and a pulpit carved with saints' faces. He shivered and he felt her shiver beside him.

They were very close together under the yew boughs.

He had a strange feeling that they were quite alone in the world and that they had been brought here for the working out of some destiny. He lifted his eyes, and turning to her, met hers. He expected her to smile but instead her face was grave, yet full of wonder and a kind of fear. He felt in himself, without analysing it, the emotion he saw in her eyes. The scent of the roses was intoxicating, fresh and unbearably sweet.

Then he got to his feet quickly, a little quelled by the stiffness of his knees. For a moment he had felt like a boy; his body betrayed him as bodies always do.

She said rather brightly, 'Have a look inside while I put these flowers on the grave. I won't be long.'

He went softly up the aisle and stood before the altar. Anyone watching him might have taken him for an atheist, so cool and appraising was his glance. Back again to look at the unassuming little font, the inscriptions on wall plaques. He put two half-crowns in the box and signed his name in the visitors' book. His hand was shaking so badly that the signature looked like that of an old man.

When he came out once more into the churchyard she was nowhere to be seen. The lettering on the older stones had been obliterated by time and weather. He walked into the new part, reading the last messages of relatives to their dead.

As he came to the end of the path where the hedge was and on the other side of the hedge a meadow, a name that seemed familiar caught his eye. Grace, John Grace. He reflected, searching his mind. It was not a common name and until quite recently he had associated it only with the great cricketer. Of course—a boy had lain dying in the road and that death and that boy's request had reminded Wexford of another, similar tragedy. Wexford had told him about it in the court. 'Must be all of twenty years . . .'

Archery looked to the engraved words for confirmation.

Sacred to the Memory of
John Grace
Who departed This Life
February 16th, 1945
In the Twenty-First Year
of His Age
Go, Shepherd, to your rest;
Your tale is told.
The Lamb of God takes
Shepherds to his fold.

A pleasant, if not brilliant, conceit, Archery thought. It was apparently a quotation, but he didn't recognise it. He looked round as Imogen Ide approached. The leaf shadows played on her face and made a pattern on her hair so that it looked as if it was covered by a veil of lace.

'Are you reminding yourself of your mortality?' she asked him gravely.

'I suppose so. It's an interesting place.'

'I'm glad to have had the opportunity of showing it to you. I'm very patriotic—if that's the word—about my county though it hasn't been mine for long.'

He was certain she was going to offer herself as his guide on some future occasion and he said quickly: 'My son is coming tomorrow. We'll have to explore together.' She smiled politely. 'He's twenty-one,' he added rather fatuously.

Simultaneously their eyes turned to the inscription on the stone.

'I'm ready to go if you are,' she said.

She dropped him outside the Olive and Dove. They said good-bye briskly and he noticed she said nothing about hoping to see him again. He didn't feel like tea and went straight upstairs. Without knowing why he took out the photograph he had of Painter's daughter. Looking at the picture, he wondered why he had thought her so lovely. She was just a pretty girl with the prettiness of youth. Yet while he looked he seemed to realise for the first time why Charles longed so passionately to possess her. It was a strange feeling and it had little to do with Tess, with Tess's appearance or with Charles. In a way it was a universal diffused empathy, but it was selfish too and it came from his heart rather than from his mind.

10

And if he hath not before disposed of his goods, let him be admonished to make his will . . . for the better discharging of his conscience and the quietness of his executors.

The Visitation of the Sick

'You don't seem to have got very far,' said Charles. He sat down in an armchair and surveyed the pleasant lounges. The maid who was operating a floor polisher thought him very handsome with his rather long fair hair and his scornful expression. She decided to give the lounge a more than usually thorough do. 'The great thing is to be businesslike about it. We haven't got all that long. I start at the brewery on Monday week.' Archery was rather nettled. His own parochial duties were being overlooked. 'I'm sure there's something fishy about that fellow Primero, Roger Primero. I rang him up before I got here last night and I've got a date to see him this morning at half eleven.'

Archery looked at his watch. It was almost ten.

'You'd better get a move on, then. Where does he live?'

'You see? Now if I'd been in your shoes that's the first thing I'd have found out. He lives at Forby Hall.

I suppose he fancies himself as the lord of the manor.' He glanced at his father and said quickly, 'Be all right if I have the car?'

'I suppose so. What are you going to tell him, Charles? He might have you thrown out.'

'I don't think he will,' Charles said thoughtfully. 'I've found out a bit about him and it seems he's mad keen on publicity. Always trying to create an image.' He hesitated, then added boldly, 'I told him I was the top features man on the *Sunday Planet* and we were doing a series on tycoons. Rather good, don't you think?'

'It doesn't happen to be true,' said Archery.

Charles said rapidly, 'The end justifies the means. I thought I could put across a line about his early life being dogged by misfortune, father dying, grandmother murdered, no prospects—that sort of thing. And look at him now. You never know what will come out. He's supposed to be very forthcoming to the Press.'

'We'd better go and get the car out.'

It was as hot as ever, but more sultry. A thin mist covered the sun. Charles wore an open necked white shirt and rather tapering trousers. Archery thought he looked like a Regency duellist.

'You won't want to start yet,' he said. 'Forby's only about four miles away. Would you like to look round the place?'

They walked up to the High Street and over the Kingsbrook bridge. Archery was proud to have his son beside him. He knew they were very much alike but he didn't for a moment deceive himself they might be taken for brothers. The heavy muggy weather had brought on a twinge of lumbago and today he had utterly forgotten what it felt like to be twenty-one.

'You're reading English,' he said to Charles. 'Tell me where this comes from.' His memory hadn't begun to fail, at any rate. He was word perfect in the little verse.

' "Go, Shepherd, to your rest;
Your tale is told.
The lamb of God takes
Shepherds to his fold." '

Charles shrugged. 'Sounds vaguely familiar, but I can't place it. Where did you see it?'

'On a gravestone in Forby churchyard.'

'You really are the end, Father. I thought you wanted to help me and Tess and all you've been doing is messing about in cemeteries.'

Archery controlled himself with difficulty. If Charles was going to take everything into his own hands there seemed no reason why he shouldn't just go back to Thringford. There was nothing to keep him in Kingsmarkham. He wondered why the prospect of returning to the vicarage seemed ineffably dull. Suddenly he stopped and nudged his son's arm.

'What's the matter?'

'That woman outside the butcher's, the one in the cape—it's that Mrs Crilling I told you about. I'd rather not come face to face with her.'

But it was too late. She had evidently seen them already, for with her cape flying, she came bearing down upon them like a galleon.

'Mr Archery! My dear friend!' She took both his hands in hers and swung them as if she were about to partner him in an eightsome reel. 'What a lovely surprise! I was only saying to my daughter this morning, I do hope I shall see that dear man again so that I can thank him for ministering to me in my wretched affliction.'

This was a new mood. She was like a dowager at a successful garden party. The cape was familiar but the dress she wore under it was an ordinary cotton frock, simple and dowdy, somewhat splashed with gravy stains on its front. She gave a broad, calm and gracious smile.

'This is my son, Charles,' Archery muttered. 'Charles, this is Mrs Crilling.'

To his surprise Charles took the outstretched, none-too-clean hand and half-bowed over it.

'How do you do?' Over her head he gave his father an angry glance. 'I've heard so much about you.'

'Nice things, I hope.' If it occurred to her that Archery had seen nothing nice about her to relate she gave no sign of it. She was quite sane, gay, even frivolous. 'Now, don't refuse to gratify my little whim. I want you both to come into the Carousel and take a wee cup of coffee with me. My treat, of course,' she added archly.

'Our time,' said Charles grandiloquently—absurdly, Archery thought, 'is quite at your disposal. Until eleven fifteen, that is. Don't let us discuss anything so absurd as treats in the company of a lady.'

Evidently it was the right line to take with her. 'Isn't he *sweet?*' she gurgled. They went into the café. 'Children are such a blessing, don't you think? The crown of the tree of life. You must be proud of him, even though he quite puts you in the shade.'

Charles pulled out a chair for her. They were the only customers and for a while no one came to take their order. Mrs Crilling leant confidingly towards Archery.

'My baby has got herself a situation and she starts tomorrow. An operative in a ladies' wear establishment, I understand the prospects are excellent. With her intelligence there's no knowing how far she can go. The trouble is she's never had a real chance.' She had been speaking in a low genteel voice. Suddenly she turned her back on him, banged the sugar basin on the table and screamed loudly in the direction of the kitchen:

'Service!'

Charles jumped. Archery shot him a glance of triumph.

'Always having her hopes raised and then it comes to nothing,' she went on just as if the scream had never happened. 'Her father was just the same—struck down with T.B. in the flower of his age and dead within six months.' Archery flinched as she jerked away from him once more. 'Where the flaming hell are those bloody girls?' she shouted.

A woman in a green uniform with Manageress embroidered on the bodice came out from the kitchen. The look she gave Mrs Crilling was bored and withering.

'I asked you not to come in here again, Mrs Crilling, if you can't behave yourself.' She smiled frostily at Archery, 'What can I get you, sir?'

'Three coffees, please.'

'I'll have mine black,' said Charles.

'What was I talking about?'

'Your daughter,' said Archery hopefully.

'Oh, yes, my baby. It's funny really she should have had such a bad break because when she was a little tot it looked as if everything in the garden was lovely. I had a dear old friend, you see, who simply doted on my baby. And she was rolling in money, kept servants and all that kind of thing . . .'

The coffee came. It was the espresso kind with foam on the top.

'You can bring me some white sugar,' said Mrs Crilling sulkily. 'I can't stomach that demerara muck.' The waitress flounced away, returned with another sugar bowl and banged it down on the table. Mrs Crilling gave a shrill little shriek as soon as she was out of earshot. 'Silly bitch!'

Then she returned to her theme. 'Very old my friend was and beyond being responsible for her actions. Senile, they call it. Over and over again she told me she wanted to do something for my baby. I passed it off, of course, having an absolute revulsion about stepping into dead men's shoes.' She stopped suddenly and dropped four heaped teaspoonsful of sugar into her coffee.

'Naturally,' said Charles. 'The last thing anyone would call you is mercenary, Mrs Crilling.'

She smiled complacently and to Archery's intense

amusement, leant across the table and patted Charles's cheek.

'You dear,' she said. 'You lovely, understanding dear.' After a deep breath she went on more practically, 'Still, you have to look after your own. I didn't press it, not till the doctor told me Mr Crilling had only got six months to live. No insurance, I thought in my despair, no pension. I pictured myself reduced to leaving my baby on the steps of an orphanage.'

For his part, Archery was unable to picture it. Elizabeth had been a sturdy youngster of five at the time.

'Do go on,' said Charles. 'It's most interesting.'

'You ought to make a will, I said to my friend. I'll pop down the road and get you a will form. A thousand or two would make all the difference to my baby. You know how she's gladdened your last years, and what have those grandchildren of yours ever done for you? Damn all, I thought.'

'But she didn't make a will?' Archery said.

'What do you know about it? You let me tell it in my own way. It was about a week before she died. I'd had the will form for weeks and weeks and all the time poor Mr Crilling was wasting away to a shadow. But would she fill it in? Not her, the old cow. I had to use all my most winning powers of persuasion.

Every time I said a word that crazy old maid of hers would put her spoke in. Then that old maid—Flower, her name was—she got a bad cold and had to keep to her bed. "Have you thought any more about disposing of your temporal estates?" I said to my friend in a light-hearted, casual manner. "Maybe I should do something for Lizzie," she said and I knew my opportunity was at hand.

'Back across the road I flew. I didn't like to witness it myself, you know, on account of my baby being a beneficiary. Mrs White, my neighbour, came over and the lady who helped with her housework. They were only too delighted. You might say it brought a ray of sunshine into their humdrum lives.'

Archery wanted to say, 'But Mrs Primero died intestate.' He didn't dare. Any hint that he knew whom she was talking about and the whole narrative might be brought to a halt.

'Well, we got it all written out. I'm a great reader, Mr Archery, so I was able to put it in the right language. "Blood is thicker than water", said my old friend—she was wandering in her mind—but she only put the grandchildren down for five hundred a-piece. There was eight thousand for my baby and I was to have charge of it till she was twenty-one, and a bit left over for the Flower woman. My friend was crying bitterly. I reckon she realised how wicked she'd been in not doing it before.

'And that was that. I saw Mrs White and the other lady safely off the premises—more fool I, though I didn't know it at the time. I said I'd keep the will safe and I did. She wasn't to mention it to anybody. And —would you believe it?—a week later she met with her death.'

Charles said innocently, 'That was a good start for your daughter, Mrs Crilling, whatever misfortunes came afterwards.'

He started as she got up abruptly. Her face had blanched to the whiteness it had worn in court and her eyes blazed.

'Any benefits she got,' she said in a choking voice, 'came from her dead father's people. Charity it was, cold charity. "Send me the school bills, Josie," her uncle'd say to me. "I'll pay them direct, and her auntie can go with her to get her uniform. If you think she needs treatment for her nerves her auntie can go with her to Harley Street, too." '

'But what about the will?'

'That bloody will!' Mrs Crilling shouted. 'It wasn't legal. I only found out after she was dead. I took it straight round to Quadrants, the solicitors that were in the High Street. Old Mr Quadrant was alive then. "What about these alterations?" he said. Well, I looked and, lo and behold, the old cow had scribbled in a lot of extra bits while I was at the front door with

Mrs White. Scribbled in bits and scratched out bits too. "These invalidate the whole thing," said Mr Quadrant. "You have to get the witnesses to sign them, or have a codicil. You could fight it," he said, looking me up and down in a nasty way, knowing I hadn't got a bean. "But I wouldn't say much for your chances." '

To Archery's horror she broke into a stream of obscenities, many of which he had never heard before. The manageress came out and took her by the arm.

'Out you go. We can't have this in here.'

'My God,' said Charles, after she had been hustled away. 'I see what you mean.'

'I must confess her language shook me a bit.'

Charles chuckled. 'Not fit for your ears at all.'

'It was most enlightening, though. Are you going to bother with Primero now?'

'It can't do any harm.'

Archery had to wait a long time in the corridor outside Wexford's office. Just as he was beginning to think he would have to give up and try again later, the main entrance doors opened and a little bright-eyed man in working clothes came in between two uniformed policemen. He was plainly some sort of criminal, but everyone seemed to know him and find him a source of ironic amusement.

'I can't stand these contemporary-type nicks,' he said impudently to the station sergeant. Wexford came out of his office, ignoring Archery, and crossed to the desk. 'Give me the old-fashioned kind every time. I've got a slummy mind, that's my trouble.'

'I'm not interested in your views on interior decoration, Monkey,' said Wexford.

The little man turned to him and grinned.

'You've got a nasty tongue, you have. Your sense of humour's sunk as you've gone up. Pity, really.'

'Shut up!'

Archery listened in admiration. He wished that he had the power and the authority to talk like that to Mrs Crilling, or that such authority could be vested in Charles, enabling him to question Primero without the inhibitions of subterfuge. Wexford, talking silkily about bombs and attempted murder, ushered the little man into his office and the door closed on them. Such things did go on, Archery thought. Perhaps his own new-forming theories were not so far-fetched after all.

'If I could just see Inspector Burden for a moment,' he said more confidently to the station sergeant.

'I'll see if he's free, sir.'

Eventually Burden came out to him himself.

'Good morning, sir. Doesn't get any cooler, does it?'

'I've got something rather important to tell you. Can you spare me five minutes?'

'Surely.'

But he made no move to take him into a more private place. The station sergeant occupied himself with perusing a large book. Sitting on a ridiculous spoon-shaped chair outside Wexford's office, Archery felt like a school boy, who having waited a long time to see the headmaster, is compelled to confide in and perhaps take his punishment from an underling. Rather chastened, he told Burden briefly about Mrs Crilling.

'Most interesting. You mean that when Mrs Primero was murdered the Crilling woman thought the will was valid?'

'It amounts to that. She didn't mention the murder.'

'We can't do anything. You realise that?'

'I want you to tell me if I have sufficient grounds to write to the Home Secretary.'

A constable appeared from somewhere, tapped on Wexford's door and was admitted.

'You haven't any circumstantial evidence,' Burden said. 'I'm sure the Chief Inspector wouldn't encourage it.'

A roar of sardonic laughter sounded through the thin dividing wall. Archery felt unreasonably piqued.

'I think I shall write just the same.'

'You must do as you please, sir.' Burden got up. 'Been seeing much of the country round here?'

Archery swallowed his anger. If Burden intended to

terminate the interview with small talk, small talk he should have. Hadn't he promised his old friend Griswold and, for that matter, the Chief Inspector, not to make trouble?

'I went to Forby yesterday,' he said. 'I was in the churchyard and I happened to notice the grave of that boy Mr Wexford was talking about in court the other day. His name was Grace. Do you remember?'

Burden's face was a polite blank but the station sergeant glanced up.

'I'm a Forby man myself, sir,' he said. 'We make a bit of a song and dance about John Grace at home. They'll tell you all about him in Forby for all it was twenty years ago.'

'All about him?'

'He fancied himself as a poet, poor kid, wrote plays too. Sort of religious mystic he was. In his day he used to try and sell his verses from door to door.'

'Like W. H. Davis,' said Archery.

'I daresay.'

'Was he a shepherd?'

'Not as far as I know. Baker's roundsman or something.'

Wexford's door swung open, the constable came out and said to Burden, 'Chief Inspector wants you, sir.'

Wexford's voice roared after him, 'You can come back in here, Gates, and take a statement from Guy Fawkes. And give him a cigarette. He won't blow up.'

'It seems I'm wanted, sir, so if you'll excuse me . . .'

Burden went with Archery to the entrance doors.

'You had your chat with Alice Flower just in time,' he said. 'If you had it, that is.'

'Yes, I talked to her. Why?'

'She died yesterday,' said Burden. 'It's all in the local rag.'

Archery found a newsagent. The *Kingsmarkham Chronicle* had come out that morning and fresh stacks of papers lay on the counter. He bought a copy and found the announcement at the bottom of the back page.

'Death of Miss A. Flower.'

He scanned it and took it back with him to the terrace of the hotel to read it properly.

'The death occurred today . . .' That meant yesterday, Archery thought, looking at the dateline. He read on. 'The death occurred today of Miss Alice Flower at Stowerton Infirmary. She was eighty-seven. Miss Flower, who had lived in the district for twenty-five years, will be best remembered for the part she played in the notorious Victor's Piece murder trial. She as for many years maid and trusted friend of Mrs Primero . . .'

There followed a brief account of the murder and the trial.

'The funeral will take place at Forby parish church on Monday. Mr Roger Primero has expressed a wish that the last rites may be celebrated quietly and that there will be no sightseers.'

Roger Primero, faithful to the end, Archery thought. He found himself hoping that Charles had done nothing to distress this kindly and dutiful man. So Alice Flower was dead at last, death had waited just long enough to let her tell him, Archery, all she knew. Again he seemed to feel the working of destiny. Well done, thou good and faithful servant. Enter thou into the joy of thy Lord!

He went in to lunch, feeling jaded and depressed. Where on earth was Charles? He had been gone more than two hours. By now Primero had probably seen through that absurd cover story and . . .

His imagination showing him his son being interrogated by Wexford at his nastiest, he was just picking at his fruit salad and warm ice cream when Charles burst into the dining room, swinging the car keys.

'I was wondering where you'd got to.'

'I've had a most instructive morning. Anything happened here?'

'Nothing much. Alice Flower is dead.'

'You can't tell me anything about that. Primero was full of it. Apparently he was at her bedside for hours yesterday.' He threw himself into a chair next to his father's. 'God, it was hot in that car! As a matter of fact, her dying like that was a help if anything. Made it easier to get him on to the murder.'

'I didn't think you could be so callous,' said Archery distastefully.

'Oh, come off it, Father. She'd had her allotted span plus seventeen. She can't have wanted to live. Don't you want to hear what I got out of him?'

'Of course.'

'You don't want any coffee, do you? Let's go outside.'

There was no one on the terrace. A yellow climbing rose had shed its petals all over the ground and the battered cane chairs. What residents there were had left possessions out here as if to reserve permanent perches, magazines, library books, a roll of blue knitting, a pair of glasses. Ruthlessly Charles cleared two chairs and blew away the rose petals. For the first time Archery noticed that he looked extremely happy.

'Well,' he said when they had sat down, 'the house first. It's quite a place, about ten times the size of Thringford Manor, and it's all built of grey stone with a kind of pediment thing over the front door. Mrs Primero lived there when she was a girl and Roger bought it when it came up for sale this spring. There's a park with deer in it and a vast drive coming up from a pillared entrance. You can't see the house from the road, only the cedars in the park.

'They've got an Italian butler—not so classy as an English one, d'you think? But I suppose they're a dying race. Anyway, this butler character let me in and kept me hanging about for about ten minutes in a hall the size of the ground floor of our house. I was a bit nervous because I kept thinking, suppose he's rung up the *Sunday Planet* and they've said they've never heard of me? But he hadn't and it was all right. He was in the library. Superb collection of books he's got and some of them looked quite worn, so I suppose someone reads them, though I shouldn't think he does.

'It was all furnished in leather, black leather. You know that rather sexy modern stuff. He asked me to sit down and have a drink . . .'

'A bit early, wasn't it?'

'People like that, they slosh it down all day. If they were working class they'd be alcoholics, but you can get away with anything when you've got a butler and about fifty thousand a year. Then his wife came in. Rather a nice-looking woman—a bit past it, of course —but magnificent clothes. Not that I'd want Tess to dress like that . . .' His face fell and Archery's heart moved with pity. 'If I ever get a say in what Tess wears,' he added dolefully.

'Go on.'

'We had our drinks. Mrs Primero wasn't very talkative, but her husband was most expansive. I didn't have to ask him much, so you needn't get all steamed up about your conscience, and he got on to the murder, quite naturally. He kept saying he wished he hadn't left Victor's Piece so early that Sunday evening. He could easily have stayed.

' "I was only going to meet a couple of chaps I knew at a pub in Sewingbury," he said. "And, as it happened, it was a dead loss because they never turned up. Or, at least, they did turn up but I got the wrong pub. So I waited about for an hour or so and then I went back to my lodgings. I wonder," he said, "how many times I've cursed myself for not staying at Victor's Piece."

'What d'you think of that? I thought it was fishy.'

'He didn't have to tell you,' Archery said. 'In any case the police must have questioned him.'

'Maybe they did and maybe they didn't. He didn't say.' Charles lounged back in his chair, and swinging his feet up poked them through the trellis. 'Then we got on to money,' he said. 'Money, I may add, is the mainspring of his existence.'

Inexplicably, Archery felt himself marked out as Primero's defender. Alice Flower had painted him in

such glowing colours. 'I had the impression he was
rather a nice sort of man,' he said.

'He's all right,' Charles said indifferently. 'He's very
modest about his success and about his money.' He
grinned. 'The kind of character who cries all the way
to the bank. Anyway, now we come to the crux of
the whole thing.

'Just before Mrs Primero was killed some mate of
his asked him if he'd like to go into business with him.
Importing or exporting. I don't quite know what it
was but it doesn't matter. The friend was to put up ten
thousand and so was Primero. Well, Primero hadn't got
it, hadn't got a smell of it. As far as he was concerned
it was hopeless. Then Mrs Primero died.'

'We know all this,' Archery objected. 'Alice Flower
told me as much . . .'

'All right, wait for it. Alice Flower didn't know this
bit. "That was the making of me," he said very breezily. "Not that I wasn't devastated by my grandmother's
death," he added as a sort of hasty afterthought. His
wife was sitting there all the time with a blank look
on her face. He kept looking at her uneasily.

' "I put up the money and we were away," he said,
talking rather fast. "And since then I've never looked
back."

'I was in a bit of a dilemma. Everything was going
so smoothly and I didn't want to mess things up. I
thought he was looking defiant and suddenly I realised
why. *He didn't know how much I knew about Mrs
Primero's money*. She'd died intestate, it was sixteen
years ago, I was a newspaper reporter and for all he
knew I was interested in him, not his grandmother.'

'A lot to read into a defiant look,' said Archery.

'Perhaps there was a bit of hindsight in that. But
just wait a minute. Then I asked a question. It was a
shot in the dark but it came off.

' "So you got your ten thousand just when you
needed it?" I said casually. Primero didn't say anything, but his wife looked at me and said, "Just the
exact sum after death duties. You should really be

asking me. Roger's told me about it so often I know it better than he does."

'Well, I couldn't leave it there. I persisted. "I understand you've got two sisters, Mr Primero," I said. "I suppose they inherited similar amounts?" He began to look terribly suspicious. After all, it wasn't my business and it had nothing to do with the story I was supposed to be writing. "Are they successful in business too?" I asked, trying to justify myself. It was a stroke of genius. Sorry to be big-headed but it was. I could actually see him relax.

' "I really don't see much of them," he said. "Oh, Roger," said his wife, "you know we *never* see them." Primero gave her an icy look. "One's married," he said, "and the other has a job in London. They're much younger than I am." "It must be nice to inherit ten thousand pounds when you're still a child," I said. "I imagine it's always nice," he said, "but I've never had the pleasure of inheriting any more. Shall we leave the subject and get on with the story of my life?"

'I pretended to take notes. I was doodling really but he thought it was shorthand. When we'd finished he got up and shook hands and said he'd keep his eye open for the *Sunday Planet*. I felt a bit awkward at that and I didn't quite know what to say but his wife saved me by asking me to lunch. So I accepted and we had a splendid lunch, smoked salmon and enormous steaks, great sides of oxen they were, and raspberries in framboise liqueur.'

'You've got a nerve,' said Archery in grudging admiration. He pulled himself up. 'It was very wrong of you. Most unethical.'

'All in a good cause. You do see the point, don't you?'

Why do one's children always think one senile yet childish, dully practical yet irrational, capable of supporting them but unintelligent to the point of imbecility?

'Of course I do,' Archery said irritably. 'Alice Flower and Mrs Crilling both said Mrs Primero had only ten thousand to leave, but apparently Roger Primero didn't get only a third of that, he got the whole ten thousand.'

Charles jerked round to face him, scattering more rose petals from the trellis. 'Now, why? There definitely wasn't a will. I've checked on that. And there were just the three heirs, Roger, Angela and Isabel. Mrs Primero hadn't another relative in the world and according to the law it should have been divided between the three grandchildren. But Roger got the lot.'

'I can't understand it.'

'Neither can I—yet. Maybe I shall when I've seen the sisters. I couldn't ask Roger where they lived, but Primero isn't a common name and the single one may be in the London phone directory. I haven't quite made up my mind about the line I'll take with them, but I've got the glimmerings of an idea. I might say I've come from the Inland Revenue . . .'

'Facilis descensus Averni.'

'In matters of this kind,' Charles said crisply, 'you have to be bloody, bold and resolute. Can I have the car again tomorrow?'

'If you must.'

'I thought you might like to go out to Victor's Piece,' Charles said in a hopeful tone, 'and just have a look round. See if you can see if Primero could have hidden himself anywhere, sneaked upstairs or something, instead of letting himself out of the front door that Sunday night.'

'Aren't you letting your imagination run away with you?'

'It's a family failing.' His eyes clouded suddenly and to Archery's dismay he put his head in his hands. Archery didn't know what to do. 'Tess hasn't spoken to me for two days,' the boy said. 'I can't lose her, I can't.' If he had been ten years younger his father would have taken him in his arms. But if he had been ten years younger the whole thing would never have happened.

'I don't give a damn,' Charles said, controlling him-

self, 'what her father was or what he did. I don't care
if every one of her ancestors was hanged. But you
do and she does and . . . Oh, what's the use?' He got
up. 'Sorry to make an exhibition of myself.' Still looking down, he scuffed his feet against the eddies of
petals. 'You're doing all you can,' he said with a dreadful prim gravity, 'but you can't be expected to understand at your age.' Without looking at his father, he
turned and went into the hotel.

11

From fornication, and all other deadly sin; and
from all the deceits of the world, the flesh and
the devil,
    Good Lord, deliver us.

The Litany

ANGELA Primero lived in a flat at Oswestry Man-
sions, Baron's Court. She was twenty-six years old and
the elder of Mrs Primero's granddaughters. That was
all Charles Archery knew about her—that and her
telephone number which he had easily found. He rang
her up and asked if he could see her on the following
morning. Thinking better of his original plan, he said
he represented the *Sunday Planet,* and the death of
Alice Flower having brought once more into prom-
inence Mrs Primero's murder, his newspaper was running a feature on the fate of the other people concerned
in the case. He was rather pleased with that. It had
the ring of verisimilitude.

Miss Primero had a grim voice for so young a woman. It was gravelly, abrupt, almost masculine. She

would be glad to see him, but he did realise, didn't
he, that her recollection of her grandmother was slight?
Just a few childhood memories were what he wanted,
Miss Primero, little touches to add colour to his story.

She opened the door to him so quickly that he wondered if she had been waiting behind it. Her appearance surprised him for he had kept a picture of her
brother in his mind and he had therefore expected
someone small and dark with regular features. He had
seen a photograph of the grandmother too, and though
the old face was both wizened and blurred by age,
there were still to be seen vestiges of an aquiline
beauty and a strong resemblance to Roger.

The girl whose flat this was had a strong plain face
with bad skin and a big prognathous jaw. Her hair
was a dull flat brown. She wore a neat dark blue frock
bought at a chain store and her figure, though over-
large, was good.

'Mr Bowman?'

Charles was pleased with the name he had invented
for himself. He gave her a pleasant smile.

'How do you do, Miss Primero?'

She showed him into a small very sparsely furnished
sitting room. He could not help adding to the mystery
by contrasting this with the library at Forby Hall. Here
there were no books, no flowers, and the only ornaments were framed photographs, half a dozen perhaps,
of a young blonde girl and a baby.

She followed his gaze towards the studio portrait
of the same girl that hung above the fireplace. 'My
sister,' she said. Her ugly face softened and she
smiled. As she spoke there came from the next room
a thin wail and the murmur of a voice. 'She's in my
bedroom now, changing the baby's napkin. She always
comes over on Saturday mornings.'

Charles wondered what Angela Primero did for a
living. A typist perhaps, or a clerk? The whole set-up
seemed too scanty and poor. The furniture was brightly
coloured but it looked cheap and flimsy. In front of

the hearth was a rug woven out of woollen rags. Needy
nothing trimmed in jollity . . .

'Please sit down,' said Angela Primero.

The little orange chair creaked as it took his weight.
A far cry, he thought, from the brother's voluptuous
black leather. From the floor above he could hear
music playing and someone pushing a vacuum cleaner.

'What do you want me to tell you?'

There was a packet of Weights on the mantelpiece.
She took one and handed them to him. He shook his
head.

'First, what you remember of your grandmother.'

'Not much. I told you.' Her speech was brusque
and rough. 'We went there to tea a few times. It was a
big dark house and I remember I was afraid to go
to the bathroom alone. The maid used to have to take
me.' She gave a staccato, humourless laugh and it was
an effort to remember she was only twenty-six. 'I never
even saw Painter if that's what you mean. There was
a child across the road we used to play with sometimes and I believe Painter had a daughter. I asked
about her once but my grandmother said she was
common, we weren't to have anything to do with her.'

Charles clenched his hands. He felt a sudden desperate longing for Tess, both for himself, and also to set
her beside this girl who had been taught to despise her.

The door opened and the girl in the photographs
came in. Angela Primero jumped up at once and took
the baby from her arms. Charles's knowledge of babies was vague. He thought this one might be about
six months old. It looked small and uninteresting.

'This is Mr Bowman, darling. My sister, Isabel
Fairest.'

Mrs Fairest was only a year younger than her sister, but she looked no more than eighteen. She was
very small and thin with a pinkish-white face and enormous pale blue eyes. Charles thought she looked like
a pretty rabbit. Her hair was a bright gingery gold.

Roger's hair and eyes were black, Angela's hair
brown and her eyes hazel. None of them was in the

least like either of the others. There was more to
genetics than met the eye, Charles thought.

Mrs Fairest sat down. She didn't cross her legs but
sat with her hands in her lap like a little girl. It was
difficult to imagine her married, impossible to think
of her as having given birth to a child.

Her sister scarcely took her eyes off her. When she
did it was to coo at the baby. Mrs Fairest had a small
soft voice, tinged with cockney.

'Don't let him tire you, darling. Put him down in
his cot.'

'You know I love holding him, darling. Isn't he
gorgeous? Have you got a smile for your auntie? You
know your auntie, don't you, even if you haven't seen
her for a whole week?'

Mrs Fairest got up and stood behind her sister's
chair. They both gurgled over the baby, stroking its
cheeks and curling its fingers round their own. It was
obvious that they were devoted to each other, but
whereas Angela's love was maternal to both sister and
nephew, Isabel showed a clinging dependence on the
older girl. Charles felt that they had forgotten he was
there and he wondered how Mr Fairest fitted into the
picture. He coughed.

'About your early life, Miss Primero . . . ?'

'Oh, yes. (Mustn't cry, sweetie. He's got wind, darling.) I really can't remember any more about my
grandmother. My mother married again when I was
sixteen. This is the sort of thing you want, is it?'

'Oh, yes.'

'Well, as I say, my mother married again and she
and my stepfather wanted us to go out to Australia
with them. (Up it comes! There, that's better.) But
I didn't want to go. Isabel and I were still at school.
My mother hung it out for a couple of years and then
they went without us. Well, it was their life, wasn't it?
I wanted to go to training college but I gave that up.
Isabel and I had the house, didn't we, darling? And
we both went out to work. (Is he going to have a
little sleep, then?)'

It was an ordinary enough tale, fragmentary and very clipped. Charles felt that there was far more to it. The hardship and the privation had been left out. Money might have changed it all but she had never mentioned money. She had never mentioned her brother either.

'Isabel got married two years ago. Her husband's in the Post Office. I'm a secretary in a newspaper office.' She raised her eyebrows, unsmiling. 'I'll have to ask them if they've ever heard of you.'

'Yes, do,' said Charles with a suavity he didn't feel. He must get on to the subject of the money but he didn't know how to. Mrs Fairest brought a carry-cot in from the other room, they placed the baby in it, bending tenderly over him and cooing. Although it was nearly noon neither of them had mentioned a drink or even coffee. Charles belonged to a generation that has accustomed itself to almost hourly snacks, cups of this, glasses of that, bits and pieces from the refrigerator. So, surely, did they. He thought wistfully of Roger's hospitality. Mrs Fairest glanced up and said softly.

'I do like coming here. It's so quiet.' Above them the vacuum cleaner continued to whirr. 'My husband and me, we've only got one room. It's nice and big but it's awfully noisy at weekends'.

Charles knew it was impertinent but he had to say it.

'I'm surprised your grandmother didn't leave you anything.'

Angela Primero shrugged. She tucked the blanket round the baby and stood up. 'That's life,' she said in a hard voice.

'Shall I tell him, darling?' Isabel Fairest touched her arm and looked timidly into her face, waiting for guidance.

'What's the point? It's of no interest to him.' She stared at Charles and then said intelligently, 'You can't put that sort of thing in newspapers. It's libel.'

Damn, damn, damn! Why hadn't he said he was

from the Inland Revenue? Then they could have got on to money at once.

'But I think people ought to know,' said Mrs Fairest, showing more spirit than he had thought her capable of. 'I do, darling. I always have, ever since I understood about it. I think people ought to know how he's treated us.'

Charles put his notebook away ostentatiously.

'This is off the record, Mrs Fairest.'

'You see, darling? He won't say anything. I don't care if he does. People ought to know about Roger.'

The name was out. They were all breathing rather heavily. Charles was the first to get himself under control. He managed a calm smile.

'Well, I *will* tell you. If you put it in the paper and I have to go to prison for it, I don't care! Granny Rose left ten thousand pounds and we should all have had a share, but we didn't. Roger—that's our brother —he got it all. I don't quite know why but Angela knows the ins and outs of it. My mother had a friend who was a solicitor where Roger worked and he said we could try and fight it, but Mother wouldn't on account of it being awful to have a court case against your own son. We were just little kids, you see, and we didn't know anything about it. Mother said Roger would help us—it was his moral duty, even if it wasn't legally—but he never did. He kept putting it off and then Mother quarrelled with him. We've never seen him since I was ten and Angela was eleven. I wouldn't know him now if I saw him in the street.'

It was a puzzling story. They were all Mrs Primero's grandchildren, all equally entitled to inherit in the event of there being no will. And there had been no will.

'I don't want to see all this in your paper, you know,' Angela Primero said suddenly. She would have made a good teacher, he thought, reflecting on waste, for she was tender with little children, but stern when she had to be.

'I won't publish any of it,' Charles said with perfect truth.

'You'd better not, that's all. The fact is, we couldn't fight it. We wouldn't have stood a chance. In law Roger was perfectly entitled to it all. Mind you, it would have been another story if my grandmother had died a month later.'

'I don't quite follow you,' said Charles, by now unbearably excited.

'Have you ever seen my brother?'

Charles nodded, then changed it to a shake of the head. She looked at him suspiciously. Then she made a dramatic gesture. She took her sister by the shoulders and pushed her forward for his inspection.

'He's little and dark,' she said. 'Look at Isabel, look at me. We don't look alike, do we? We don't look like sisters because we aren't sisters and Roger isn't our brother. Oh, Roger is my parents' child all right and Mrs Primero was his grandmother. My mother couldn't have any more children. They waited eleven years and when they knew it was no good they adopted me. A year later they took Isabel as well.'

'But . . . I . . .' Charles stammered. 'You were legally adopted, weren't you?'

Angela Primero had recovered her composure. She put her arm round her sister who had begun to cry.

'We were legally adopted all right. That didn't make any difference. Adopted children can't inherit when the dead person has died without making a will—or they couldn't in September 1950. They can now. They were making this Act at the time and it became law on October 1st, 1950. Just our luck, wasn't it?'

The photograph in the estate agent's window made Victor's Piece look deceptively attractive. Perhaps the agent had long given up hope of its being sold for anything but its site value, for Archery, enquiring tentatively, was greeted with almost fawning exuberance. He emerged with an order to view, a bunch of keys and permission to go over the house whenever he chose.

No bus was in sight. He walked back to the stop by the Olive and Dove and waited in the shade. Presently he pulled the order to view out of his pocket and scanned it. 'Splendid property of character,' he read, 'that only needs an imaginative owner to give it a new lease of life . . .' There was no mention of the old tragedy, no hint that violent death had once been its tenant.

Two Dewingbury buses came and one marked Kingsmarkham Station. He was still reading, contrasting the agent's euphemisms with the description in his transcript, when the silver car pulled into the kerb.

'Mr Archery!'

He turned. The sun blazed back from the arched wings and the glittering screen. Imogen Ide's hair made an even brighter silver-gold flash against the dazzling metal.

'I'm on my way to Stowerton. Would you like a lift?'

He was suddenly ridiculously happy. Everything went, his pity for Charles, his grief for Alice Flower, his sense of helplessness against the juggernaut machinery of the law. An absurd dangerous joy possessed him and without stopping to analyse it, he went up to the car. Its body work was as hot as fire, a shivering silver glaze against his hand.

'My son took my car,' he said. 'I'm not going to Stowerton, just to a place this side of it, a house called Victor's Piece.'

She raised her eyebrows very slightly at this and he supposed she knew the story just as everyone else did, for she was looking at him strangely. He got in beside her, his heart beating. The continual rhythmic thudding in his left side was so intense as to be physically painful and he wished it would stop before it made him wince or press his hand to his breast.

'You haven't got Dog with you today,' he said.

She moved back into the traffic. 'Too hot for him,'

she said. 'Surely you're not thinking of buying Victor's Piece?'

His heart had quietened. 'Why, do you know it?'

'It used to belong to a relative of my husband's.'

Ide, he thought, Ide. He couldn't remember hearing what had become of the house after Mrs Primero's death. Perhaps it had been owned by some Ides before it became an old people's home.

'I have a key and an order to view, but I'm certainly not going to buy. It's just—well . . .'

'Curiosity?' She could not look at him while she was driving but he felt her thoughts directed on him more powerfully than any eyes. 'Are you an amateur of crime? It would have been natural to have used his name, to end the question with it. But she didn't. It seemed to him that she had omitted it because 'Mr Archery' had suddenly become too formal, his Christian name still too intimate. 'You know, I think I'll come over it with you,' she said. 'I don't have to be in Stowerton until half-past twelve. Let me be your guide, may I?'

Imogen Ide will be my guide . . . It was a stupid jingle and it tinkled in his ears on a minor key like an old, half-forgotten madrigal. He said nothing but she must have taken his silence for assent, for instead of dropping him at the entry she slowed and turned into the lane where dark gables showed between the trees.

Even on this bright morning the house looked dark and forbidding. Its yellow-brown bricks were crossed with fretted half-timbering and two of its windows were broken. The resemblance between it and the agent's photograph was as slight as that of a holiday postcard to the actual resort. The photographer had cunningly avoided or else subsequently removed the weeds, the brambles, the damp stains, the swinging rotted casements and the general air of decay. He had also succeeded in somehow minimising its rambling size. The gates were broken down and she drove straight through the gap, up the drive and stopped directly before the front door.

This moment should have been important to him, his first sight of the house where Tess's father had committed—or had not committed—his crime. His senses should have been alert to absorb atmosphere, to note details of place and distance that the police in their jaded knowledge had overlooked. Instead he was conscious of himself not as an observer, a note-taker, but only as a man living in the present, dwelling in the moment and discarding the past. He felt more alive than he had done for years and because of this he became almost unaware of his surroundings. Things could not affect him, not recorded fact. His emotions were all. He saw and experienced the house only as a deserted place into which he and this woman would soon go and would be alone.

As soon as he had thought this in so many words he knew that he should not go in. He could easily say that he only wanted to look at the grounds. She was getting out of the car now, looking up at the windows and wrinkling her eyelids against the light.

'Shall we go in?' she said.

He put the key in the lock and she was standing close beside him. He had expected a musty smell from the hall but he was hardly aware of it. Shafts of light crossed the place from various dusty windows and motes danced in the beams. There was an old runner on the tiled floor and catching her heel in it, she stumbled. Instinctively he put out his hand to steady her and as he did so he felt her right breast brush his arm.

'Mind how you go,' he said, not looking at her. Her shoe had sent up a little cloud of dust and she gave a nervous laugh. Perhaps it was just a normal laugh. He was beyond that kind of analysis, for he could still feel the soft weight against his arm as if she had not stepped quickly away.

'Terribly stuffy in here,' she said. 'It makes me cough. That's the room where the murder was committed—in there.' She pushed open a door and he saw a deal board floor, marble fireplace, great bleached patches on the walls where pictures had hung. 'The stairs are behind here and on the other side is the kitchen where poor old Alice was cooking the Sunday dinner.'

'I don't want to go upstairs,' he said quickly. 'It's too hot and dusty. You'll get your dress dirty.' He drew a deep breath and, moving far from her, stood against the mantelpiece. Here, just on this spot, Mrs Primero had felt the first blow of the axe; there the scuttle had stood, here, there, everywhere, the old blood had flowed. 'The scene of the crime,' he said fatuously.

Her eyes narrowed and she crossed to the window. The silence was terrible and he wanted to fill it with chatter. There was so much to say, so many remarks even mere acquaintances could make to each other on such a spot. The noonday sun cast her shadow in perfect proportion, neither too tall nor grossly dwarfed. It was like a cut-out in black tissue and he wanted to fall to his knees and touch it, knowing it was all he would get.

It was she who spoke first. He hardly knew that he had expected her to say, but not this—certainly not this.

'You are very like your son—or he's like you.'

The tension slackened. He felt cheated and peeved. 'I didn't know you'd met,' he said.

To this she made no reply. In her eyes was a tiny gleam of fun. 'You didn't tell me he worked for a newspaper.'

Archery's stomach turned. She must have been there, at the Primeros'. Was he expected to sustain Charlie's lie?

'He's so very like you,' she said. 'It didn't really click, though, until after he'd gone. Then, taking his appearance and his name together—I suppose Bowman's his pseudonym on the *Planet*, is it?—I guessed. Roger hasn't realised.'

'I don't quite understand,' Archery began. He would have to explain. 'Mrs Ide . . .'

She started to laugh, stopped when she saw the dismay in his face. 'I think we've both been leading each other up the garden,' she said gently. 'Ide was my maiden name, the name I used for modelling.'

He turned away, pressing the hot palm of his hand against the marble. She took a step towards him and he smelt her scent. 'Mrs Primero was the relative who owned this house, the relative who's buried at Forby?' There was no need to wait for her answer. He sensed her nod. 'I don't understand how I can have been such a fool,' he said. Worse than a fool. What would she think tomorrow when the *Planet* came out? He offered up a stupid ashamed prayer that Charles had found out nothing from the woman who was her sister-in-law. 'Will you forgive me?'

'There's nothing to forgive, is there?' She sounded truly puzzled, as well she might. He had been asking pardon for future outrages. 'I'm just as much to blame as you. I don't know why I didn't tell you I was Imogen Primero.' She paused. 'There was no deceit in it,' she said. 'Just one of those things. We were dancing—something else came up . . . I don't know.'

He raised his head, gave himself a little shake. Then he walked away from her into the hall. 'You have to go to Stowerton, I think you said. It was kind of you to bring me.'

She was behind him now, her hand on his arm. 'Don't look like that. What are you supposed to have done? Nothing, nothing. It as just a—a social mistake.'

It was a little fragile hand but insistent. Not knowing why, perhaps because she too seemed in need of comfort, he covered it with his own. Instead of withdrawing it, she left her hand under his and as she sighed it trembled faintly. He turned to look at her, feeling shame that was as paralysing as a disease. Her face was only a foot from his, then only inches, then no distance, no face but only a soft mouth.

The shame went in a wave of desire made the more terrible and the more exquisite because he had felt nothing like it for twenty years, perhaps not ever. Since coming down from Oxford he had never kissed any woman but Mary, scarcely been alone with any but the old, the sick or the dying. He did not know how to end the kiss, nor did he know whether this in itself was inexperience or the yearning to prolong something that was so much more, but not enough more, than touching a shadow.

She took herself out of his arms quite suddenly, but without pushing or struggling. There was nothing to struggle against. 'Oh, dear,' she said, but she didn't smile. Her face was very white.

There were words to explain that kind of thing away. 'I don't know what made me do that' or 'I was carried away, the impulse of the moment . . .' He was sick of even the suggestion of lying. Truth itself seemed even more compelling and urgent than his desire and he thought he would speak it even though tomorrow and in the days to come it too would appear to her as a lie.

'I love you. I think I must have loved you from the first moment I saw you. I think that's how it was.' He put his hands up to his forehead and his fingertips, though icy cold, seemed to burn just as snow can burn the skin. 'I'm married,' he said. 'You know that—I mean my wife is living—and I'm a clergyman. I've no right to love you and I promise I'll never be alone with you again.'

She was very surprised and her eyes widened, but which of his confessions had surprised her he had no idea. It even occurred to him that she might be amazed at hearing from him lucid speech, for up to now he had been almost incoherent. 'I mustn't suppose,' he said, for his last sentence seemed like vanity, 'that there's been any temptation for you.' She started to speak, but he went on in a hurry, 'Will you not say anything but just drive away?'

She nodded. In spite of his prohibition, he longed for her to approach him again, just touch him. It was an impossible hunger that made him breathless. She made a little helpless gesture as if she too were in the grip of an overpowering emotion. Then she turned, her face held awkwardly away from him, ran down the hall and let herself out of the front door.

After she had gone it occurred to him that she had asked no questions as to his reasons for coming to the house. She had said little and he everything that mattered. He thought that he must be going mad, for he could not understand that twenty years of discipline could fall away like a lesson imparted to a bored child.

The house was as it had been described in the transcript of the trial. He noticed its layout without emotion or empathy, the long passage that ran from the front door to the door at the back where Painter's coat had hung, the kitchen, the narrow, wall-confined stairs. A kind of cerebral paralysis descended on him and he moved towards that back door, withdrawing the bolts numbly.

The garden was very still, overgrown, basking under a brazen sky. The light and the heat made him dizzy. At first he could not see the coach house at all. Then he realised he had been looking at it ever since he stepped into the garden, but what he had taken for a great quivering bush was in fact solid bricks and mortar hidden under a blanket of virginia creeper. He walked towards it, not interested, not in the least curious. He walked because it was something to do and because this house of a million faintly trembling leaves was at least a kind of goal.

The doors were fastened with a padlock. Archery was relieved. It deprived him of the need for any action. He leant against the wall and the leaves were cold and damp against his face. Presently he went down the drive and through the gateless entrance. Of course, the silver car would not be there. It wasn't. A bus came almost immediately. He had quite forgotten that he had omitted to lock the back door of Victor's Piece.

Archery returned the keys to the estate agent and lingered for a while looking at the photograph of the

house he had just come from. It was like looking at
the portrait of a girl you had known only as an old
woman, and he wondered if it had perhaps been taken
thirty years before when Mrs Primero had bought the
house. Then he turned and walked slowly back to the
hotel.

Half-past four was usually a dead time at the Olive
and Dove. But this was a Saturday and a glorious
Saturday at that. The dining room was full of trippers,
the lounge decorously crowded with old residents and
new arrivals, taking their tea from silver trays. Archery's heart began to beat fast as he saw his son in
conversation with a man and a woman. Their backs
were towards him and he saw only that the woman
had long fair hair and that the man's head was dark.

He made his way between the armchairs, growing
hot with trepidation and weaving among beringed
fingers holding teapots, little asthmatic dogs, pots of
cress and pyramids of sandwiches. When the woman
turned he should have felt relief. Instead bitter disappointment ran through him like a long thin knife. He
put out his hand and clasped the warm fingers of Tess
Kershaw.

Now he saw how stupid his first wild assumption had
been. Kershaw was shaking hands with him now and
the man's lively face, seamed all over with the wrinkles
of animation, bore no resemblance at all to Roger
Primero's waxen pallor. His hair was not really dark
but thin and sprinkled with grey.

'Charles called in on us on his way back from town,'
Tess said. She was perhaps the worst dressed woman
in the room in her white cotton blouse and navy serge
skirt. As if explaining this, she said quickly, 'When
we heard his news we dropped everything and came
back with him.' She got up, threaded her way to the
window and looked out into the bright hot afternoon.
When she came back she said, 'It feels so strange. I
must have walked past here lots of times when I was
little, but I can't remember it at all.'

Hand in hand with Painter perhaps. And while they

walked, the murderer and his child, had Painter
watched the traffic go by and thought of the way he
could become part of that traffic? Archery tried not
to see in the fine pointed face opposite his own, the
coarse crude features of the man Alice Flower had
called Beast. But then they were here to prove it had
not been that way at all.

'News?' he said to Charles and he heard the note of
distaste creep into his voice.

Charles told him. 'And then we all went to Victor's
Piece,' he said. 'We didn't think we'd be able to get in,
but someone had left the back door unlocked. We went
all over the house and we saw that Primero could easily
have hidden himself.'

Archery turned away slightly. The name was now
invested with many associations, mostly agonising.

'He said good-bye to Alice, opened and closed the
front door without actually going out of it, then he
slipped into the dining room—nobody used the dining
room and it was dark. Alice went out and . . .' Charles
hesitated, searching for a form of words to spare Tess.
'And, after the coal was brought in, he came out, put
on the raincoat that was left hanging on the back door
and—well, did the deed.'

'It's only a theory, Charlie,' said Kershaw, 'but it fits
the facts.'

'I don't know . . .' Archery began.

'Look, Father, don't you want Tess's father cleared?'

Not, thought Archery, if it means incriminating *her*
husband. Not that. I may already have done her an
injury, but I can't do her that injury.

'This motive you mentioned,' he said dully.

Tess broke in excitedly, 'It's a marvellous motive, a
real motive.' He knew exactly what she meant. Ten
thousand pounds was real, solid, a true temptation,
while two hundred pounds . . . Her eyes shone, then
saddened. Was she thinking that to hang a man wrong-
fully was as bad as killing an old woman for a bag of
notes? And would that too remain with her all her

life? No matter which way things fell out, could she ever escape?

'Primero was working in a solicitor's office,' Charles was saying excitedly. 'He would have known the law, he had all the facilities for checking. Mrs Primero might not have known about it, not if she didn't read the papers. Who knows about all the various Acts of Parliament that are going to be passed anyway? Primero's boss probably had a query about it from a client, sent him to look it up, and there you are. Primero would have known that if his grandmother died intestate before October 1950 all the money would come to him. But if she died after the Act his sisters would get two-thirds of it. I've been looking it all up. This is known as the Great Adoption Act, the law that gave adopted children almost equal rights with natural ones. *Of course* Primero knew.'

'What are you going to do?'

'I've been on to the police but Wexford can't see me before two on Monday. He's away for the weekend. I'll bet the police never checked Primero's movements. Knowing them, I'd say it's likely that as soon as they got hold of Painter they didn't trouble with anyone else.' He looked at Tess and took her hand. 'You can say what you like about this being a free country,' he said hotly, 'but you know as well as I do that everyone has a subconscious feeling that "working class" and "criminal class" are more or less synonymous. Why bother with the respectable, well-connected solicitor's clerk when you've already got your hands on the chauffeur?'

Archery shrugged. From long experience he knew it was useless to argue with Charles when he was airing his quasi-communist ideals.

'Thank you for your enthusiastic reception,' Charles said sarcastically. 'What is there to look so miserable about?'

Archery could not tell him. A load of sorrow seemed to have descended on him and in order to answer his son, he sorted out from conflicting pain something he could express to them all.

'I was thinking of the children,' he said, 'the four little girls who have all suffered from this crime.' He smiled at Tess. 'Tess, of course,' he went on, 'those two sisters you saw—and Elizabeth Crilling.'

He did not add the name of the grown woman who would suffer more than any of them if Charles was right.

12

Is it not lawful for me to do what I will with mine own?
                    The Gospel for Septuagesima Sunday

THE man who was shown into Wexford's office at nine on Monday morning was small and slender. The bones of his hands were particularly fine and with narrow delicate joints like a woman's. The dark grey suit he wore, very expensive looking and very sleek, made him look smaller than he actually was. He seemed to be surrounded, even so early in the morning and away from his home, with a great many adjuncts of elegance. Wexford, who knew him well, was amused by the sapphire tiepin, the two rings, the key chain with its heavy drop of chased—amber, was it?—the briefcase of some kind of reptile skin. How many years, he asked himself, was Roger Primero going to need to get used to wealth?

'Lovely morning,' said Wexford. 'I've just had a couple of days at Worthing and the sea was like a millpond. What can I do for you?'

'Catch a con man,' said Primero, 'a lousy little squirt posing as a journalist.' He unclipped the briefcase and flicked a Sunday newspaper across Wexford's desk. It slipped on the polished surface and fell to the floor. Raising his eyebrows, Wexford let it lie.

'Hell,' said Primero. 'There's nothing for you to see, anyway.' His glazed eyes had a sore look in the handsome expressionless face. The man's vanity had made him rebel against glasses at last, Wexford thought, blinking slightly behind his own heavy tortoiseshell frames. 'Look here, Chief Inspector, I don't mind telling you, I'm hopping mad. This is how it was. Mind if I smoke?'

'Not at all.'

A gold cigarette case spilled out from his pocket, followed by a holder and a lighter in peculiar black and gold mosaic. Wexford watched this production of props, wondering when it was going to end. The man is furnished like a room, he thought.

'This is how it was,' he said again. 'Character rang me up on Thursday, said he was on the *Planet* and wanted to do an article about me. My early life. You get the picture? I said he could come along on Friday and he did. I gave him a hell of a long interview, all the dope and the upshot of it was my wife asked him to lunch.' He screwed up his mouth and nose like a man smelling something offensive. 'Hell,' he said, 'I don't suppose he's ever seen a lunch like that in all his life . . .'

'But no article appeared and when you rang the *Planet* this morning they'd never heard of him.'

'How did you know?'

'It happens,' said Wexford dryly. 'I'm surprised at you, sir, a man of your experience. The time to ring the *Planet* was *Friday* morning.'

'It makes me feel such a frightful ass.'

Wexford said airily, 'No money passed, I daresay?'

'Hell, no!'

'Just the lunch, then, and you told him a lot of things you'd rather have left unsaid.'

'That's the thing.' His expression had been sulky, but suddenly he smiled and it was a likeable smile. Wexford had always rather liked him. 'Oh, hell's bells, Chief Inspector . . .'

'Hell's bells, as you say. Still, you were wise to come to us, though I don't know that we can do anything unless he makes a move . . .'

'A move? What d'you mean, a move?'

'Well, let me give you an example. Nothing personal, you understand. Just supposing a wealthy man, a man who is somewhat in the public eye, says something a shade indiscreet to a reputable journalist. Ten to one he can't use it because he's laying his paper open to libel action.' Wexford paused and gave the other man a penetrating look. 'But if he says those same indiscreet things to an impostor, a confidence trickster . . .' Primero had grown very pale. 'What's to stop the impostor following a few leads and ferreting out something really damaging. Most people, Mr Primero, even decent law-abiding people, have something in their pasts they'd rather not have known. You have to ask yourself, if he's not on the level, what's he up to? The answer is either he's after your money or else he's crazy.' He added more kindly, 'In my experience nine out of ten of them are just crazy. Still, if it'll help to set your mind at rest perhaps you could give us a description. I suppose he gave you his name?'

'It wouldn't be his real name.'

'Naturally not.'

Primero leant confidingly towards him. During the course of his long career Wexford had found it valuable to make himself *au fait* with perfumes and he noticed that Primero smelt of Lentheric's Onyx.

'He seemed nice enough,' Primero began. 'My wife was quite taken with him.' His eyes had begun to water and he put his fingers very cautiously up to them. Wexford was reminded of a weeping woman who dare not rub her eyes for fear of smudging mascara. 'I haven't told her about this, by the way. I passed it off. Wouldn't want to upset her. He was well-spoken, Oxford accent and all that. A tall fair fellow, said his name was Bowman, Charles Bowman.'

'A-ha!' said Wexford but not aloud.

'Chief Inspector?'

'Mr Primero?'

'I've just remembered something. He was—well, he was extraordinarily interested in my grandmother.'

Wexford almost laughed.

'From what you've told me I think I can assure you there won't be any serious repercussions.'

'You think he's a nut?'

'Harmless, anyway.'

'You've taken a load off my mind.' Primero got up, retrieved his briefcase and picked up the newspaper. He did it rather awkwardly as if he was unused to performing even so simple a service for himself. 'I'll be more careful in future.'

'An ounce of prevention, you know.'

'Well, I won't take up any more of your time.' He pulled a long, but possibly sincerely sad face. The watering eyes added to his look of melancholy. 'Off to a funeral, as a matter of fact. Poor old Alice.'

Wexford had noticed the black tie on which the sapphire glowed darkly. He showed Primero to the door. Throughout the interview he had kept a solemn face. Now he permitted himself the indulgence of gargantuan, though almost silent, laughter.

There was nothing to do until two o'clock except sight-seeing. Charles had been out early and bought a guide book. They sat in the lounge studying it.

'It says here,' said Tess, 'that Forby is the fifth prettiest village in England.'

'Poor Forby,' said Charles. 'Damned with faint praise.'

Kershaw began organising them.

'How about all piling into my car . . .' He stuck his finger on the map '. . . and going down the Kingsbrook Road to Forby—keep clear of Forby Hall, eh, Charlie?—have a quick look at the church, and then on to Pomfret. Pomfret Grange is open every weekday in the summer—we might have a look over it—and back into Kingsmarkham along the main road.'

'Lovely,' said Tess.

Kershaw drove and Archery sat beside him. They followed the same route he had taken with Imogen Ide when she had come to put flowers on old Mrs Primero's grave. As they came within sight of the Kingsbrook he remembered what she had said about the implacability of water and how, notwithstanding the efforts of man, it continues to spring from the earth and seek the sea.

Kershaw parked the car by the green with the duck-pond. The village looked peaceful and serene. Summer was not as yet so far advanced as to dull the fresh green of the beech trees or hang the wild clematis with its frowsty greyish beard. Knots of cottage surrounded the green and on the church side was a row of Georgian houses with bow windows whose dark panes glistened, showing chintz and silver within. There were just three shops, a post office, a butcher's with a canopy and white colonnade, and a place selling souvenirs for tourists. The cottagers' Monday morning wash hung drying in the windless warm air.

They sat on the seat on the green and Tess fed the ducks from a packet of biscuits she had found on the shelf under the dashboard. Kershaw produced a camera and began taking photographs. Suddenly Archery knew he did not want to go any further with them. He almost shivered with distaste at the thought of trailing round the galleries of Pomfret Grange, gasping with false pleasure at the china and pretending to admire family portraits.

'Would you mind if I stayed here? I'd like to have another look at the church.'

Charles glared. 'We'll all go and look at the church.'

'I can't, darling,' said Tess. 'I can't go into a church in jeans.'

'Not in these trousers,' Kershaw quipped. He put

away his camera. 'We'd better get moving if we're going to see the stately home.'

'I can easily go back on the bus,' said Archery.

'Well, for God's sake, don't be late, Father.'

If it was going to be any more than a sentimental journey, he too would need a guide. When the car had gone he made his way into the souvenir shop. A bell rang sweetly as he opened the door and a woman came out from a room at the back.

'We don't keep a guide to St Mary's, but you'll find them on sale inside the church door.'

Now he was here he ought to buy something. A postcard? A little brooch for Mary? That, he thought, would be the worst kind of infidelity, to commit adultery in your heart every time you saw your wife wearing a keepsake. He looked drearily at the horse brasses, the painted jugs, the trays of costume jewellery.

A small counter was devoted entirely to calendars, wooden plaques with words on them in pokerwork, framed verses. One of these, a little picture on a card, showing a haloed shepherd with a lamb, caught his eye because the words beneath the drawing were familiar.

'Go, Shepherd, to your rest . . .'

The woman was standing behind him.

'I see you're admiring the efforts of our local bard,' she said brightly. 'He was just a boy when he died and he's buried here.'

'I've seen his grave,' said Archery.

'Of course a lot of people who come here are under the impression he was a shepherd, you know. I always have to explain that at one time shepherd and poet meant the same thing.'

'Lycidas,' said Archery.

She ignored the interruption. 'Actually he was very well-educated. He'd been to High School and everyone said he should have gone to college. He was killed in a road accident. Would you like to see his photograph?'

She produced a stack of cheap framed photographs

from a drawer beneath the counter. They were all
identical and each bore the legend: John Grace, Bard
of Forby. Those whom God loves, die young.

It was a fine ascetic face, sharp-featured and ultra-
sensitive. It also, Archery considered, gave the impression that its owner suffered from pernicious anaemia.
He had a curious feeling that he had seen it somewhere
before.

'Was any of his work published?'

'One or two bits in magazines, that's all. I don't
know the ins and outs of it because I've only been here
ten years, but there was a publisher who had a weekend cottage here and he was very keen on making his
poetry into a book when the poor boy died. Mrs Grace
—his mother, you know—was all for it, but the thing
was most of the stuff he'd written had disappeared.
There were just these bits you see here. His mother said
he'd written whole plays—they didn't rhyme, if you
know what I mean, but they were kind of like Shake-
speare. Anyway, they couldn't be found. Maybe he'd
burnt them or given them away. It does seem a shame,
though, doesn't it?'

Archery glanced out of the window towards the little
wooden church. 'Some mute inglorious Milton here
may rest . . .' he murmured.

'That's right,' said the woman. 'You never know,
they may turn up, like the Dead Sea Scrolls.'

Archery paid five and sixpence for the picture of
the shepherd and the lamb and strolled up towards the
church. He opened the kissing gate and, walking in a
clockwise direction, made for the door. What was it
she had said? 'You must never go widdershins around
a church. It's unlucky.' He needed luck for Charles and
for himself. The irony was that however things fell
out, one of them would lose.

There was no music coming from the church, but
as the door opened he saw that some sort of service
was in progress. For a moment he stood, looking at
the people and listening to the words.

'If after the manner of men I have fought with beasts

at Ephesus, what advantageth it me, if the dead rise not?'

It was a funeral. They were almost exactly half way through the service for the burial of the dead.

'Let us eat and drink for tomorrow we die . . .'

The door gave a slight whine as he closed it. Now, as he turned, he could see the funeral cars, three of them, outside the other gate. He went to look again at Grace's grave, passed the newly dug trench where this latest coffin was to be laid, and finally sat down on a wooden seat in a shady corner. It was a quarter to twelve. Give it half an hour, he thought, and then he would have to go for his bus. Presently he dozed.

The sound of gentle footfalls awakened him. He opened his eyes and saw that they were carrying the coffin out of the church. It was supported by four bearers, but it was a small coffin, a child's perhaps or a short woman's. On it were a few bunches of flowers and a huge wreath of madonna lilies.

The bearers were followed by a dozen people, the procession being headed by a man and a woman walking side by side. Their backs were towards Archery and besides that the woman, dressed in a black coat, wore a large black hat whose brim curved about her face. But he would have known her anywhere. He would have known her if he were blind and deaf, by her presence and her essence. They could not see him, had no idea they were watched, these mourners who had come to bury Alice Flower.

The other followers were mostly old, friends of Alice's perhaps, and one woman looked as if she must be the matron of the Infirmary. They gathered at the graveside and the vicar began to speak the words that would finally commit the old servant to the ground. Primero bent down and, taking rather fastidiously a handful of black earth, cast it on to the coffin. His shoulders shook and a little hand in a black glove reached out and rested on his arm. Archery felt a savage stab of jealousy that took away his breath.

The vicar spoke the Collect and blessed them. Then
Primero went a little way apart with him, they spoke
together and shook hands. He took his wife's arm and
they walked slowly towards the gate where the cars
were. It was all over.

When they were out of sight Archery got up and
approached the gradually filling grave. He could smell
the lilies five yards off. A card was attached to them
and on it someone had written simply: 'From Mr and
Mrs Roger, with love.'

'Good day,' he said to the sexton.

'Good day, sir. Lovely day.'

It was gone a quarter past twelve. Archery hurried
towards the kissing gate, wondering how often the
buses ran. As he came out from under the arch of
trees, he stopped suddenly. Charles was striding towards him up the sandy lane.

'Good thing you didn't come,' Charles called. 'The
place was shut for redecorating. Can you beat it? We
thought we might as well drift back and pick you up.'

'Where's the car?'

'Round the other side of the church.'

They would be gone by now. Just the same Archery
wished he were safely back at the Olive and Dove
eating cold beef and salad. As they rounded the yew
hedge a black car passed them. He forced himself to
look towards the gate. The Primeros were still there,
talking to the matron. His throat grew suddenly dry.

'Let's cut across the green,' he said urgently.

'Mr Kershaw happens to be waiting on this side.'

They were now only a few yards from the Primeros.
The matron shook hands and stepped into a hired
limousine. Primero turned and his eyes met those of
Charles.

He grew first white, then a curious vinegary purple.
Charles went on walking towards him and then Primero too began to move. They were approaching each
other menacingly, ridiculously, like two gunmen in a
Western.

'Mr Bowman, of the *Sunday Planet*, I believe?'

Charles stopped and said coolly. 'You can believe what you like.'

She had been talking to the women in the car. Now she withdrew her head and the car began to move off. They were alone, the four of them, in the centre of the fifth prettiest village in England. She looked at Archery first with embarrassment, then with a warmth that conquered her awkwardness.

'Why, hallo, I . . .'

Primero snatched at her arm. 'Recognise him? I shall need you for a witness, Imogen.'

Charles glared. 'You what?'

'Charles!' said Archery sharply.

'Do you deny that you made your way into my home under false pretences?'

'Roger, Roger . . .' She was still smiling, but her smile had grown stiff. 'Don't you remember we met Mr Archery at the dance? This is his son. He's a journalist, but he uses a pseudonym, that's all. They're here on holiday.'

Charles said rigidly, 'I'm afraid that isn't quite true, Mrs Primero.' She blinked, her lashes fluttering like wings, and her gaze came to rest softly on Archery's face. 'My father and I came here with the express purpose of collecting certain information. That we have done. In order to do it we had to make our way into your confidence. Perhaps we have been unscrupulous, but we thought the end justified the means.'

'I'm afraid I don't understand.' Her eyes were still on Archery and he was unable to draw his own away. He knew that his face registered a tremendous plea for forgiveness, a disclaimer of Charles's statement, and also registered the agony of love. There was, however, no reason why she should read there anything but guilt. 'I don't understand at all. What information?'

'I'll tell you . . .' Charles began, but Primero interrupted him.

'Since you're so frank, you won't have any objection

to coming down to the police station right now and laying your "information" before Chief Inspector Wexford.'

'None at all,' Charles drawled, 'except that it happens to be my lunchtime and in any case I have an appointment with the Chief Inspector already. At two sharp. I intend to tell him, Mr Primero, just how opportunely for you your grandmother died, how—oh, perfectly legally, I admit—you managed to cheat your sisters out of their inheritance, and how you concealed yourself in Victor's Piece on a certain evening in December sixteen years ago.'

'You're out of your mind!' Primero shouted.

Archery found his voice. 'That's enough, Charles.' He heard her speak, a tiny disembodied sound.

'It isn't true!' And then, terribly afraid. 'It isn't true, is it?'

'I'm damned if I'll argue it out in the street with this crook!'

'Of course it's true.'

'It was all above board.' Primero suddenly broke. They were all hot, standing there in the noon sun, but only Primero's face showed actual sweat, water drops on the cheesy sallow skin. 'Hell, it was a matter of law,' he blustered. 'What's it got to do with you, anyway? Who *are* you?'

Without taking her gaze from Archery, she took her husband's arm. All the gaiety had left her face and she looked almost old, a faded blonde who was effaced by her black clothes. Because she had become ugly she suddenly seemed for the first time within Archery's reach, yet she had never been farther from it. 'Let's go home, Roger.' Her mouth trembled and cobweb lines had appeared at its corners. 'In the course of your enquiries, Mr Archery,' she said, 'I hope you managed to combine pleasure with business.'

Then they were gone. Charles gave a great gasp.

'I must say I rather enjoyed that. I suppose by pleasure she meant the lunch they gave me. You can rely on these tycoons' wives to tot up every egg in the caviare. Still it was hard on her. You needn't look so shattered, Father. It's awfully middle-class to have a phobia about scenes.'

13

I deal with the thing that is lawful and right
. . . and all false ways I utterly abhor.
Psalm 119, appointed for the 26th Day

'PUBLIC General Acts and Measures, 1950.' Wexford took the book—was it a White Paper? Archery was ashamed to confess that he did not know—and read the title aloud. 'There's something here you want me to look at?'

Charles found the page for him. 'Here.' Wexford began to read. The silence was tense, almost agonised. Archery looked surreptitiously at the others, Charles who was flushed with eagerness, Kershaw trying to sit casually, but whose bright darting eyes betrayed his anxiety, Tess who looked confident, serene. Was it her mother in whom she trusted so completely or was it Charles? A good deal of Charles's poise had deserted him when, on entering the office five minutes before, he had had to introduce Tess to the Chief Inspector.

'Miss Kershaw,' he had said, 'my . . . the girl I'm going to marry. I . . .'

'Ah, yes.' Wexford had been very urbane. 'Good afternoon, Miss Kershaw, Mr Kershaw. Won't you sit down? Heatwave's coming to an end at last, I'm afraid.'

And indeed a change had come over the bright blue un-English sky. It had begun just after lunch with the appearance of a cloud that was truly no bigger than

a man's hand, and this cloud had been followed by
more, driven by a sudden wind. Now, as Wexford,
frowning a little, read steadily, Archery contemplated
the window from which the yellow blind had been fully
raised, and through it the lumpy blotchy mass of cu-
mulus, hollowed and pock-marked with grey.

'Very interesting,' said Wexford, 'and new to me.
I didn't know the Primero sisters were adopted. Convenient for Primero.'

'Convenient?' said Charles. Archery sighed within
himself. He could always tell when his son was going
to be rude or what Charles himself called forthright.
'Is that all you've got to say?'

'No,' said Wexford. Few people have the confidence
and the restraint to say 'yes' or 'no' without qualifica-
tion. Wexford was big and heavy and ugly; his suit
had seen better days, too many wet ones and too many
hot dusty ones, but he radiated strength. 'Before we go
any further on this tack, Mr Archery,' he said to
Charles, 'I'd like to say that I've had a complaint about
you from Mr Primero.'

'Oh, that.'

'Yes, that. I've been aware for some days that your
father had made the acquaintance of the Primeros.
Perhaps it wasn't a bad idea and I'm sure it wasn't an
unpleasant one to do so through Mrs Primero.' Archery knew his face had become white. He felt sick. 'And
let me say in all fairness,' Wexford went on, 'that I
told him it was all right as far as I was concerned to
make contact with the people concerned in the Primero case.' He glanced briefly at Tess who didn't move.
'Make contact, I said, not make trouble. Your little
escapade on Friday is what I call making trouble and
that I won't have!'

Charles said sulkily, 'All right, I'm sorry.' Archery
saw that he had to justify himself before Tess. 'You're
not going to tell me that your people don't occasionally
invent a cover story to get what they want.'

'My people,' Wexford snapped, 'happen to have the
law on their side.' He added grandiloquently, 'They *are*

the law.' The frown thawed. 'Now we've got the lec-
ture over you'd better tell me just what you and your
father have found out.'

Charles told him. Wexford listened patiently, but
as the evidence against Primero mounted, instead of
surprise, his face registered a strange blankness. The
heavy features had become brutish, like those of an
old bull.

'Of course, you'll say he had an alibi,' said Charles.
'I realise your people would have checked his alibi and
after all these years it's going to be difficult to crack,
but . . .'

'His alibi was not checked,' said Wexford.

'What did you say?'

'His alibi was not checked.'

'I don't understand.'

'Mr Archery . . .' Wexford got up and rested his
massive hands on the desk, but he didn't move away
from behind it. 'I am quite happy to discuss this
whole matter with you, answer any questions you may
like to ask.' He paused. 'But not in the presence of
Miss Kershaw. If I may say so, I think you were un-
wise to bring her with you.'

Now it was Charles's turn to get to his feet.

'Miss Kershaw is going to be my wife,' he said
hotly. 'Anything you say to me you can say to her.
I won't have any secrets from her in this.'

Casually Wexford sat down again. He drew a bunch
of papers from a desk drawer and began to study them.
Then he lifted his eyes slowly and said: 'I'm sorry
this has been a fruitless interview for you. With a little
co-operation I think I could have saved you a lot of
useless enquiry. But, if you'll forgive me, I'm a very
busy man so I'll say good afternoon.'

'No,' said Tess suddenly. 'I'll go. I'll wait in the car.'

'Tess!'

'Of course I'm going, darling. Don't you see? He
can't talk about my father in front of me. Oh, darling,
be your age!'

He is being his age, thought Archery miserably.

Wexford knew something—something that was going
to be horrible. But why was he playing this pouncing
cat and mouse game with them all, why had he played
it with Archery all along? Confidence and strength—
but did it cover a fierce inverted snobbism, a fear that
the Archeries might shake his authority and trouble
the still waters of his district? And yet the man held
such sway and was, beyond a doubt, a good, just man.
He would never lie or even shift truth to cover a lapse.
'His alibi was not checked . . .' If only they would stop
fencing!

Then, suddenly, Wexford stopped it.

'No need to leave the building, Miss Kershaw,' he
said. 'If your—your father would care to take you
upstairs—straight along the corridor and turn left when
you come to the double doors—you'll find we've got
quite a reasonable canteen, even for a lady. I suggest
a cup of strong tea and an eccles cake.'

'Thanks.' Tess turned and just touched Kershaw's
shoulder. He rose at once. Wexford closed the door
after them.

Charles took a deep breath, and making a brave attempt to lounge casually in his chair, said, 'All right,
then. What about this alibi that for some mysterious
reason was never investigated?'

'The reason,' said Wexford, 'was not mysterious. Mrs
Primero was killed between six-twenty-five and seven
o'clock on the evening of Sunday, September 24th,
1950.' He paused to allow Charles's inevitable iter-
ruption of 'Yes, yes', uttered with fierce impatience.
'She was killed in Kingsmarkham and at six-thirty
Roger Primero was seen in Sewingbury five miles
away.'

"Or, he was seen, was he?' Charles scoffed, crossing
his legs. 'What do you think, Father? Does it seem
remotely possible to you that he could have fixed it
beforehand that he'd be "seen"? There's always some
shifty mate who'll perjure himself and say he's seen
you for twenty quid.'

'Some shifty mate, eh?' Wexford was now hardly bothering to conceal his amusement.

'Somebody saw him. All right. Who saw him?'

Wexford sighed and the smiled was erased.

'I saw him,' he said.

It was a blow in the face. Archery's love for his son, dormant over the past days, rose within his breast in a hot tide. Charles said nothing, and Archery who had been doing this sort of thing rather a lot lately, tried hard not to hate Wexford. He had taken an unconscionable time coming to the point, but this, of course, was his revenge.

The big elbows rested on the desk, the fingers meeting and pressing together in an implacable pyramid of flesh. The law incarnate. If Wexford had seen Primero that night, there was no gainsaying it, for here was incorruptibility. It was almost as if God had seen him. Horrified, Archery pulled himself up in his chair and gave a dry painful cough.

'You?' said Charles at last.

'I,' said Wexford, 'with my little eye.'

'You might have told us before!'

'I would have,' said Wexford mildly and, oddly enough, believably, "if I'd had the remotest idea you suspected him. Chatting up Primero about his grandmother was one thing, pinning murder on him quite another.'

Polite now, stiff and very formal, Charles asked, 'Would you mind telling us the details?'

Wexford's courtesy matched his. 'Not at all. I intend to. Before I do, however, I'd better say that there was no question of hindsight. I knew Primero. I'd seen him in court with his chief on a good many occasions. He used to go along with him to learn the ropes.' Charles nodded, his face set. Archery thought he knew what was going on in his mind. Loss was something he knew about, too.

'I was in Sewingbury on a job,' Wexford continued, 'and I'd got a date to meet a man who sometimes gave

us a bit of information. What you might call a shifty
mate, but we never got twenty quidsworth out of him.
The appointment was for six at a pub called the Black
Swan. Well, I had a word with my—my friend, and I
was due back in Kingsmarkham at seven. I walked out
of the public bar at just on half past six and ran slap
bang into Primero.

' "Good evening, Inspector," he said, and I thought
he looked a bit lost. As well he might. I found out
afterwards that he'd been going to meet some pals, but
he'd got the wrong pub. They were waiting for him at
The Black Bull. "Are you on duty?" he said. "Or can
I buy you a short snort?" '

Archery nearly smiled. Wexford had given a very
fair imitation of the absurd slang Primero still affected after sixteen years of affluence.

' "Thanks all the same," I said, "but I'm late as it
is." "Good night to you, then," he said and he went
up to the bar. I'd only been in Kingsmarkham ten
minutes when I got called out to Victor's Piece.'

Charles got up slowly and extended a stiff, mechani-
cal hand.

'Thank you very much, Chief Inspector. I think
that's all anyone can say on the subject, don't you?'
Wexford leaned across the desk and took his hand. A
faint flash of compassion softened his features, weakened them, and was gone. 'I'm sorry I wasn't very
polite just now,' Charles said.

'That all right,' said Wexford. 'This is a police station, not a clerical garden party.' He hesitated and
added, 'I'm sorry, too.' And Archery knew that the
apology had nothing to do with Charles's ill manners.

Tess and Charles began to argue even before they
had all got into the car. Certain that they had said it
all or something very like it before, Archery listened
to them indifferently. He had kept silent for half an
hour and still there was nothing he could say.

'We have to be realistic about it,' Charles was saying. 'If I don't mind and Mother and Father don't

mind, why can't we just get married and forget you
ever had a father?'

'Who says they don't mind? That's not being realistic, anyway. I'm being realistic. One way and another I've had a lot of luck . . .' Tess flashed a quick
watery smile at Kershaw. 'I've had more than anyone
would have thought possible, but this is one bit I have
to dip out on.'

'And what does that mean exactly?'

'Just that—well, it was ridiculous ever to imagine
we could be married, you and I.'

'You and I? What about all the others who'll come
along and fancy you? Are you going to go through the
same melodrama with them or d'you think you'll
weaken when the thirties rear their ugly heads?'

She winced at that. Archery thought Charles had
almost forgotten they were not alone. He pushed her
into the back seat of the car and banged the door.

'I'm curious, you see,' Charles went on, bitterly
sarcastic. 'I'd just like to know if you've taken a vow
of perpetual chastity. O God, it's like a feature in the
Sunday Planet—Condemned to lonely spinsterhood
for father's crime! Just for the record, since I'm supposed to be so far above you morally, I'd like to know
the qualifications the lucky man has to have. Give me
a specification, will you?'

Her mother had built up her faith, but the Archery
family with their doubts had knocked it down; still it
had lived until Wexford had killed it. Her eyes were
fixed on Kershaw who had given her reality. Archery
was not surprised when she said hysterically:

'I suppose he'd have to have a murderer for a father.'
She gasped, for she was admitting it to herself for the
first time. 'Like me!'

Charles tapped Archery's back. 'Just nip out and
knock someone off,' he said outrageously.

'Oh, shut up,' said Kershaw. 'Give it a rest, Charlie,
will you?'

Archery touched his arm. 'I think I'll get out, if you
don't mind. I need some air.'

'Me too,' said Tess. 'I can't stand being boxed up in here any longer and I've got a ghastly head. I want some aspirins.'

'Can't park here.'

'We'll walk back to the hotel, Daddy. If I don't get out I'll pass out.'

Then they were all three on the pavement, Charles's face as black as thunder. Tess swayed a little and Archery caught her arm to steady her. Several passers-by gave them curious looks.

'You said you wanted aspirins,' said Charles.

It was only a few yards to the nearest chemist's, but Tess was shivering in her thin clothes. The air was heavy and cloying. Archery noticed that all the shop-keepers had furled their sunblinds.

Charles seemed about to begin again but she gave him a pleading look, 'Don't let's talk about it any more. We've said it all. I needn't see you again till October, not then if we're careful . . .'

He frowned silently, made a little gesture of repudiation. Archery held the shop door open for Tess to pass through.

There was no one inside but the assistant and Elizabeth Crilling.

She did not appear to be buying anything, just waiting and gossiping with the shopgirl. It was the middle of a weekday afternoon and here she was shopping. What had become of the job in the 'ladies' wear establishment'? Archery wondered if she would recognise him and how he could avoid this happening, for he did not want to have to introduce her to Tess. It gave him a little thrill of awe when he realised what was happening in this small town shop, a meeting after sixteen years of the child who was Painter's daughter and the child who had discovered Painter's crime.

While he hovered near the door. Tess went up to the counter. They were so close together that they were almost touching. Then Tess reached across in front of Liz Crilling to select one of the aspirin bottles, and in doing so brushed her sleeve.

'I beg your pardon.'

'That's O.K.'

Archery could see Tess had nothing smaller than a ten shilling note. His trepidation, his fears for the effect of illumination on Tess at this moment were so great, that he almost cried aloud, 'Never mind. Leave it! Only, please God, let us all get away and hide ourselves!'

'Haven't you anything smaller?'

'I'm sorry.'

'I'll just go and see if we've got any change.'

The two young women stood side by side in silence. Tess stared straight in front of her, but Liz Crilling was playing nervously with two little scent bottles displayed on a glass shelf, moving them about as if they were chessmen.

Then the pharmacist in his white coat came out from the back.

'Is there a Miss Crilling waiting for a prescription?'

Tess turned, her face flooded with colour.

'This is a repeat prescription, but I'm afraid it's no longer valid . . .'

'What d'you mean, no longer valid?'

'I mean that it can only be used six times. I can't let you have any more of these tablets without a fresh prescription. If your mother . . .'

'The old cow,' said Liz Crilling slowly.

The swift animation on Tess's face died as if she had been struck. Without opening her purse she tumbled the change loose into her handbag and hurried out of the shop.

The old cow. It was her fault, everything bad that had ever happened to you was her fault—beginning with the beautiful pink dress.

She was making it for you and she worked at the sewing machine all day that cold wet Sunday. When it was finished you put it on and Mummy brushed your hair and put a ribbon in it.

'I'll just pop over and show you off to Granny Rose,' Mummy said and she popped over, but when she came back she was cross because Granny Rose was asleep and hadn't heard when she'd tapped on the window.

'Give it half an hour,' Daddy said, 'and maybe she'll be awake then.' He was half asleep himself, lying in bed, white and thin on the pillows. So Mummy had stayed upstairs with him, giving him his medicine and reading to him because he was too weak to hold a book.

'You stay in the sitting room, Baby, and mind you don't get that frock dirty.'

You had done as you were told but it made you cry just the same. Of course you didn't care about not seeing Granny Rose, but you knew that while she was talking to Mummy you could have slipped out into the passage and down the garden to show it to Tessie, now, while it was brand-new.

Well, why not? Why not put on a coat and run across the road? Mummy wouldn't come down for half an hour. But you would have to hurry, for Tessie always went to bed at half-past six. Auntie Rene was strict about that. 'Respectable working class,' Mummy said, whatever that meant, and although she might let you into Tessie's bedroom she wouldn't let you wake her up.

But why, why, why had you gone?

Elizabeth Crilling came out of the shop and walked blindly towards the Glebe Road turning, bumping into shoppers as she went. Such a long way to go, past the hateful little sand houses that were like desert tombs in this spectral form light, such a long long way . . . And there was only one thing left to do when you got to the end of the road.

14

It is lawful for Christian men . . . to wear
weapons and serve in the wars.

The Thirty-nine Articles

THE letter with the Kendal postmark was awaiting
Archery on the hall table when they got back to the
Olive and Dove. He glanced at it uncomprehendingly,
then remembered. Colonel Cosmo Plashet, Painter's
commanding officer.

'What now?' he said to Charles when Tess had gone
upstairs to lie down.

'I don't know. They're going back to Purley tonight.'

'Do we go back to Thringford tonight?'

'I don't know, Father. I tell you I don't know.' He
paused, irritable, pink in the face, a lost child. 'I'll
have to go and apologise to Primero,' he said, the child
remembering its manners. 'It was a bloody awful way
to behave to him.'

Archery said it instinctively, without thinking. "I'll
do that, if you like. I'll ring them.'

'Thanks. If he insists on seeing me I'll go. You've
talked to her before, haven't you? I gathered from
something Wexford said.'

'Yes, I've talked to her, but I didn't know who she
was.'

'That,' said Charles, severe again, 'is you all over.'

Was he really going to ring her up and apologise?
And why should he have the vanity to suppose that
she would even come to the phone? 'In the course of
your enquiries, Mr Archery, I hope you managed to

combine pleasure with business.' She was bound to
have told her husband what she had meant by that.
How the middle-aged clergyman had suddenly gone
sentimental on her. He could hear Primero's reply,
his colloquialism, 'Didn't actually make the old pass,
did he?' and her light dismissive laughter. His soul
cringed. He went into the empty lounge and ripped
open Colonel Plashet's letter.

It was handwritten on rough white vellum almost as
thick as cartridge paper. By the occasional fading of
the ink from deep black to pale grey Archery could
tell that the writer had not used a fountain pen. An
old man's hand, he thought, a military man's address,
'Srinagar,' Church Street, Kendal . . .

Dear Mr. Archery, he read,
*I was interested to receive your letter and will do
my best to provide you with what information I can
on Private Herbert Arthur Painter. You may be aware
that I was not called to give evidence as to character at
Painter's trial, though I held myself in readiness to do
so should it have been necessary. Fortunately I have
retained in my possession certain notes I then made.
I say fortunately, for you will appreciate that Private
Painter's war service covered a period of from twenty-
three to twenty years ago, and my memory is no longer
what I should like it to be. Lest you should be under
the impression, however, that I am the possessor of
information sympathetic to Painter's relatives, I must
reluctantly disabuse your mind. In deciding not to call
me, Painter's defending counsel must have been aware
that any statement I could truthfully have made would,
instead of assisting their cause, have merely made the
task of prosecution easier.*

That was it, then. There would follow only another
loathsome catalogue to Painter's propensities. Colonel
Plashet's very idiosyncratic style and writing brought
home to him more forcibly than the cold print of the
transcript had done, the kind of man Charles was pre-

pared to accept as a father-in-law. Curiosity, not hope, made him read on,

Painter had been serving with His Majesty's Forces for one year when he entered my regiment. This was shortly prior to our embarkation for Burma as part of the Fourteenth Army. He was a most unsatisfactory soldier. We saw no action until we had been in Burma for three months, during which time Painter was twice put on a charge for being drunk and disorderly and sentenced to seven days' detention for gross insolence on an officer.

In action his manner and bearing improved considerably. He was a naturally pugnacious man, brave and aggressive. Soon after this, however, an incident occurred in the village in which we had our camp and a young Burmese woman was killed. A Court Martial was held before which Painter was charged with her manslaughter. He was found not guilty. I think I had better say no more on this matter.

In February 1945, six months before the cessation of hostilities in the Far East, Painter succumbed to a certain tropical affliction which manifests itself in severe ulceration of the legs, accelerated, I am told by his complete disregard of certain elementary hygenic precautions and his refusal to take a proper diet. He became seriously ill and responded badly to treatment. There was at this time a troopship lying off Calcutta, and as soon as Painter's condition allowed, he and certain other sick men were transported there by air. This troopship reached a United Kingdom port during the latter part of March, 1945.

I have no further information as to Painter's fate except that I believe he was shortly afterwards demobilised on health grounds.

If you have any other questions whatsoever to put to me regarding Painter's war service, you may be assured of my willingness to answer them to the best of my ability and discretion. You have my full permission to publish this letter. May I, however, ask your

indulgence to an old man's whim, and request a copy of
your book when it comes out?
                    Yours sincerely,
                            Cosmo Plashet

They all assumed he was writing a book. Archery
smiled a little at the colonel's grandiose style, but
there was nothing to smile at in the brief lines about
the Burmese woman's death. The colonel's guarded, 'I
think I had better say no more on this matter . . .'
told him more than a page of explanations.

Nothing new, nothing vital. Why, then, did he have
this urgent sensation of having missed something of
importance? But no, he couldn't see it . . . He looked
again, not knowing what he was looking for. Then, as
he stared at the spidery loops and whorls, he was
engulfed by a hot wave of trepidation and longing. He
was afraid to speak to her, yet he longed to hear her
voice.

He looked up, surprised to find how dark it had become. The summer afternoon sky simulated dusk with
its covering of slate-coloured cloud. Over the housetops
away to the east it was leaden tinged with angry purple
and as Archery began to fold the letter, a vivid flash
of lightning shocked across the room, flashing the
words on the paper into relief and bleaching his hands
livid white. The thunder followed it as he reached
the stairs, and echoes were still curling and growling
round the old building when he entered his bedroom.

She could only refuse to speak to him. She wouldn't
even have to do that herself, for she could send the
Italian butler. There was no question of her berating
or reproaching him personally—she could do it with
far more crushing effect by proxy.

'Forby Hall. Mr Primero's residence.'

It *was* the butler. The Italian accent distorted every
word except the name to which it gave true Latin
emphasis.

'I should like to speak to Mrs Primero.'

'What name shall I say, sir?'

'Henry Archery.'

Perhaps she would not be with her husband when the message came. People situated as they were in an enormous house of many rooms tended to live individual lives, he in the library, she in the drawing room. She would send the butler back with a message. As a foreigner the butler would be without that intimate feel for the nuances of English and that would give her scope. She could tell him to say something subtle and apparently polite and he would not appreciate the cutting sting that underlay the words. He heard footsteps, echoing footsteps across the big hall Charles had described. The phone crackled, perhaps because of the storm.

'Hallo?'

Out of a bone-dry throat he tried to speak. Why hadn't he rehearsed something? Because he had been so sure she wouldn't come?

'Hallo, are you still there?'

'Mrs Primero . . .'

'I thought you might have got fed-up with waiting. Mario took so long about it.'

'Of course I waited.' Rain burst against his window, smacking and sobbing at the glass. 'I want to apologise to you for this morning. It was unforgivable.'

'Oh, no,' she said. 'I've forgiven you—for this morning. You didn't really take any part in it, did you? It was the other times that seem so—well, not unforgivable, just incomprehensible.'

He could imagine her little helpless gesture, the white hands spreading out.

'One doesn't like to feel one's been used, you see. It's not that I'm hurt. I'm not likely to be hurt because I'm really very tough, much tougher than Roger. But I am a bit spoilt and I feel as if I've been kicked off my pedestal. Good for me, I expect.'

Archery said slowly, 'There's so much to explain. I thought I could explain on the phone, but now I find I can't.' And yet the violence of the storm made it easier for him. He could hardly hear his own words. 'I want to *see* you,' he said, forgetting his promise.

Apparently she had forgotten it too. 'You can't come here,' she said practically, 'because Roger's somewhere about and he might not look on your apology in the same light as I do. And I can't come to you because the Olive and Dove, being a respectable hostelry, doesn't allow visitors in residents' bedrooms.' He made an inarticulate murmur. 'That's the second cheap thing I've said to you today,' she said. 'Oh, my dear, you wouldn't want to talk in the lounge among all the fuddy-duddies, would you? I know, what about Victor's Piece?'

'It's locked,' he said, adding stupidly, 'and it's raining.'

'I've got a key. Roger's always kept one. Shall we say eight? The Olive will be only too happy if you have an early dinner.'

He dropped the receiver almost guiltily as Charles put his head round the door. And yet the telephone call had not been clandestine but made at Charles's instigation.

'I think I've made it all right with the Primeros,' he said, and he reflected on words from an unremembered source. God gave men tongues that they might conceal their thoughts.

But Charles, with the quixotry of youth, had lost interest. 'Tess and her father are just off,' he said.

'I'll come down.'

They were standing in the hall, waiting. For what? Archery wondered. The storm to cease? A miracle? Or just to say good-bye?

'I wish we hadn't seen Elizabeth Crilling,' Tess said. 'And yet now I wish I'd talked to her.'

'Just as well you didn't,' said Archery. 'You're worlds apart. The only thing you'd have in common is your age. You're both twenty-one.'

'Don't wish away my life,' Tess said oddly and he saw there were tears in her eyes. 'I'm not twenty-one till October.' She picked up the duffel bag that served her as a weekend case and held out her hand to Archery.

'We must love you and leave you,' said Kershaw. 'Doesn't seem anything more to be said, does there, Mr Archery? I know you hoped things would work out, but it wasn't to be.'

Charles was gazing at Tess. She kept her eyes averted.

'For God's sake say I can write to you.'

'What's the use?'

'It would give me pleasure,' he said tightly.

'I shan't be at home. I'm going to Torquay to stay with my aunt the day after tomorrow.'

'You won't be camping on the beach, will you? This aunt, doesn't she have an address?'

'I haven't got a piece of paper,' said Tess and Archery saw that she was near to tears. He felt in his pocket, pulled out first Colonel Plashet's letter—not that, not for Tess to see—then the illuminated card with the verse and the picture of the shepherd. Her eyes were misted and she scrawled the address quickly, handing it to Charles without a word.

'Come on, lovey,' said Kershaw. 'Home, and don't spare the horses.' He fished out his car keys. 'All fifteen of them,' he said, but no one smiled.

15

If he hath offended any other . . . ask them
forgiveness; and where he hath done injury or
wrong to any man . . . make amends to the
uttermost of his power.

The Visitation of the Sick

IT was raining so heavily that he had to dash from the
car into the dilapidated porch and even there the rain
caught him, blown by the gusty wind and tossed in icy
droplets off the evergreens. He leant against the door
and staggered because it gave with his weight and
swung noisily open.

She must have arrived already. The Flavia was nowhere to be seen and he felt a shiver of self-disgust
and trepidation when it occurred to him that she was
being purposely discreet. She was well known in the
district, she was married and she was having a secret
meeting with a married man. So she had hidden her
conspicuous car. Yes, it was cheap, cheap and sordid,
and he, a priest of God, had engineered it.

Victor's Piece, dry and rotten in drought, smelt wet
and rotten now the rain had come. It smelt of fungus
and dead things. There were probably rats under these
knotted flaking floorboards. He closed the door and
walked a little way down the passage, wondering where
she was and why she had not come out to him when she
heard the door. Then he stopped, for he as facing the
back door where Painter's raincoat had hung, and
there was a raincoat hanging there now.

Certainly nothing had hung there on his previous

visit to the house. He moved up to the raincoat, fascinated and rather horrified.

Of course, it was obvious what had happened. Someone had bought the place at last, the workmen had been in and one of them had left his raincoat. Nothing to be alarmed about. His nerves must be very bad.

'Mrs. Primero,' he said, and then, because you do not call women with whom you have secret assignations by their surnames, 'Imogen! Imogen!'

There was no answer. And yet he was sure he was not alone in the house. What about knowing her if you were deaf and blind, jeered a voice within him, what about knowing her by her essence? He opened the dining room door, then the drawing room. A damp cold smell came to meet him. Water had leaked under the window sill and formed a spreading pool, dark in colour, hideously evocative. This and the rusty veining on the marble of the fireplace recalled to him splashed blood. Who would buy this place? Who could bear it? But someone had bought it for there was a workman's coat hanging behind the door . . .

Here she had sat, the old woman, and bade Alice go to church. Here she had sat, her eyes closing easily into sleep, when Mrs Crilling had come tapping at the window. Then he had come, whoever he was, with his axe and perhaps she had still been sleeping, on and on over the threats and the demands, over the blows of the axe, on and on into endless sleep. Endless sleep? *Mors janua vitae.* If only the gateway to life had not been through an unspeakable passage of pain. He found himself praying for what he knew was impossible, that God should change history. Then Mrs Crilling tapped on the window.

Archery gave a start so violent and galvanic that he seemed to feel a hand squeeze his heart with slippery fingers. He gasped and forced himself to look.

'Sorry I'm late,' said Imogen Ide. 'What a ghastly night.'

She should have been on the inside, he thought, pulling himself together. But she had been outside, tapping, tapping, because she had seen him standing there like a lost soul. This way it altered the aspect of things, for she had not hidden the car. It stood on the gravel beside his own, wet, silver, glittering, like something alive and beautiful from the depths of the sea.

'How did you get in?' she said in the hall.

'The door was open.'

'Some workman.'

'I suppose so.'

She wore a tweed suit and her pale hair was wet. He had been silly enough—bad enough, he thought—to imagine that when they met she would run to him and embrace him. Instead she stood looking at him gravely, almost coldly, two little frown lines between her brows.

'The morning room, I think,' she said. 'There's furniture in there and besides it doesn't have—associations.'

The furniture consisted of two kitchen stools and a caneback chair. From the window, heavily encrusted with grime, he could see the conservatory to whose walls of cracked glass the tendrils of a dead vine still clung. He gave her the chair and sat down on one of the stools. He had a strange feeling—but a feeling not without a charm of its own—that they had come here to buy the house, he and she, had come early and were reduced to wait thus uncomfortably until the arrival of the agent who would show them round.

'This could be a study,' he would say. 'It must be lovely on a fine day.'

'Or we could eat in here. Nice and near the kitchen.'

'Will you be able to bear getting up in the morning to cook my breakfast?' (My love, my love . . .)

'You were going to explain,' she said, and of course, there would never be a shared bed or a shared breakfast or any future at all. This was their future, this interview in a damp morning room, looking at a dead vine.

He began to tell her about Charles and Tess, about Mrs Kershaw's belief. Her face grew even harder and colder when he came to the bit about the inheritance and before he had finished, she said:

'You really meant to pin the murder on Roger?'

'What could I do? I was torn between Charles,' he said, 'and you.' She shook her head quickly, the blood running into her face. 'I beg you to believe I didn't try to know you because you were his wife.'

'I believe you.'

'The money . . . his sisters . . . you didn't know about that?'

'I knew nothing. Only that they existed and that he never saw them. Oh God!' She screwed up her face, pushed her hands over her cheeks, across her eyes and up to the temples. 'We've been talking about it all day. He can't see that he was morally obliged to help them. Only one thing matters to him, that Wexford won't take it seriously as a motive for murder.'

'Wexford saw him himself that night at the crucial time in Sewingbury.'

'He doesn't know or he's forgotten. He's going to go through hell until he can pluck up courage to ring Wexford. Some people might say that's his punishment.' She sighed. "Are his sisters very badly off?"

'One of them is. She lives in a single room with her husband and her baby.'

'I've got Roger to agree to let them have what they should have had in the first place, three thousand, three hundred odd each. I think I'd better go to see them myself. He won't even notice it's gone. It's funny, you know, I knew he was unscrupulous. You can't make that amount of money without being, but I didn't know he'd stoop to that.'

'It hasn't made you . . . ?' He hesitated, wondering what he had destroyed.

'Never feel the same about him again? Oh, my dear, you are funny. Listen, I'll tell you something. Seven years ago it was and the month of June. My face was on the cover of six separate magazines that month. The most photographed girl in Britain.'

He nodded, puzzled and out of his depth.

'If you reach a peak there's nothing left but to go downhill. In June of the next year I had my face on one magazine. So I married Roger.'

'You didn't love him?'

'I liked him, you know. He saved me in a way and all the time I'm saving him.' Archery knew what she meant, recalling her soft tranquillity in the Olive dining room, her hand touching a mourner's trembling arm. He expected always from her calm serenity and he was shocked when she raged suddenly: 'How was I was to know there was a middle-aged clergyman waiting for me—a clergyman with a wife and a son and a guilt complex as big as a mountain?'

'Imogen!'

'No, you're not to touch me! It was stupid to come here and I should never have done it. Oh God, how I hate these sentimental scenes!'

He got up and walked as far from her as the little room allowed. It had stopped raining but the sky was sludge-coloured and the vine was as dead as a doornail.

'What will they do now,' she said, 'your son and this girl?'

'I don't think they know themselves.'

'And you, what will you do?'

' "Go to the wife of my bosom," ' he quoted, ' "the same as I ought to go." '

'Kipling!' She gave a hysterical laugh, and he was pained by the depths he was discovering too late. 'Kipling! That's all I need.'

'Good-bye,' he said.

'Good-bye, dear Henry Archery. I've never known what to call you. Do you know that?' She lifted his hand, kissed the palm.

'Perhaps it's not a name for dalliance,' he said ruefully.

'But it sounds well with Rev. in front of it.'

She went out, closing the door soundlessly behind her.

'Jenny kissed me,' he said to the vine. Jenny could just be short of Imogen. 'So what?'

Presently he came out into the hall and he wondered why the place seemed emptier and more lifeless than before. Perhaps it was his own fresh sense of loss. He turned towards the back door and then he saw. It was not an imagined but an actual diminishing. The raincoat had gone.

Had it ever been there or was his fancy, morbid and hypersensitive, creating hallucinations? It was a vision that might naturally come to someone involved as he was in Painter's story. But if the raincoat had never been there what would account for those penny-sized puddles on the floor, made surely by rain rivulets running from a sleeve?

He had no belief in the vulgar supernatural. But now as he stood looking at the hook where the raincoat had hung, he remembered how he had jumped at the tap on the window and had likened the marble veining to blood. It was not impossible that some evil hung over places such as this, fermenting the imagination and re-creating on the mind's retina images from a past tragedy.

The door was glazed in square panes. All were dirty yet all glinted faintly in the evening light—all but one. He peered, then smiled wryly at his absurd fancies. The glass had been completely removed from the frame nearest to the lock. An arm could have passed through it to turn the key and slide back the bolts.

It was unbolted now. He stepped out on to the flagged yard. Beyond, the garden lay enveloped in thin wet mist. The trees, the bushes, the lush blanket of weed sagged under their weight of water. Once he would have left the responsible citizen's anxiety as to the whereabouts of whoever had broken that window, might even have considered going to the police. Now he was simply apathetic, indifferent.

Imogen filled his mind, but even on this subject, his thoughts were no longer passionate or ashamed. He would give her five more minutes to get away and then he would return to the Olive. Mechanically he stooped down and for something to do began carefully picking up the shards of broken glass, stacking them against the wall where no one, not even the burglar, might tread on them.

His nerves were bad, he knew that, but surely that was a footfall, the sound of indrawn breath.

She was coming back! But she must not—it was more than he could stand. The sight of her would be joy, but anything she said could only mean a fresh parting. He set his teeth, tightened the muscles of his hands and before he could stop himself his fingers had closed on a sliver of glass.

The blood came before the pain. He stood up, looking stupidly and aloud in that empty place, and he turned to meet the tap-tap of high heels.

Her scream burst in his face.

'Uncle Bert! Uncle Bert! Oh, my God!'

His hand was all bloody but he put it out, the hurt hand and the other to catch Elizabeth Crilling as she fell.

'You ought to have it stitched,' she said. 'You'll get tetanus. You'll have an awful scar.'

He wrapped the handkerchief more tightly about the wound and sat grimly on the step, watching her. She had come round in seconds but her face was still white. A little gust of wind flicked through the tangled mass of green and showered them with water drops. Archery shivered.

'What are you doing here?' he asked.

She lay back in the chair he had fetched her from the morning room, her legs stretched out and limp. He noticed how thin they were, thin as the legs of an Oriental, the stockings wrinkled at the ankles.

'I've had a row with my mother,' she said.

He said nothing, waiting. For a moment she remained inert, then her body seemed to snap forwards, a trap with a steel spring. Instinctively, he shifted a little away from her, for she had brought her face towards his, her hands clutching each other between knees and breast. Her mouth moved before the words found sound.

'Oh Christ!' He kept still, controlling his inevitable reaction to the oath. 'I saw you with blood on you,' she said, 'and then you said it, what he said. "I've cut myself." ' A great shudder rocked her as if she had been grasped and shaken by an invisible force. Amazed, he watched her slacken again and heard her say in cold contrast, 'Give me a cigarette.' She tossed her bag to him. 'Light it!' The flame guttered in the damp air and the tugging wind. She cupped her thin hands with their big knuckles around it. 'Always snooping, aren't you?' she said, drawing back. 'I don't know what you thought you'd find, but this is it.'

Bewildered, he found himself staring at the garden, up at the overhanging gables, down at the wet broken paving.

'Me, I mean,' she said with savage impatience. 'You've been telling tales to the police about me and you don't even know what it's all about.' Again she snapped forward and shamelessly—he was horrified —pulled up her skirt and exposed her thigh above her stocking top. The white skin was covered all over with needle punctures. 'Asthma, that's what it's about. Asthma tablets. You dissolve them in water—and that's a hell of a job on its own—and then you fill up a hypodermic.'

Archery did not think himself easily shocked. But he was shocked now. He felt the blood run into his face. Embarrassment silenced him, then gave place to pity for her and a kind of diffused indignation with humanity.

'Does it have any effect?' he asked as coolly as he could.

'It gives you a lift, if you follow me. Much the same as you get from singing psalms, I expect,' she jeered. 'There was this man I lived with, he put me on to it. I was in the right place for getting supplies, you see. Until you sent that bastard Burden down and he put the fear of God into my mother. She's got to get a new prescription every time she wants them now and she's got to collect them herself.'

'I see,' he said, and hope went. So that was what Mrs Crilling had meant. In prison there would be no tablets, no syringe, and because she had become addicted to them she would have to reveal her addiction or . . .

'I don't think the police can do anything to you,' he said, not knowing whether they could or not.

'What would you know about it? I've got twenty left in a bottle so I came here. I've made myself a bed upstairs and . . .'

He interrupted her. 'It's your raincoat?'

The question surprised her, but only for a moment, then scorn returned to make her look twice her age.

'Sure it is,' she said scathingly. 'Whose did you think it was, Painter's? I went out for a bit to get something from my car, left the door on the latch and when I came back you were here with that tarty piece.' He kept his eyes on her, controlling himself. For the only time in his life he felt an urge to strike another person's face. 'I didn't dare come back for a bit,' she said, returning to the only other mood she had, a self-pitying childishness. 'But I had to get my raincoat—the tablets were in the pocket.'

She inhaled deeply and flung the cigarette away from her into the wet bushes.

'What the hell were you doing, returning to the scene of the crime? Trying to get under his skin?'

'Whose skin?' he whispered urgently.

'Painter's of course. Bert Painter's. My Uncle Bert.' She was defiant again, but her hand shook and her eyes glazed. It was coming now. He was like a man awaiting bad news, knowing it was inevitable, knowing even exactly that it was going to be, but still hoping that there would be some detail, some fact to mitigate it. 'That night,' she said, 'he stood there just like you. Only he was holding a piece of wood and there was blood on it and all over him. "I've cut myself," he said. "Don't look, Lizzie, I've cut myself."'

16

When the unclean spirit is gone out of a man,
he walketh through dry places seeking rest and
finding none. He saith, I will return unto my
house whence I came out.

The Gospel for the Fourth Sunday in Lent

SHE told it in the second person, 'You did this,' 'You
did that.' Archery realised he was hearing what no
parent and no psychiatrist had ever heard, and he
marvelled. The peculiar use of the pronoun seemed to
draw his own mind into the child's body so that he
could see with her eyes and feel with her overweening
terror.

She sat in the damp dusk on the spot where it had
all begun for her, utterly still now. Only her eyelids
moved. Sometimes, at agonising moments in the narrative, she would close her eyes then open them again
with a slow exhalation of breath. Archery had never
been to a seance—would indeed have disapproved of
such a thing as being theologically untenable—but he
had read of them. Elizabeth Crilling's steady outpour-
ing of terrible events told in a flat monotone was
reminiscent, he thought, of mediumistic revelation.
She was coming to the end now and a weary relief
crossed her face as of one shedding a load.

. . . You put your coat on, your best coat because
it was your best frock, and you ran across the road,
down the sideway and past the greenhouse. Nobody
saw you because there was no one about. Or was there?
Surely that was the back door closing softly.

You came very quietly around the side of the house and then you saw it was only Uncle Bert who had come out of the house into the garden.

'Uncle Bert, Uncle Bert! I've got my best frock on. Can I go and show it to Tessie?'

Suddenly you were very frightened, more frightened than you had ever been in all your life, because Uncle Bert was breathing in such a funny way, gasping and coughing like Daddy did when he had one of his attacks. Then he turned round and there was red stuff all over him, on his hands and all down the front of his coat.

'I've cut myself,' he said. 'Don't look, Lizzie. I've just cut myself.'

'I want Tessie! I want Tessie!'

'Don't you go up there!'

'You're not to touch me. I've got my new dress on. I'll tell my mummy.'

He just stood there with the red stuff on him and his face was like the face of a lion, big thick mouth, thick nose, curly tawny hair. Yes, it was like the lion in that picture book Mummy said you must not look at . . .

The red stuff had splashed on to his face and trickled to the corner of his mouth. He brought that dreadful face down close to yours and shouted right at you:

'You tell her, Lizzie Crilling, you stuck-up little snob, and d'you know what I'll do? Wherever I am—wherever, d'you hear me?—I'll find you and I'll give you what I gave the old girl.'

It was over. He could tell that by the way she came out of her trance, sat up and gave a kind of moan.

'But you went back,' Archery murmured. 'You went back with your mother?'

'My mother!' Weeping would not have surprised him. This violent bitter laughter did. On a high discordant peal, she stopped suddenly and rushed into her answer. 'I was only five, only a kid. I didn't know what he meant, not then. I was much more frightened of letting her know I'd been over there.' He noted that 'her' and knew intuitively she would not mention her mother by name again. 'You see, I didn't even know it was blood and I reckon I must have thought it was paint.

'Then we went back. I wasn't afraid of the house and I didn't know what he meant by the old girl. I think when he said about giving me what he'd given the old girl I thought he meant his wife, Mrs Painter. He knew I'd seen him hit her. I found the body. You knew that? God, it was terrible. I didn't understand, you see. D'you know what I thought at first? I thought she'd sort of burst.'

'Don't,' said Archery.

'If you can't take it now, what d'you think it was like for me? I was *five*. Five, my Christ! They put me to bed and I was ill for weeks. Of course, they'd arrested Painter, but I didn't know that. You don't tell children that sort of thing. I didn't know what had happened at all, only that Granny Rose had burst open and he had made it happen and if I said I'd seen him he'd do the same to me.'

'But afterwards. Didn't you tell anyone then?'

She had talked about finding the body and said it was terrible, but then there had been affectation in her voice. A child finding a murdered woman, he thought. Yes, all the world would recoil in shock from that. Yet for her that had not been the worst. Now as he asked her about afterwards he saw the trance begin once more to mist her face as the spectre of Painter—Painter on this very spot—rose before it.

'He'd find you,' she mumbled. 'He'd find you wherever you were, wherever he was. You wanted to tell *her,* but she wouldn't listen to you. "Don't think about it, Baby, put it out of your mind." But it wouldn't go *out . . .*' Her features worked and the blank eyes flickered.

'Miss Crilling, let me take you home.'

She was standing up now, moving mechanically towards the house wall, a robot whose programming has failed. When her hands touched the bricks she stopped and spoke again, talking to him but into the house itself.

'It wouldn't go out. It went in and in, till it was just a little black wheel spinning and playing the same thing over and over again.'

Had she realised she was speaking in metaphor? He had thought of a medium's utterances, but now he knew it had been more like a discordant record, playing the same horror each time it was pricked by the stylus of association. He touched her arm and was surprised when she followed him meekly and limply back to the chair. They sat in silence for some minutes. She was the first to speak and she was almost her normal self.

'You know Tessie, don't you? She's going to marry your son?' He shrugged. 'I think she was the only real friend I ever had,' she said quietly. 'It was her birthday the next week. She was going to be five, and I thought I'd give her one of my old dresses. Sneak it round when *she* was with the old girl. Generous little beast, wasn't I? I never saw her again.'

Archery said gently, 'You saw her this afternoon in the chemist's.'

Her new tranquillity was very finely balanced. Had he pushed it too far?

'In the white blouse?' she said in a dead even voice, so low that he had to lean forward and strain to catch it. He nodded.

'That girl who hadn't got any change?'

'Yes.'

'She was standing beside me and I never knew.' There was a long silence. The only sound was the faint rustling of wet bushes, water-loaded gleaming leaves on the coach-house walls. Then she tossed her head. 'I reckon I don't notice women much,' she said. 'I saw you all right and the boy that was with you. I remember I thought the talent's looking up in this dump.'

'The talent,' Archery said, 'is my son.'

'Her boy-friend? I never would have told you!' She gave a low cry of exasperation. 'And, my God, I never would have told her—not if you hadn't caught me out like that.'

'It was chance, coincidence. Perhaps it's better that I do know."

'You!' she said. 'That's all you think about, you and your precious son. What about me?' She stood up, looked at him and moved towards the door with the broken pane. It was true he thought, ashamed. He had been prepared to sacrifice all these other people to save Charles, the Crillings, Primero, even Imogen— but his quest had been doomed from the beginning because history could not be changed.

'What will they do to me?' Her face was turned away from him and she spoke softly. But there was such urgency and such fear in those six short words that their impact was as if she had shouted.

'Do to you?' He could do no more than get to his feet and stand helplessly behind her. 'Why should they do anything to you?' He remembered the dead man on the crossing and he remembered the needle punctures, but he said only, 'You've been more sinned against than sinning.'

'Oh, the Bible!' she cried. 'Don't quote the Bible to me.' He said nothing for he had not done so. 'I'm going upstairs now,' she said strangely. 'When you see Tess would you give her my love? I wish,' she said, 'I wish I could have given her something for her birthday.'

By the time he had found a doctor's house he felt all hand, nothing but hand, a throbbing thing that beat like a second heart. He recognised Dr Crocker at once and saw that he, too, was remembered.

'You must be enjoying your holiday,' Crocker said. He stitched the finger, filled a syringe with anti-tetanus serum. 'First that dead boy and now this. Sorry, but this may hurt. You've got thick skin.'

'Really?' Archery could not help smiling as he bared his upper arm. 'I want to ask you something.' Without stopping to explain he put the question that had been troubling him all the way from Victor's Piece. 'Is it possible?'

'Beginning of October?' Crocker looked closely and not unsympathetically at him. 'Look, how personal is this?'

Archery read his thoughts and managed a laugh. 'Not that personal,' he said. 'I am, as they say, enquiring for a friend.'

'Well, it's extremely unlikely.' Crocker grinned. 'There have been cases, very few and far between. They make minor medical history.'

Nodding, Archery got up to go.

'I shall want to see that finger again,' the doctor said. 'Or your local G.P. will. You'll need another couple of injections. See to it when you get home, will you?'

Home . . . yes, he would be home tomorrow. His stay in Kingsmarkham had not been a holiday, anything but that, yet he had that curious end-of-a-holiday feeling when the resort one has stayed in becomes more familiar than home.

He had walked along this High Street every day, more frequently even than he trod the main village street at Thringford. The order of the shops, chemist, grocer, draper, were as well known to him as to the housewives of Kingsmarkham. And the place was certainly pretty. Suddenly it seemed sad that he should hardly have noticed its prettiness—more than that really, for prettiness does not go with grace and dignity —but would associate it for ever with a lost love and a failed search.

Street lamps, some of them of ancient design and with wrought iron casings, showed him alleys winding between stone walls, coaching yards, flowers in a few cottage gardens. The weak yellow light bleached these flowers to a luminous pallor. Half an hour ago it had been just light enough to read print by; now the darkness had come down and lamps appeared in windows fronting the street. The sky had a rainy look and stars

showed only in the crevices between bulbous bloated
cloud. There was no moon.

The Olive and Dove was brightly lit and the car park
full. Glass doors separated the hall from the cocktail
bar and he saw that it was crowded. There were groups
and pairs of young people, sitting on high stools,
gathered round the small black oak tables. Archery
thought he would give everything he possessed to see
Charles among them, throwing back his head in
laughter, his hand resting on the shoulder of a pretty
girl. Not a beautiful, intellectual, tainted girl—just
someone pretty and dull and uncomplicated. But
Charles was not there. He found him alone in the
lounge writing letters. Only a few hours had elapsed
since his parting from Tess, but already he was
writing . . .

'What on earth have you done to your hand and
where have you been?'

'Hacking away at the past.'

'Don't be cryptic, Father. It doesn't suit you.' His
tone was bitter and sullen. Archery wondered why
people say that suffering improves the character, why
indeed he had sometimes thoughtlessly said it to his
own parishioners. He listened to his son's voice, carp-
ing, querulous and selfish. 'I've been wanting to address
this envelope for the past two hours, but I couldn't
because I don't know where Tess's aunt lives.' Charles
gave him a sour accusing look. 'You wrote it down.
Don't say you've lost it.'

'Here.' Archery took the card from his pocket and
dropped it on the table. 'I'm going to phone your
mother, tell her we'll be home in the morning.'

'I'll come up with you. This place goes dead at
night.'

Dead? And the bar crowded with people, some of
whom were surely as exacting as Charles. If Tess had
been with them it would not have been dead. Quite
suddenly Archery made up his mind that Charles must
be made happy, and if happiness meant Tess, he should

have Tess. Therefore the theory he was formulating
would have to be made to work.

He paused on the threshold of his bedroom, put his
hand to the light switch but did not press it. There in
the darkness with Charles behind him there flashed
across his brain a picture of himself and Wexford that
first day at the police station. He had been firm then.
'Bitterly, bitterly against this marriage,' he had told
the Chief Inspector. How utterly he had come round!
But then he had not known what it was to crave for
a voice and a smile. To understand all was not merely
to forgive all, it was utter identification of the spirit and
the flesh.

Over his shoulder Charles said, 'Can't you find the
switch?' His hand came up and met his father's on the
dry cold wall. The room flooded with light. 'Are you
all right? You look worn-out.'

Perhaps it the the unaccustomed gentleness in his
voice that did it. Archery knew how easy it is to be
kind when one is happy, how nearly impossible to feel
solitude in the midst of one's own misery. He was
suddenly filled with love, an overflowing diffused love
that for the first time in days had no specific object
but included his son—and his wife. Hoping unreasonably that her voice would be soft and kind, he moved
towards the telephone.

'Well, you are a stranger,' were the first words he
heard and they were sharp with resentment. 'I was
beginning to wonder what had happened to you.
Thought you must have eloped.'

'I wouldn't do that, darling,' he said, sick at heart.
And then, because he had to set his foot back on the
path of constancy, he took a grotesque echo, 'Kingsmarkham isn't conspicuous for its talent. I've missed
you.' It was untrue and what he was going to say next
would also be a lie. 'It'll be good to be home with you
again.' That lie would have to be changed into truth.
He clenched his hand till the hurt finger burned with
pain, but as he did so he thought that he and time
could make it true . . .

'You do use some extraordinary expressions,' Charles said when he had rung off. 'Talent, indeed. Very vulgar.' He was still holding the card, staring at it with utter absorption. A week ago Archery would have marvelled that a woman's address and a woman's handwriting could provide such a fascination.

'You asked me on Saturday if I'd ever seen this before. You asked me if I'd heard it. Well, now I've *seen* it, it's rung a bell. It's part of a long religious verse play. Part of it's in prose but there are songs in it—hymns really—and this is the last verse of one of them.'

'Where did you see it? In Oxford? In a library?'

But Charles was not listening to him. He said as if he had been meaning to say it for the past half-hour, 'Where did you go tonight? Had it any connection with me and—and Tess?'

Must he tell him? Was he obliged to root out those last vestiges of hope before he had anything real and proven to put in their place?

'Just to have a last look at Victor's Piece.' Charles nodded. He appeared to accept this quite naturally. 'Elizabeth Crilling was there, hiding.' He told him about the drugs, the wretched attempts to secure more tablets, but he did not tell him everything.

Charles's reaction was unexpected. 'Hiding from what?'

'The police, I suppose, or her mother.'

'You didn't just leave her there?' Charles asked indignantly. 'A crazy kid like that? God knows what she might do. You don't know how many of those tablets would poison her. She might take them deliberately to that end. Have you thought of that?'

She had accused him of not considering her but even that taunt had not prompted him. It had simply not crossed his mind that he was doing something irresponsible in leaving a young girl alone in an empty house.

'I think we ought to go to Victor's Piece and try to get her to come home,' Charles said. Observing the sudden animation on his son's face, Archery wondered how sincere he was and how much of this spurt of energy was due to a desire to do something, anything, because he knew that if he went to bed he would not sleep. Charles put the card away in his pocket. 'You won't like this,' he said, 'but I think we ought to take the mother with us.'

'She's quarrelled with her mother. She behaves as if she hates her.'

'That's nothing. Have you ever seen them together?'

Only a glance across a courtroom, a glance of indecipherable passion. He had never seen them together. He knew only that if Charles were alone somewhere and miserable, on the verge perhaps of taking his own life, he, Archery, would not want strangers to go to his succour.

'You can drive,' he said and he tossed the keys to his son.

The church clock was striking eleven. Archery wondered if Mrs Crilling would be in bed. Then it occurred to him for the first time that she might be worrying about her daughter. He had never attributed to the Crillings ordinary emotions. They were different from other people, the mother deranged, the girl delinquent. Was that why, instead of being merciful, he had merely used them? As they turned into Glebe Road he felt a new warmth stir within him. It was not too late—especially now she had found some release—to bring Elizabeth back, to heal that old wound, to retrieve something out of chaos.

Outwardly he was cold. He was coatless and the night was chilly. You expect a winter's night to be cold, he thought. There was something depressing and wrong about a cold summer night. November with flowers, a November wind that ruffled the ripe leaves of summer. He must not find omens in nature.

'What d'you call it,' he said to Charles, 'when you ascribe emotions to nature? What's the expression?'

'The Pathetic Fallacy,' Charles said. Archery shivered.

'This is the house,' he said. They got out. Number twenty-four was in darkness upstairs and down.

'She's probably in bed.'

'Then she'll have to get up,' said Charles and rang the bell. He rang again and again. "Pointless," he said. 'Can we get round the back?'

Archery said, 'Through here,' and led Charles through the sandy arch. It was like a cavern, he thought, touching the walls. He expected them to be clammy but they were dry and prickly to the touch. They emerged into a dark pool among patches of light which came from french windows all along the backs of houses. A yellow square segmented by black bars lay on each shadowed garden but none came from Mrs Crilling's window.

'She must be out,' said Archery as they opened the little gate in the wire fence. 'We know so little about them. We don't know where she'd go or who her friends are.'

Through the first window the kitchen and the hall showed dark and empty. To reach the french windows they had to push through a tangle of wet nettles which stung their hands.

'Pity we didn't bring a torch.'

'We haven't *got* a torch,' Archery objected. He peered in. 'I've got matches.' The first he struck showed him the room as he had seen it before, a muddle of flung-down clothes and stacked newspapers. The match died and he dropped it on wet concrete. By the light of a second he saw that on the table were the remains of a meal, cut bread still in its paper wrapping, a cup and saucer, a jam jar, a single plate coated with something yellow and congealed.

'We might as well go,' he said. 'She isn't here.'

'The door's not locked,' said Charles. He lifted the latch and opened it quietly. There came to them at once a peculiar and unidentifiable odour of fruit and of alcohol.

'You can't go in. There isn't the slightest justification for breaking in.'

'I haven't broken anything.' Charles's foot was over the threshold, but he stopped and said over his shoulder

to his father, 'Don't you think there's something odd
here? Don't you feel it?'

Archery shrugged. They were both in the room now.
The smell was very strong but they could see nothing
but the dim outlines of cluttered furniture.

'The light switch is on the left by the door,' he said.
'I'll find it.' He had forgotten that his son was a man,
that his son's adult sense of responsibility had brought
them there. In that dark, evilly scented place, they were
just a parent and his child. He must not do as Mrs
Crilling had done and let the child go first. 'Wait there,'
he said. He felt his way along the side of the table,
pushed a small armchair out of his path, squeezed behind the sofa and felt for the switch. 'Wait there!' he
cried again, much more sharply and in a spasm of real
fear. Previously in his passage across the room his
feet had come into contact with debris on the floor, a
shoe, he thought, a book dropped face downwards. Now
the obstruction was larger and more solid. His scalp
crept. Clothes, yes, and within those clothes something
heavy and inert. He dropped to his knees, thrusting
forward hands to palpate and fumble. 'Dear God . . . !'

'What is it? What the hell *is* it? Can't you find the
light?'

Archery could not speak. He had withdrawn his
hands and they were wet and sticky. Charles had
crossed the room. Light pouring into and banishing
that darkness was a physical pain. Archery closed his
eyes. Above him he heard Charles make an inarticulate
sound.

He opened his eyes and the first thing he saw was
that his hands were red. Charles said, 'Don't look!' and
he knew that his own lips had been trying to frame
those words. They were not policemen, not used to
sights such as this, and each tried to save the other
from seeing.

Each had to look. Mrs Crilling lay spread on the
floor between the sofa and the wall and she was quite
dead. The chill of her body came up to Archery's
hands through the pink flounces that covered it from

neck to ankles. He had seen that neck and at once had looked away from the stocking that made a ligature around it.

'But she's all over blood,' said Charles, 'It's as if— God!—as if someone had sprinkled her with it.'

17

I held my tongue and spake nothing; I kept silence, yea, even from good words; but it was pain and grief to me.

Psalm 39. *The Burial of the Dead*

'IT isn't blood,' said Wexford. 'Don't you know what it is? Couldn't you smell it?' He lifted the bottle someone had found under the sideboard and held it aloft. Archery sat on the sofa in Mrs Crilling's living room, worn, tired, utterly spent. Doors banged and footsteps sounded as Wexford's two men searched the other room. The people upstairs had come in at midnight, Saturday night happy, the man a little drunk. The woman had had hysterics during Wexford's questioning.

They had taken the body away and Charles moved in his chair round so that he could not see the crimson splashes of cherry brandy.

'But why? Why did it happen?' he whispered.

'Your father knows why.' Wexford stared at Archery, his grey gimlet eyes deep and opaque. He squatted opposite them on a low chair with wooden arms. 'As for me, I don't know but I can guess. I can't help feeling I've seen something like this before, a long, long time ago. Sixteen years to be exact. A pink frilly dress that a little girl could never wear again because it was spoilt with blood.'

Outside the rain had begun again and water lashed against the windows making them rattle. It would be cold now inside Victor's Piece, cold and eerie like a deserted castle in a wood of wet trees. The Chief Inspector had an extra uncanny sense that almost amounted to telepathy. Archery willed his thoughts to alter course lest Wexford should divine them, but the question came before he could rid his mind of its pictures.

'Come on, Mr Archery, where is she?'

'Where is who?'

'The daughter.'

'What makes you think I know?'

'Listen to me,' said Wexford. 'The last person we've talked to who saw her was a chemist in Kingsmarkham. Oh, yes, we went to all the chemists first naturally. This one remembers that when she was in the shop there were two men and a girl there too, a young man and an elder one, tall, fair, obviously father and son.'

'I didn't speak to her then,' Archery said truthfully. The smell sickened him. He wanted nothing but sleep and peace and to get out of this room where Wexford had kept them since they had telephone him.

'Mrs Crilling's been dead six or seven hours. It's ten to three now and you left the Olive at a quarter to eight. The barman saw you come in at ten. Where did you go, Mr Archery?'

He sat silent. Years and years ago—Oh, centuries ago!—it had been like this in school. You own up, you betray someone, or everyone suffers. Funny, once before he had thought of Wexford as a kind of head-master.

'You know where she is,' Wexford said. His voice was loud, threatening, ominous. 'D'you want to be an accessory? Is that what you want?'

Archery closed his eyes. Quite suddenly he knew why he was prevaricating. He wanted the very thing that Charles had warned him might happen and although it was contrary to his religion, wicked even, he wanted it with all his heart.

Charles said, 'Father . . .' and when he got no reply shrugged, turned his dull shocked eyes to Wexford. 'Oh, what the hell? She's at Victor's Piece.'

Archery realised that he had been holding his breath. He let it out in a deep sigh. 'In one of the bedrooms,' he said, 'looking at the coach house and dreaming of a heap of sand. She asked what they would do to her and I didn't understand. What will they do to her?'

Wexford got up. 'Well, sir . . .' Archery noted that 'sir' as one might notice the re-assuming of a velvet glove. 'You know as well as I do that it's no longer lawful to punish with death for certain . . .' His eyes flickered over the place where Mrs Grilling had lain. '. . . certain heinous and grievous offences.'

'Will you let us go now?' Charles asked.

'Until tomorrow,' said Wexford.

The rain met them at the front door like a wave or a wall of spray. For the past half hour it had been drumming on the roof of the car and seeping in through the half-open quarter light. There was water lying in a small pool at Archery's feet but he was too tired to notice or care.

Charles came with him into his bedroom.

'I shouldn't ask you now,' he said. 'It's almost morning and God knows what we'll have to go through tomorrow, but I have to know. I'd rather know. But what else did she tell you, that girl at Victor's Piece?'

Archery had heard of people pacing a room like caged beasts. He had never imagined himself so strung with tension that in spite of utter exhaustion he would have to find released by crossing and re-crossing a floor, picking up objects, replacing them, his hands shaking. Charles waited, too wretched even for impatience. His letter to Tess lay in its envelope and the dressing table and beside it the card from the gift shop. Archery picked it up and kneaded it in his hands, crumpling the deckle edging. Then he went up to his

son, put his hands gently on his shoulders and looked
into the eyes that were young replicas of his own.

'What she told me,' he said, 'needn't matter to you.
It would be like—well, someone else's nightmare,'
Charles did not move. 'If you will only tell me where
you saw the verse that is printed on this card.'

The morning was grey and cool, such a morning as
occurs perhaps three hundred time a year out of the
three hundred and sixty-five, when there is neither
rain nor sun, frost nor fog. It was a limbo of a morning. The policeman on the crossing had covered his
shirt sleeves with his dark jacket, the striped shop blinds
were rolled up and sluggish steps had grown brisk.

Inspector Burden escorted Archery along the drying
pavements to the police station. Archery was ashamed
to answer Burden's kindly question as to how he had
slept. He had slept heavily and soundly. Perhaps he
would also have slept dreamlessly had he known what
the inspector now told him, that Elizabeth Crilling was
alive.

'She came with us quite willing,' Burden said and
added rather indiscreetly, 'To tell you the truth, sir,
I've never seen her so calm and sane and—well, at
peace, really.'

'You want to go home, I suppose,' Wexford said
when Burden had left them alone in the blue and yellow office. "You'll have to come back for the inquest
and the magistrates' court hearing. You found the
body.'

Archery sighed. 'Elizabeth found a body sixteen
years ago. If it hadn't been for her mother's self-seek-
ing-vanity, greed for something she had no claim to—
that would never have happened. You might say that
that greed reached out and destroyed long after its
original purpose had been frustrated. Or you might say
that Elizabeth bore her mother a grudge because Mrs
Crilling would never let her talk about Painter and
bring her terrors to the light of day.'

'You might,' said Wexford. 'It could be all those

things. And it could be that when Liz left the chemist's she went back to Glebe Road, Mrs Crilling was afraid to ask for another prescription, so Liz, in the addict's frenzy, strangled her.'

'May I see her?'

'I'm afraid not. I'm beginning to guess just what she saw sixteen years ago and what she told you last night.'

'After I'd talked to her I went to see Dr Crocker. I want you to look at this.' Archery gave Wexford Colonel Plashet's letter, silently indicating the relevant passage with his bandaged finger. 'Poor Elizabeth,' he murmured. 'She wanted to give Tess a dress for her fifth birthday. Unless Tess has changed a lot it wouldn't have meant much to her.'

Wexford read, closed his eyes briefly and then gave a smile. 'I see,' he said slowly and restored the letter to its envelope.

'I am right, aren't I? I'm not juggling things, imagining things? You see, I can't trust my own judgment any more. I have to have an opinion from an expert in deduction. I've been to Forby, I've seen a photograph, I've got a letter and I've talked to a doctor. If you had the same clues would you have come to the same conclusions?'

'I'm sure you're very kind, Mr Archery.' Wexford gave a broad ironic grin. 'I get more complaints than compliments. Now, as to clues and conclusions, I would, but I'd have been on to it a whole lot sooner.

'You see, it all depends on what you're looking for and the fact is, sir, you didn't know what you *were* looking for. All the time you were trying to disprove something in the face of—well, you said it—expert deduction. What you've found now achieves the same result as the other thing would have. For you and your son, that is. But it hasn't changed what for justice is *status quo*. We would have made sure we knew precisely what we were looking for at the start, the basic thing. When you come down to that, it doesn't matter a damn to you who committed the crime. But you were looking through a pair of spectacles that were too big for you.'

'A glass darkly,' said Archery.

'I can't say I envy you the coming interview.'

'Strange,' said Archery thoughtfully as he got up to go, 'that although we both held such opposing opinions in the end we were both right.'

Wexford had said he must come back. He would make his visits short, though, short and blind, his eyes opening only in the court he could see out of this window, his words mere evidence. He had read stories of people transported to strange places, blindfolded and in shuttered cars, so that they should not see the country through which they passed. In his case he would be prevented from seeing visions and associations with those visions, by the presence of those he was legitimately allowed to love. Mary should come with him and Charles and Tess to be his shutters and his hood. Certainly he would never see this room again. He turned to give it a last glance, but if he hoped to have the last word he was disappointed.

'Both right,' said Wexford, giving Archery's hand a gentle clasp. 'I by reason and you by faith. Which, taken all in all,' he added, 'is only what one might expect.'

She opened the door to them carefully, grudgingly, as if expecting to see gypsies or a brush salesman from a disreputable firm.

'I hope you'll forgive us, Mrs Kershaw,' Archery said with too loud heartiness. 'Charles wanted to see Tess and as we were coming this way . . .'

It is difficult to greet callers, even unwelcome callers, without some kind of a smile. Irene Kershaw did not smile, but she made muttering noises in which he caught the occasional word: 'very welcome, I'm sure,' 'unexpected . . .' and 'not really prepared . . .' They got into the hall, but it was an awkward manoeuvre and it almost involved pushing past her. She had grown rather red and she said to Charles, now quite coherently:

'Tess has popped down to the shops to get a few last-minute things for her holiday.' Archery could see that she was angry and that she did not know how to vent her anger on people who were at the same time adults and from a different background from her own. 'You've quarrelled haven't you?' she said. 'What are you trying to do, break her heart?' Apparently she was capable of emotion, but once she had shown it, not capable of control. Tears welled into her eyes. 'Oh dear . . . I didn't mean to say that.'

Archery had explained everything to Charles in the car. He was to find Tess, get her alone and tell her. Now he said, 'You might go down the hill, Charles, and see if you can meet her coming up, She'll be glad of a hand with her basket.'

Charles hesitated, possibly because he was at a loss to answer Mrs Kershaw's accusation and could not bring himself to echo so exaggerated an expression as 'a broken heart'. Then he said, 'I'm going to marry Tess. That's what I've always wanted.'

The colour died out of her face and now that there was no occasion for them the tears trickled down her cheeks. Archery would, under other circumstances, have been embarrassed. Now he realised that this mood of hers, tears, a lukewarm resentment that might be her nearest approach to passion, would make her receptive to what he had to say. A tired tigress apparently lurked under that dull suburban exterior, a mother beast capable of being roused only when its young was threatened.

Charles let himself out of the front door. Archery, left alone with her, wondered where the other children were and how soon Kershaw himself would return. Again he was finding himself, when in the sole company of this woman, at a loss for words. She made no effort to help him, but stood stiff and expressionless, dabbing at the tearmarks with the tips of her fingers.

'Perhaps we could sit down?' He made a gesture

towards the glass door. 'I should like to have a talk, settle things, I . . .'

She was recovering fast, tunnelling back into the sanctuary of her respectability. 'You'd like some tea?'

The mood must not be allowed to peter out into small-talk over the cups. 'No,' he said, 'no, really . . .'

She went before him into the living room. There were the books, the Reader's Digests, the dictionaries and the works on deep sea fishing. The portrait of Jill on the easel was finished and Kershaw had made the amateur's mistake of not knowing when to stop, so that the likeness had been lost in last-minute touches. In the garden which was spread before him with the unreality and the garish colours of a cushion cover in gros point, the Paul Crampel geraniums burned so brightly that they hurt his eyes.

Mrs Kershaw sat down genteelly and crimped her skirt over her knees. Today, now that it was cold again, she wore a cotton dress. She was that kind of woman, Archery thought, who would wear her winter clothes on and on cautiously until she was sure a heatwave was fully established. Then, just as the hot weather was ending and the storm about to break, then at last the carefully laundered thin dress would be brought out.

The pearls had been restrung. She put her hand up to them and drew it away quickly, curbing temptation. Their eyes met and she gave a tiny nervous giggle, perhaps aware that he had noticed her tiny vice. He gave a small inner sigh, for all her emotion had gone and her face showed only the natural bewilderment of a hostess who does not know the purpose of a call and is too discreet to question the caller.

He must—he *must*—awaken something from behind that pale lined brow. All his carefully prepared openings died. In a moment she would begin on the weather or the desirability of white weddings. But she did not quite do that. He had forgotten the other stock remark that is so handy a conversation starter between strangers.

'And how did you enjoy your holiday?' said Irene Kershaw.

Very well. That would do as well as anything.

'Forby is your native village, I believe,' he said. 'I went to see a grave while I was there.'

She touched the pearls with the flat of her hand. 'A grave?' For an instant her voice was as raw as when she had talked of a broken heart, then all passionless Purley again as she added, 'Oh, yes, Mrs Primero is buried there, isn't she?'

'It wasn't her grave I saw.' Softly he quoted, ' "Go, shepherd to your rest . . ." Tell me, why did you keep all the works he left behind him?'

That there would be reaction and that that reaction might be anger he had expected. He was prepared for a flouncing hauteur or even that damning, dulling response so dear to the heart of the Mrs Kershaws of this world: 'We needn't discuss that.' He had not thought she would be frightened and at the same time stricken with a kind of awe. She cowered a little in the armchair—if cowering is compatible with perfect stillness—and her eyes wide and glistening now, had the utter immobility of the dead.

Her fear had the effect of frightening him. It was as communicable as a yawn. Suppose she were to have a fit of hysterics? He went on very gently:

'Why did you keep them hidden away in the dark? They might have been published, they might have been acted. He could have had posthumous fame.'

She made no answer at all, but now he knew what to do, the answer came to him like a gift of God. He only had to go on talking, gently, mesmerically. The words tumbled out, platitudes and clichés, praise of work he had never seen and had no reason to suppose he would admire, assurances and unfounded promises he might never be able to honour. All the time, like a hypnotist, he kept his eyes on her, nodding when she nodded, breaking into a wide fatuous smile when for the first time a tiny vague one trembled on her lips.

'May I see them?' he dared. 'Will you show me the works of John Grace?'

He held his breath while with torturing slowness she mounted a stool and reached for the top of the book case. They were in a box, a large cardboard grocer's box that had apparently once contained a gross of tinned peaches. She handled it with a peculiar reverence, her care all concentrated on it, so that she let the magazines which had been stacked on it cascade to the floor.

There must have been a dozen of them but only one cover picture splashed at Archery like acid on the eyes. He blinked away from the beautiful photographed face, the pale hair under a hat of June roses. He had waited for Mrs Kershaw to speak now and her words pulled him out of shock and misery.

'I suppose Tess told you,' she whispered. 'It was supposed to be our secret.' She lifted the lid of the box so that he was able to read the writing on the topmost sheet of manuscript. *The Fold. A Prayer in Dramatic Form* by John Grace.' 'If you'd told me before I would have shown them to you. Tess said I should show them to anyone who would be interested and would understand.'

Again their eyes met and Irene Kershaw's tremulous stare was caught and steadied in his strong one. He knew his face was mobile and expressive of his thoughts. She must have read them for she said, thrusting the box towards him, 'Here, have them. You can have them.' He drew away his hands and his body, horrified and ashamed. At once he had realised what she was doing, that she was trying to pay him off with her most precious material possession. 'Only don't ask me.' She gave a little thin cry. 'Don't ask me about him!'

Impulsively, because he could not bear those eyes, he covered his own with his hands. 'I've no right to be your inquisitor,' he murmured.

'Yes, yes . . . It's all right.' Her fingers touching his shoulder were firm with a new strength. 'But don't ask me about him. Mr Kershaw said you wanted to know about Painter—Bert Painter, my husband. I'll tell you everything I can remember, anything you want to know.'

Her inquisitor and her tormentor . . . Better a swift knife thrust than this interminable twisting on the rock. He clenched his hands till the only pain he could feel came from the wound where the glass had gone in and he faced her across the yellowing sheets of verse.

'I don't want to know about Painter any more,' he said. 'I'm not interested in him. I'm interested in Tess's father . . .' The moan she gave and the feel of those fingers scrabbling at his arm could not stop him now. 'And I've known since last night,' he whispered, 'that Painter *couldn't* have been her father.'

18

. . . As ye will answer at the dreadful day of judgment when the secrets of all hearts shall be disclosed.

The Solemnisation of Matrimony

SHE lay on the floor and wept. To Archery, standing by helpless, it was some measure of her total breakdown that she had come so far wide of her conventional limits as to lie there prone and shake with sobs. Archery had never in his life reached such a nadir of despair. He pitied with an anxiety that had something of panic in it this woman who cried as if the power to weep had long fallen into disuse, as if she were experimenting with some new and shattering exercise.

He did not know how long this abandonment to grief had lasted or would last. This room with all its apparatus for living what some call a 'full life' contained no clock and he had removed his watch to make room for the wrist anchorage of the bandage. Just as he was beginning to feel that she would never stop, she made a curious humping movement so that she rested like a flogged overburdened beast.

'Mrs. Kershaw . . .' he said. 'Mrs. Kershaw, forgive me.'

She got up slowly, her breast still heaving. The cotton dress was creased into a faded rag. She said something but he could not hear her at all and he realised what had happened. She had utterly exhausted her voice.

'Can I get you a glass of water, some brandy?'

Her head shook as if it were not part of her body but a separate thing quivering on a pivot. Her voice came in a hoarse croak. 'I don't drink.' Then he knew that nothing could fully pierce the layers of respectability. She fell into the chair from which his questions had prised her and let her arms hang limply over its sides. When he came back from the kitchen and gave her the glass of water she had recovered sufficiently to sip it and to rub with the old refinement at the corners of her lips. He was afraid to speak.

'Does she have to know?' The words had a hollow sound to them but the roughness had gone. 'My Tessie, does she have to know?'

He did not dare to tell her that Charles would have told her already. 'It's nothing these days,' he said, and shed with a word two thousand years' teaching of his faith. 'Nobody thinks anything of it any more.'

'Tell me what you know.' He knelt at her feet, praying that all his guesses would approximate to the truth and that there would be few gaps for her to fill. If only he could deal well with this last task and save her the shame of confession.

'You and John Grace,' he said, 'you lived close together in Forby. You were in love with each other, but he was killed . . .'

On an impulse he took the manuscript in his hands and laid it gently in her lap. She took it as a religious takes a talisman or a relic and she said softly:

'He was so clever. I couldn't understand the things he wrote, but they were beautiful. His teacher wanted him to go to college but his mother wouldn't let him. You see, his father had a bakery business and he had to go into that.' Let her go on, he prayed, edging away to squat on the edge of his chair. 'He still wrote his poems and his plays,' she said, 'and in the evenings he used to study for some exam. He wasn't strong enough to go into the forces, anaemia or something he had.' Her fingers tightened on the manuscript but her eyes were dry and drained. Archery had a quick vision of the pale pointed face in the souvenir shop picture, only now it was blending into and becoming one with Tess's.

He let his eyes linger on Irene Kershaw for a brief moment with painful compassion. They had reached a point in this telling where she must, unless he could save her, touch on that which would humiliate her most.

'You were going to be married,' he said.

Perhaps she was afraid to hear the words he might choose. 'We never did anything wrong but the once,' she cried. 'Afterwards—well, he wasn't nasty like other boys, and he was just as ashamed as me.' Justifying herself, her head turned from him, she whispered, 'I've had two husbands and then there was John, but I've never been much for that side of things.' Her head swung back and her face was aflame. 'We were engaged, we were going to be married . . .'

Archery knew he must rush on with his conjectures. 'After he was killed you knew you were going to have a child?' She nodded, silent now with the enormity of her embarrassment. 'You had nowhere to go, you were afraid so you married Painter. Let me see, John Grace was killed in February 1945 and Painter got home from Burma at the end of March. You must have known him before,' he said, guessing, improvising.

'Perhaps he was stationed at Forby before he went to the Far East?' A tiny nod rewarded him and he was prepared to go on, drawing someone else's story out of an inspired imagination, out of a letter from Kendal, a photographed face, the bruises on a woman's arm. He lifted his eyes from her and clasped his hands tightly to stop the sound that might have been no more than a sigh. Even a sigh would tell her. At the open french window, against the blaze of red petals, Kershaw was standing, silent, still and powerfully alert. How long had he been there? How much had he heard? Archery, transfixed, sought momentarily in his expression for suffering or anger and saw a sweetness that brought a sudden strength to his heart.

Perhaps he was betraying this woman, perhaps he was doing the unforgivable. It was too late for such recriminations.

'Let me try to finish,' he said, and he had no idea whether he kept his voice on the same level he had used before. 'You were married and you let him think he was Tess's father. But he suspected and that was why he never loved her as a father loves his child? Why didn't you tell Mr Kershaw?'

She leant forward and he could tell she had not heard the man behind her move almost soundlessly into the room. 'He never asked me about my life with Bert,' she said. 'But I was so ashamed of it, of being married to a man like that. Mr. Kershaw's so good—you don't know him—he never asked me, but I had to tell him some of it, didn't I?' She was suddenly eloquent. 'Think what I had to tell him, think what I had to bring him —nothing! People used to point to me out in the streets like I was a freak. He had to take that on his shoulders—Mr Kershaw who'd never touched dirt in all his life. He said he'd take me away and give me a new life where no one'd know, he said I wasn't to blame, I was innocent. D'you think I was going to give up the one chance I'd ever had by telling him Tess was —was illegitimate?'

Archery gasped and staggered to his feet. By the

power of his eyes and his will he had been trying to force the man behind her chair to retreat the way he had come. But Kershaw remained where he was, still, a man apparently without breath or heartbeats. His wife had been rapt, her own story dulling all outer stimuli, but now she seemed to sense the atmosphere in the room, the soundless passion of two other people whose sole desire was to help her. She twisted in her chair, sketched a strange little gesture of pleading and rose to confront her husband.

The scream Archery expected never came. She lurched a little, but whatever she was trying to gasp out was lost and muffled by Kershaw's strong embrace. He heard her say only, 'Oh, Tom, Oh, Tom!' but his energy was so drained that his brain was filled with just one foolish thought. It was the first time he had ever heard Kershaw's christian name.

She did not come downstairs again for that time. Archery supposed that he would not see her again until they all met among flowers and bridesmaids and wedding cake. Tess sat palefaced and almost shy, her hand clasped in that of Charles, the manuscript on her knees.

'I feel so strange,' she said. 'I feel I have a new identity. It's as if I had three fathers and the most remote of them was really my father . . .'

Charles said tactlessly, 'Well, wouldn't you choose to have had this one, a man who could write like this?' But Tess lifted her eyes momentarily to the man Archery would have to learn to call Tom and he knew she had made her choice.

Then she thrust the heavy stack of paper towards Archery. 'What can we do with them?'

'I could show them to a publisher I know. I once wrote part of a book myself . . .' He smiled. 'On Abyssinian cats. I do know someone who might be interested. Something I can do to make amends,' he said.

'You? You've got nothing to reproach yourself with.' Kershaw moved to stand between him and the lovers.

Only marred one marriage to make another, Archery
thought. 'Listen,' said Kershaw, his face scored with the
lines of effort to make himself understood. 'You did
nothing but what I should have done years ago, talked
to her. I couldn't, you see. I wanted to get off on the
right foot. Now I can see you can be too tactful, too
damned diplomatic. Oh, there were a thousand little
things, how she'd never cared for Painter but he'd
been pestering her to marry him. I never asked her
what made her change her mind when he came home
from Burma. God help me, I thought it wasn't my
business! She didn't want me to tell Tess about Painter
and I went through agony trying to put that across to a
kid of twelve.' Here, unafraid of sentimentality, he
caught his stepdaughter's free hand and held it briefly.
'I remember I even got mad at Rene because she seemed
to be contradicting every blessed word I said.

Tess quoted softly. ' "Never mind what Daddy says.
Your father was no murderer." '

'And she was right but I turned a deaf ear. She'll
talk to me now as she's never talked in all these years.
She'll talk to you, Tess, if you'll go up to her now.'

Like a child she hesitated and her lips trembled into
a nervous smile of indecision. But obedience—happy,
reasonable obedience—was natural in that house.
Archery had seen an instance of it before.

'I don't know what to say, how to begin,' she said,
getting slowly to her feet. 'I'm so desperately afraid of
hurting her.'

'Begin with your wedding, then,' Kershaw said ro-
bustly. Archery watched him stoop to the floor where
the magazines had fallen. 'Show her this and let her
dream of seeing you in something like it.'

Tess was in jeans and a white shirt, an Olivia or a
Rosalind finding her lost birthright and with it a new
womanhood. She took the magazine from Kershaw
and glanced at the cover picture, the hat that was a
pyramid of flowers crowning the most photographed
face in Britain.

'That's not for me,' she said, but she took it with her

and Archery watched them depart together, Charles's flesh and blood love and his own, a paper fantasy. Not for me, not for me . . .

'We must go soon,' he said to his own. 'It's time we shared all this with your mother.'